A PERFECT FLOCK

A PERFECT FLOCK
Mike Bogue

To Dad, whose dreams saw him through the darkest
nights of the soul.

"Be ye therefore perfect, even as your Father which is in heaven is perfect." Matthew 5:48, KJV

Chapter 1

Tuck Jameson's next words would either heal or crush Avery Olson.

Tuck scooted his university office chair before Avery's. "Son, your family is wrong."

Avery looked down. "They say I'm too dumb to pass college. Say I'll have to work the farm the rest of my life."

"Bat dung. You've got B's in most of your classes."

"But I have a D in Algebra. If I flunk the final, it's adios, financial aid, adios college."

"Tutoring can prevent that. Arkansas River Valley University has the best tutors around." He chuckled. "I should know—I trained them."

"What if I bomb the final anyways?"

Gently, Tuck said, "Avery, look at me."

The student lifted his head, his eyes glistening.

"If worse comes to worst, and you fail the algebra final, you have options for the spring. You could take out a personal loan."

"A student can do that?"

"Yes. You'd just need to find someone to co-sign for it."

Avery frowned. "Oh."

"But your algebra final isn't until next week. I'll reserve you some time with our best math tutor." In the past, Tuck would have prayed for the student, but since Dad's death, he no longer knocked on heaven's door. He summoned good thoughts and handed Avery the Algebra tutor printout.

"Mr. Jameson, can I go now?"

"Sure." He smiled and gave Avery a thumbs up. "Best of luck on your algebra final. You can do this."

Avery nodded, but his shoulders slumped as he left.

Had Tuck's pep talk done the trick? Poor kid had his heart set on being a game warden—but if he didn't return in the spring, where would he end up? Tuck ground his teeth. Maybe he should offer to co-sign for a loan.

Minutes later, his phone pinged and displayed a one-digit text:

4

Dread clutched his insides. His friend Ham Crouch had used their emergency text code only twice before, most recently for the passing of Tuck's father.

Ham arrived and greeted Tuck with a handshake and an elbow grasp, which knotted Tuck's stomach. Something terrible must have happened, maybe a death in the family. Tuck offered a chair, and Ham squeezed his three hundred pounds into creaking leather. He stank of cigarettes.

A grin flit across Ham's broad face and died, always a sign he wished he could be elsewhere. "It's your brother. He's becoming a Perfect. Told me this morning God's leading him to join The Body."

"A Perf?" Tuck slammed a fist on his desk. "Clay wouldn't, couldn't."

"His initiation is in a few days."

Heat flooded Tuck's face. "I lost Dad to those self-proclaimed sinless freaks. I'm not losing Clay too."

"What are you going to do?"

"Set him straight ASAP." Tuck hated to strong-arm his little brother, but Clay didn't know what was good for him. He had ignored Tuck's advice in the past. But not anymore.

Ham leaned forward, his chair squeaking. "You could

make things worse. Let's talk this through."

"I get that Clay resents me—"

"I've never heard Clay say one bad thing about you."

"He never says a bad thing about anybody." But Tuck wondered how Clay viewed him these days. They'd argued over Dad's funeral—Clay wanted Perfs to attend, Tuck didn't. Mom decided on a private family ceremony. Since then, Clay had drifted.

Tuck's watch beeped noon—time for Clay's usual Salvation Army stint.

He rose and snatched his overcoat, and Ham fell in step beside him. Meeting Clay meant he'd have to skip the Student Government Association lunch. He texted the SGA president to inform her.

Tobacco stench continued to waft from Ham, and Tuck sidestepped away. "You've started smoking again."

"Not now, okay?"

They marched into the Arkansas River Valley University parking lot across from Bailey Coliseum. Shivering, Tuck turned up his collar and frowned at the tomb gray sky. No doubt ARV's four thousand students weathering December finals hoped for snow, but not him. Too often snow meant his out-of-town tutors couldn't make it to the Tutoring Center on time.

Billy Wilson, the university's oldest maintenance man, waved Tuck and Ham over between a row of parked cars. Tuck inwardly groaned. Hard to believe the poor guy now insisted on working twelve-hour days, six days a week, but the man's will was no longer his own.

"Mornin'." Billy's voice crackled with phlegm as students slammed car doors. "Lovely day for gatherin' up trash, ain't it, Dr. Rivers?"

Ham sighed. "I'm not Dr. Rivers, Billy, I'm—"

"Oh, yeah! Mr. Ham. You kick kids out of school."

"Right."

Tuck grinned. Billy often mistook Ham for Dr. Rivers

since both men resembled Mack trucks with red goatees.

"Billy," Ham said, "go home, man. You're sick."

"I'm to work for my supervisor like he's Jesus Christ himself, and a little ole cold won't stop me from working for Jesus." Billy sneezed into his bent arm.

"You'll get pneumonia, old-timer. How old are you, anyway?"

"Seventy-two years young. If the Lord wants me to die serving him as a Perfect, fine with me."

Tuck wrapped the maintenance man's scarf tighter around his neck. "Maybe this'll help."

"Much obliged, Mr. Jameson." Billy squinted. "I see you're still taller than a redwood and thin as a rail. Don't lose no more weight now."

"Thanks for your concern." He took a deep breath and chose his next words warily. "Billy, you're a good man. I hate to say this, but The Body is using you."

Billy's expression flattened. "You ought not to go there, Mr. Jameson. The Body is the Lord's church on earth like in olden days. Join us." His eyes momentarily gleamed with an eerie intensity.

Tuck's neck hairs stood at attention. Had he imagined it? "Thanks for the invite, but I'm already a Christian. Ham too."

Billy smiled, a cough drop's medicinal odor seeping between his teeth. "That's what the Evil One wants you to believe. But The Body is the only true church. It's the Lord's will none should perish but all should come to a saving knowledge of the truth."

"With all due respect, I know the Bible."

"Preacher's kids—you think you know everything." Billy wheezed and drew in a breath. "Time's running out. Especially for you."

"I don't understand what that means, and I don't care."

"You will." That weird gleam in Billy's eyes again. "Now if you gents will excuse me, I done tarried long enough." Coughing, Billy crawled under a Chevrolet pickup, snatched a Styrofoam cup crusted with hot chocolate, and stuffed it in his trash bag.

Tuck and Ham moved beyond Billy's earshot. A shudder rippled across Tuck's shoulders as he considered the grip The Body had on its followers. "You catch that? Time's running out, especially for me?"

Ham shrugged. "All the Perfects say stuff like that."

"Yeah, right." Billy had aimed his words at Tuck, but why? A veiled death threat? Something worse?

"Besides, Billy's the only Perfect on campus."

"So far."

Tuck stood beside his truck and shook his head. Should he rebuke Ham again? Probably wouldn't help. Rarely did. But despite his doubts—how he longed to make a clean break with God—he had a Christian duty to set his friend straight. "Ham, you need to stop smoking."

Ham rolled his eyes.

"You've got a family."

"I hear you. Just under a lot of stress."

"Want to talk about it after I see Clay?"

"Not today." He ran a hand over his fresh buzz cut. "Beanpole, go easy on Clay. He's your only brother."

"That's why I can't go easy on him."

"He's wrong about the Body but try to see things his way."

"I can't do that." He clenched his jaw. "No matter what it takes, Clay's going to see the light."

Tuck stole into his truck and drove clear of student pedestrians glued to their smartphones. He turned onto Highway 8 North toward Walmart. He'd scare Clay straight all right—no brother of his was going to join The Body and become a dead hero like Dad.

Chapter 2

As Tuck trod to Clay's Salvation Army station at the Walmart entrance, he rehearsed his ultimatum to his brother, who clanged the hand bell and bid passersby "Merry Christmas." Every December, Clay assisted the Salvation Army, but The Body probably disdained such service.

Upon seeing Tuck, Clay smiled, perhaps a bit too broadly.

Tuck gave him a pair of hunting gloves and a wool pullover hat. "You need these."

"Thanks, Mom."

Even though the joke wasn't that funny, Tuck chuckled to honor Clay's rare attempt at humor.

Clay sobered. "Seriously, I appreciate the cap and gloves."

"Well, we can't have you getting frostbite out here." Tuck longed to say more, but his throat tightened, and he refused to let his little brother hear his voice shake.

Clay's resemblance to Dad was scary—same stocky build and world-famous Jameson ears. He suffered the nickname "Dumbo" as a child. Any peer who'd said that in Tuck's earshot during grade school received a fist sandwich.

The Arctic wind, tinged with the sharpness of woodsmoke, whipped around Tuck, and he pulled his overcoat tighter. "Any Perfects you know of donated today?"

Clay's lip curled. "I despise that term."

"Didn't mean any offense. But isn't that what The Body claims its members can be? Perfect?"

"Not the way people think. It's a matter of biblical sanctification."

Tuck wanted to correct Clay but restrained himself. He feared his brother had changed. Clay hadn't spoken with Mom since Dad's funeral three months earlier, and he'd stopped attending choir practice.

From the parking lot, ninety-year-old Mrs. Ramona Stevens tottered up and struggled to shove a wadded bill and some loose change into the Salvation Army kettle. Garbed in a black coat, gloves, and scarf, she seemed dressed for a funeral.

"Let me help you, ma'am," Clay said.

She handed him the bill and change, and he forced the twenty into the kettle, followed by clinking coins. "Thank you so much, Clayton. Real sorry about your father. My condolences to you both."

Tuck dipped his chin, and Clay thanked her.

She smiled. "Your father died a hero. You must be very proud."

Clay nodded, but Tuck stiffened. He couldn't count the number of times he'd heard that. People didn't understand Dad had experienced a fatal heart attack because The Body had forced him to act against his will.

Refusing Clay's help, Mrs. Stevens hobbled into the store.

Tuck took a deep breath. *Showtime.* "Ham told me you plan to join The Body."

"That's right."

"Little brother, have you lost your mind?"

"I think I've found it." He folded his arms. "I need The Body."

"Why, for God's sake?"

"Because I'm scum."

Tuck rolled his eyes—not this again. Clay had never accepted that God loved him as he was.

"You don't know the thoughts I have sometimes."

"We all have those. Besides, you put up with Kenny. I'd have kicked him out weeks ago."

"I see Christ in people like Kenny."

"There you go. To quote Ham, 'you're one righteous guy.'"

Clay grinned. "Nice try. But I know the truth."

"This town needs you just the way you are."

"No, it doesn't. I can be a better Christian by joining The Body."

"Becoming a Perf didn't make Dad a better Christian. It made him a robot."

"It made him selfless."

Tuck cursed. Dad had been selfless, all right—every Arkansas TV station had shown him plowing through tornado debris in search of a buried victim until he clutched his chest and collapsed. "So, what about this initiation jazz? Just yesterday, I heard The Body is using some new technology."

Clay shook his head. "The media. Anything that smells evangelical, they label dangerous."

"Plenty of responsible news sources claim Brother Moody brainwashes his followers."

"If brainwashing means losing my free will for God's sake, so be it." Clay pointed to his chest. "The Holy Spirit has assured me joining The Body is the best thing. In time, you'll see I'm right."

Tuck's cheeks roasted, a contrast to the chill wind nipping at his ears. "Clay, how can you be so blind?"

Clay's eyes filled with apparent pity. "You need to join The Body yourself. I've been praying you would."

Tuck searched for words, found none, and stomped to his pickup. Tuck loved his little brother more than his own life—he wouldn't let The Body murder Clay like it had Dad.

He smacked the steering wheel. If only his brother, for once in his life, would listen to reason. His restrained arguments for Clay to get a Master's in Psychology had never registered either, yet his brother deserved to be more than an Assistant Public Librarian. He was too gifted to merely check out books and collect overdue fines.

Ham's words about easing up on Clay pricked Tuck's conscience. He'd been pretty rough on his brother. Only one thing to do.

Tuck trod to the Salvation Army station, but Clay was MIA—maybe he'd gone into Walmart to use the restroom. Tuck pulled five twenties from his wallet and waited. He considered putting a note with the bills, but he changed his mind and shoved them into the kettle. He could text Clay an apology later.

As Tuck drove back to the ARV campus, he tuned into Dr. Marv Gillespie's most recent podcast about The Body:

"The cult's infomercials on Arkansas TV have lured many, including folks who consider themselves Christians, into making appointments with Body counselors. Winkdale now has ten house temples where Body adherents meet and strategize about evangelizing door to door. Shades of Jehovah's Witnesses.

"On Sundays, cult members who are able drive to The Temple in Northwest Arkansas, about a hundred miles north from our fair hamlet of Winkdale. The Temple can hold thousands, but an anonymous source tells me that while it's still mostly empty, it has started filling up. The Body is using social media so skillfully that—"

Tuck switched off the podcast. The Body was growing like a cancer every day, and Clay would soon be a part of it, unless…

Brother Eli popped into Tuck's head. Clay revered Eli as a pastor and an outspoken champion for the poor, and he would no doubt take the reverend's advice. Despite its small size, Winkdale had other ministers, but Clay had never warmed to them.

Unfortunately, Tuck and Eli hadn't parted on the best of terms. They'd argued before Tuck left the church, but though Eli ruled his congregation like a despot, he loved them. More importantly, he valued Clay. That meant after work, Tuck had to chuck his pride and make nice with Eli. Oh, the things big brothers did for their siblings.

Chapter 3

D r. Van Pritchard, ARV's Vice President of Student Affairs, glared at Tuck. "Jameson, you're late."

Tuck rubbed the back of his neck. "My apologies, sir." The old warhorse was sure to bring up Brother Moody's presentation at the college tomorrow night, even though many professors objected to it since ARV was a state institution and not a private Christian school.

Dr. Pritchard tramped before his expensive oak desk. His brushed silver hair made him look grandfatherly, an image he courted for parents and alumni. "Got something important to tell you."

Tuck braced himself.

"Out of deference to your father's passing, I'm relieving you from helping with Brother Moody's presentation tomorrow."

Something was up—compassion wasn't Dr. Pritchard's style. "I appreciate your thoughtfulness."

"I am also forbidding you from attending. And don't cross your arms at me. I'm afraid you'd say something regrettable."

If he only knew. "Sir, I have a couple of questions for Brother Moody."

"Well, you'll just have to keep them to yourself, won't you?" Dr. Pritchard pulled a bourbon bottle from his desk and poured a drink. "I'd offer you a shot, but I know better.

Wouldn't even drink with us at deer camp."

Tuck ignored the taunt. "Sir, I don't believe you can bar me from attending Brother Moody's presentation."

"No, but I can sure as blazes fire you." Dr. Pritchard's smile widened to unsettling proportions. "If you bring up this conversation, I'll play dumb. I'll have Coach Phillips say he was here, that I never said a word about giving you a pink slip."

"Brother Moody is a menace, sir. Not just to Arkansas, but possibly the entire country."

Dr. Pritchard laughed and slapped Tuck's back. "Jameson, you're a hoot. Brother Moody, a menace to this country? That's melodramatic even for you."

"May I remind you, sir, my father is dead because of Brother Moody."

"That's not how my favorite op-eds see it."

"With all due respect—"

"Don't want to hear it. Brother Moody's been good for Arkansas. How can a bleeding heart like you argue against that?"

"I argue against anybody who brainwashes people."

Dr. Pritchard poured another drink and knocked it back. "Some people never learn." He pointed at Tuck. "Better watch your step tomorrow. As for today, recant your social media and newspaper accusations against The Body."

"Sir, I respect you as my superior. But you don't have the right to restrict my free speech."

"Who said anything about restricting anybody's free speech?" Dr. Pritchard moved so close his bourbon breath fouled the air. "I'm saying if you go to Brother Moody's presentation and make waves, you're toast." Dr. Pritchard brushed Tuck away. "Out of my office."

Tuck left. He ignored his smiling colleagues in the hall. He even sailed past his administrative assistant's desk without a word.

In his office, Tuck gazed at his Master of Education

diploma on the wall and felt the old fire to be ARV's next Dean of Students. Prestige with a capital "P"—"*Ladies and gentlemen, may I introduce Dean Jameson*"—plus a chance to make a bigger difference in students' lives. Even though Tuck didn't yet have his doctorate, the president had implied he would promote Tuck when the dean retired, and that had been Tuck's dream job for a decade. Plenty of Tuck's colleagues championed him to be the next dean as well. But Tuck's aspiration was toast if Dr. Pritchard fired him.

He checked his personal email—as usual, dozens of responses to his series of *Arkansas at Large* articles in which he accused The Body of brainwashing followers and sending Dad to an early grave. In addition, he included anecdotes attributed to anonymous sources that detailed the unexplained disappearances of certain Good Sams—The Body's term for its members. Despite circumstantial evidence and the suspicions of missing persons' relatives, Arkansas law enforcement had taken a hands-off approach.

Of course, Dr. Prichard and ARV wanted to keep Tuck away from Brother Moody's presentation tomorrow because alumni like T.J. LeMay were major Brother Moody supporters. ARV feared Tuck would embarrass the school with his accusations and questions, no doubt infuriating LeMay, the school's biggest donor, who had already protested Tuck's *Arkansas At Large* articles. Arkansas' major TV stations planned to report on tomorrow night's presentation, and Dr. Pritchard wouldn't countenance Tuck venting his spleen before the cameras.

Tuck rubbed his eyes. What to do? He had no alternate career plans if he lost his ARV job. Oh, sure, he could find another job, but he had rooted his career trajectory here. He also mentored several on-campus students, and he couldn't desert them. Besides, if he got canned, who would run the Tutoring Center, Early Warning, Academic Coaching?

Someone knocked. Great—just what Tuck needed.

Dr. Marv Gillespie ducked his head under the top doorframe, and Tuck's irritation faded. Seeing an old friend in times like these wrapped a smile around his face. As usual, the journalism professor sported a three-piece suit, today spiced by a blue bow tie. Despite ARV's policy of diversity, only four African Americans numbered among ARV's faculty—three women and one man, Marv. "Tuck, you don't look good. Bad day?"

Tuck smiled. "You could say that. How's The Body article coming?"

"Swimmingly. Making me more certain than ever that I'm right to be an atheist. I've even lined up an interview with Maurice."

"The Anti-Body leader?"

"The same. Might even tell me his real name. Then only one interview left—yours."

"Sorry." Marv had requested the interview months ago after Dad had become a Perf. "The Body is still a sensitive topic for me. Today it got worse." Tuck told Marv about Clay's plans to join The Body.

Marv tapped his chin, his tasteful cologne seasoning the air. "Most unfortunate."

"Dr. Pritchard told me to steer clear of Brother Moody's presentation, and to stop my one-man Arkansas media war against The Body."

"If I know you, you plan to ignore our fearless leader."

"Actually, I haven't decided."

Marv cocked his head. "Maybe I don't know you as well as I think."

"I assume you will be attending."

"Wouldn't miss it for a promotion to department dean. Brother Moody has denied my many requests for an interview. Ditto his administrators, and even most Good Sams out in the trenches." Marv arched an eyebrow. "But tomorrow night, I draw blood."

"I might join you." Tuck smiled.

"Fine, but I will be asking my questions first." Marv said it as a declaration, not a request.

Tuck inwardly sighed—once Marv had made up his mind, he had made up his mind.

"Besides," Marv continued, "my questions will make the perfect calm before the whirlwind your questions unleash."

"You seem convinced I'm going to buck Dr. Pritchard."

"Oh, but you must—I'm not ready for the world to end."

Marv left, leaving Tuck to ponder his dilemma.

Career mattered, but family mattered more. As for ARV's students, they had other mentors, such as Ham. Speaking of which, Tuck wished Ham wasn't going to Conway tomorrow night to give that campus discipline presentation—he could use Ham's support.

Should he tell Mom about Clay's plans? Not yet. He'd wait to see what happened at The Body's presentation tomorrow. Fortunately, Mom was staying with her sister in Little Rock a hundred miles away, so shouldn't hear anything for a while.

Tuck picked up Clay's graduation picture and examined it as though it were a jury summons. He, Dad, and Clay were all smiles, Dad's arms atypically draped over Tuck's and Clay's shoulders. Mom had snapped the photo. What a happy day that was. But Tuck stained it by insisting Clay should go for his Master's. The hurt in Clay's eyes—Tuck had never forgotten it, and never would. Now his brother was headed to the same spiritual slaughterhouse that had claimed Dad.

Tuck resolved to fight for his brother's soul—after all, God wouldn't.

Chapter 4

After a short drive, Tuck knocked on Brother Eli's front door, greeted by the acerbic pastor's frown. "Oh. You."

Tuck said, "Look, I regret we ended things badly." He hoped his face displayed a sincerity he didn't feel.

Resembling a balding, overgrown teddy bear, Eli drummed his fingers against his stubbled cheek. "As I recall, I am an egomaniacal pastor lording it over his flock."

Who quashes honest dissent with a heavy hand, Tuck wanted to add. "I spoke out of turn."

"I didn't think that was possible for you."

Eli wasn't making this easy. If not for the fact Clay respected this guy, Tuck would leave post-haste. But he knew Brother Eli wasn't brusque with everyone—just troublemakers like Tuck who disagreed with his vision of church government. "Look, I apologize. It shouldn't be up to me how you choose elders."

"Can I get that in writing? I'd like to have it notarized. Maybe even bronzed."

Tuck internally held his nose. "Anything if you'll help Clay."

Eli's brow furrowed. "What's up with the Clayster?"

"It concerns The Body. What's your take on Brother Moody's sect?"

Eli smiled. "Hey, I'm always game to diss Bro Moody.

And the Clayster's my favorite congregant. In case you missed it, that's permission to come on in."

Eli waved Tuck into the den. The chaotic ambience didn't surprise Tuck—the odor of burned toast filled the air, a slice of which set half-eaten on a supper tray balanced precariously on a coffee table.

"Excuse the mess," Eli said as he plopped on the couch, a newspaper crunching under him.

Tuck set his jaw. It was now or never. "Clay plans to join The Body."

Tuck expected the news would rock Eli's world, but the preacher casually arched an eyebrow. "Sorry to pop your bubble, but I already knew. Clay and I talked last night."

Though unsurprised, Tuck disliked the idea of his brother confiding in Eli. "You try to talk him out of it?"

"You know I can't tell you that."

Fine. He would play another angle. "Folks in your congregation considering joining The Body?"

"'Fraid so, despite the iron fist you say I rule them with. They've seen the videos on TV, think The Body is Habitat for Humanity on steroids. Brother Moody says all other churches are apostate, making The Body de rigueur for 'real' Christians."

"Your congregants don't worry about The Body's theology?"

"Despite my best efforts to educate them, my sheep consider theology a four-letter word. No surprise. Our society has become dazzled by the superficial, not bothering to examine what festers underneath."

Tuck popped a breath mint in his mouth. "So, you think the Body's claimed lock on salvation cons even churchgoers to join?"

"Yes. It also appeals to unchurched believers. You know how Bro Moody uses your own father's passing as a selling point. Clay's fine with that, even proud Bro Moody holds up y'all's daddy as an example to emulate."

How Clay could believe such things frustrated Tuck. He crunched his breath mint, flooding his mouth with wintergreen. "If you didn't try to talk Clay out of joining The Body already, would you do so now?"

"Sorry, no."

"You just said Brother Moody is a phony."

"He is. But I won't interfere in Clay's decision."

"You've run people like me out of your church for disagreeing on minor points of doctrine. But you'll let Clay go just like that?" Tuck snapped his fingers.

Eli leaned forward, and the couch squeaked. "You don't understand. Criticizing The Body in public can be hazardous to a Southern preacher's health."

Tuck grew chilled, as though a shadow had blocked the sun. "What are you talking about?"

"Can I confide in you, Mr. Jameson?"

In the past, before their falling out, Eli had confided a couple of personal matters to Tuck, and he had never shared them. Sounded like Eli wanted to reveal something he felt he couldn't disclose to any of his congregants, even the elders. "You can."

Eli interlocked his fingers. "Last Sunday, I broke a long-standing tradition I've held for years—during my sermon, I criticized a minister and denomination by name."

"Brother Moody and The Body?"

"Give that man a Klondike bar. Some said they enjoyed hearing me take a stand. Some dissed me. Then there was the next morning…"

The shadow over the sun deepened. "What happened?"

Eli's voice grew hushed, as though the walls could hear. "My tires had been slashed. A message spray-painted on the door said, 'Mock a man of God and you will suffer John the Baptist's fate.' I've always wanted to get ahead in life, but not that way."

"Why didn't I read about this in the Winkdale paper?"

"Because the editor's a Perfect."

Goosebumps broke out over Tuck's arms. If The Body owned Winkdale's press, what was next?

Despite his animosity toward Eli, he sympathized with the man's fear—but he didn't hesitate to use that fear to go for Eli's jugular. "You won't help me change Clay's mind because you're a coward."

"Mr. Jameson, I have a family, something a divorced man like you knows nothing about. I can't take chances."

"Then who can?"

"Looked in the mirror lately?"

"Clay won't listen to me."

"Probably wouldn't pay me any mind either."

Tuck's cheeks burned, his hands clenching into fists. "Don't you realize Clay's soul is at stake?"

Eli's face crumpled in sad resignation. "I don't like the Clayster defecting to the Dark Side any more than you do. But my wife and son trump your baby bro."

"You think Brother Moody might resort to violence?"

"Or worse."

"Like what?"

"Brainwashing."

"You assume that's what The Body is doing?"

"Is there any doubt?" Eli chuckled, but a shudder gave away his unease. "Hey, I'm just a backwater Southern preacher minding what's left of his flock."

Desperation washed Tuck's hubris aside. He considered dropping to his knees and clasping his hands. "Clay worships you, Brother Eli. Talk to him."

"I can't."

"Please." Tuck clutched Eli's arm.

Eli rocketed to his feet, the dinner tray clattering from the coffee table. "Got to get this place cleaned up. Wife gets home in ten minutes. She'll clobber me if she sees this mess."

A weight settled over Tuck as he pulled out of Eli's drive. He felt a new sympathy for the pastor. The vandalism

Eli described shocked him—it clashed with the peaceful actions of the Perfs whom Tuck had seen. Could the vandals be Brother Moody sympathizers who weren't yet Perfs? Or were they something altogether different?

Tuck's phone chimed—April was waiting for him at Pizza Palace. Oh, man, he was late for their dinner date. Hopefully, she wouldn't mind… much.

If Eli wouldn't talk sense into his brother, what about Clay's roommate Kenny? No—he was less trustworthy than a redneck lawyer.

Clay's fellow choir members? No. They weren't close.

What about April? Everyone respected her, Clay included. She'd won Best Teacher at Winkdale High two years in a row and volunteered tutoring time at ARV three days a week. Besides all that, Tuck suspected Clay had a crush on her.

Trouble was, so did Tuck. But she was engaged to David Freeman. Too often, Tuck wished she would break it off. In his worst moments, he even hoped something might happen to David.

Chapter 5

Intent on a successful mission, Tuck sprang from his truck in the Pizza Palace parking lot. After talking to Eli, Tuck's concern for Clay had escalated. But April had always been an excellent confidant, and in his dreams, more.

April waited at the Pizza Palace door. Despite her frown, she looked alluring as the wind whipped her honey blond hair across her face. It wasn't as though she'd aged well since high school—it was as though she hadn't aged at all.

"You're late," April said.

Tuck raised his hands as he stepped over a crumpled Coke cup. "*Mea culpa.*"

"What took you so long?"

"Secret mission."

"Yeah? Did it have anything to do with you becoming dean of students next year?"

"Hey, that's not a sure thing."

"Not what I've heard." She grinned slyly. "I've got my sources, you know."

Before Tuck could reply, Kaleb Olson, Winkdale's answer to Sasquatch, dashed before the restaurant door and towered over him and April. "Have you seen the light?"

Tuck scowled, but April said, "Kaleb, Tuck and I are Christians."

"Are you?" he said. "Real Christians join Brother Moody's Church of The Body of Jesus Christ on Earth. All other churches are apostate."

"No offense," Tuck said, "but I'm hungry enough to eat a Clydesdale. Please let us pass so we can enjoy our dinner in peace."

"Peace." Kaleb's smile twisted. "The days of peace in this state, in this world are numbered, my friend."

"Last time, Kaleb. Please."

Kaleb stepped aside; his eyes were enigmatic.

Inside, the garlic aroma overpowered Tuck, provoking treasured memories. Same red booths, same frayed tablecloths, same nicked-up buffet bar. But the nostalgia couldn't smother his still boiling blood.

April shook her head as Tuck marched to the cash register where Vinnie Spinelli, Pizza Palace's manager for fifteen years, smiled beneath his handlebar mustache. "How can I help the two of you this wonderful December evening?"

Tuck said, "By telling Kaleb to knock off his evangelizing routine."

Vinnie looked wounded. "Sorry, Mr. Jameson. Me, I figure all paths lead to God. But what can I say about Kaleb? He's my cousin."

"Yes, I—"

"He stayed up all night helping us pack. We're moving up by Cove Lake."

"Good for you, but—"

"I got a bad back, you know." Vinnie leaned over and put a hand on his lower spine.

"Yes, I know that too." Everyone knew—Vinnie's bad back was legendary throughout the county.

"Kaleb hasn't slept for over twenty-four hours, and he paid the tab of everyone who ate lunch today. He only asked one thing in exchange."

"Don't tell me—the right to hector customers about becoming a Perf."

"Well, I wouldn't put it that way, Mr. Jameson, but yes,

the right to express his religious beliefs."

Tuck told Vinnie what Kaleb could do with his religious beliefs.

"Tuck," April said. "What's gotten into you?"

Shame washed across Tuck in a scalding wave, and he hung his head. "I apologize, Vinnie. I had no call to say that."

"Happens to the best of us," Vinnie said, smiling as he pulled on his mustache. "Just to show there's no hard feelings, you and Ms. Showers eat free off the buffet—it's on the house."

Tuck shook his head. "Can't let you do that. Not after what I said."

"But I *want* to, Mr. Jameson!"

"Vinnie," April said, smiling, "we thank you for your generosity. We'll leave an extra-large tip."

The various castle paintings that adorned the walls usually wowed Tuck. Some of the palaces were real, such as the Dromborg Castle in Northwest Arkansas, but most were fantasy—King Arthur's Camelot, *The Lord of the Rings'* Minas Tirith, *The Chronicle of Narnia*'s Anvard. Local artist Dwight Seals had painted them, and he'd done a fine job. Evocative as they were, they failed to quench Tuck's agitation.

At April's urging, to which Tuck grunted, the two of them helped themselves to the buffet. April uncharacteristically piled her plate with pizza. Tuck stuck to one piece of Canadian bacon with a dollop of coleslaw.

They sat in a booth lit by an aromatic candle, and April sighed. "That was embarrassing, Tuck. Kaleb is a lamb—a little overbearing sometimes—but there was no reason to complain to Vinnie about him."

Tuck took a bite of coleslaw. "I was within my rights to criticize Kaleb. This whole Perf thing is getting out of hand. Next, they'll be selling their heresy like Girl Scout cookies."

"You sure it's heresy?"

Tuck stopped in mid-chew, the slaw losing its tang.

"Don't tell me you're thinking about becoming a Perf yourself?"

"No. But David joined The Body last week."

Tuck dropped his fork. "You're kidding."

"I wish." April crunched into a pizza slice. "I suspected David had leanings in that direction. He considered being a youth minister once. He's also very civic-minded."

"As every up-and-coming bank president should be," Tuck said.

April smiled. "Do I detect sarcasm?"

"Me? Not on your life. David's a good guy." *But not good enough.* Tuck hoped he'd hidden his actual feelings. If she married David, Tuck would lose another chance with her forever.

April said, "Since becoming a Good Sam, he's changed. Before we marry, he insists I become a Good Sam too."

Tuck's fears ramped to red alert—April a Perf? "How do you feel about that?"

April picked up a piece of pepperoni pizza, and as though being forced, crunched into it. "I'm not sure."

"Do you still have feelings for David?"

"Yes." She dropped her pizza. "Oh, I don't know. It's all so confusing. He's no longer himself." She frowned. "He's acting like a Pod Person."

Tuck nodded. She was referring to *Invasion of the Body Snatchers*, for in high school, she'd shared her love of old movies with Tuck, and *Body Snatchers* was one of her favorites. "I'm sorry you're going through this."

"Don't be. Mom and Dad think David hung the moon. They'd be beside themselves if I broke off the engagement. Mom says he's a good catch."

"When your mom thinks of marriage, she sees dollar signs."

"I know, I know. Breaking off my engagement to Mel almost killed her."

"I think it was the best thing for you."

April stopped chewing. "Was it? Wish I knew what was best for me."

Tuck thought he knew the answer, and it wasn't David. He gulped his tea, finding it bitter. "So, if you marry David, would you keep teaching?"

"David wants me to be a stay-at-home housewife. Wants kids as soon as possible." Passion filled her eyes. "But Tuck, I love teaching more than anything in the world. I'd hate never seeing students again."

"Sounds like you're building a case against David."

April shrugged. "Maybe. I plan to talk to my pastor about it sometime. I'm not sure who I can trust."

"Hard Truths 101—you can only trust yourself. June taught me that. So did Dad in his own way." And God most certainly had.

"Tuck, I wish things between you and June had worked out. But I don't share your cynicism." Her eyes misted. "It's sad to see your faith slipping away."

"Reality has opened my eyes, that's all. Guess you could say I've become a deist, like some of the founding fathers." He enjoyed his salty bite of Canadian bacon pizza. "That puts me in good company."

"That puts you in mistaken company. God doesn't take a hands-off approach to the world."

"No? Sure would explain the bulk of human history."

"You need to go back to church."

Tuck snickered. "Uh-huh. Or else what? 1 go to hell?"

"Of course not." April frowned. "Why do you say things like that?"

"Look, April, you're an amazing… you're great. But after all that's happened, I'm not sure I'll ever return to church."

April turned her blue eyes full force on Tuck. Her face burst into that wonderful smile that had sent dozens of male hearts fluttering back in high school, Tuck's chief among them. "Can I help?"

Tuck grinned. "Funny you should ask." He told her about Clay's plans to join The Body. "Clay is my only brother, April. I can't stand the thought of him being brainwashed the way Dad was."

"I understand."

Tuck studied his plate. "Besides, I owe Clay. I let him down once. Bad."

"What happened?"

"Not sure I should say." Tuck took a bite and chewed.

"Give me a hint—when did it happen?"

"Years ago." He struggled to swallow. "Which is why it probably doesn't matter anymore."

"It matters. Out with it."

"Okay, okay. I was thirteen, Clay about ten, when we lived in Pottsville. There was this neighborhood bully, Mason Lee, always messing with Clay. I'd tell Mason to lay off. That seemed to work."

"Doesn't sound so bad to me."

"I haven't got to the bad part. Anyway, that summer Clay believed he'd gotten 'slain in the Spirit,' so he was determined to save Mason's soul. He planned to witness to him on a certain afternoon—can't remember what day it was—and I'd decided I would be there to keep Mason in line."

"Were you?"

Tuck winced. "No. See, some of the older guys at school asked me to go with them to a Garth Brooks' concert—one of 'em had gotten sick, so he gave me his ticket, and his big brother was gonna drive us. At least, I think it was his big brother."

"Where were your parents during all this?"

"Out of town. By the time they got home, I was long gone. Anyway, before I left—and I'll never forget this— Clay said, 'You may never see me again.' I said something like, 'Yeah, whatever.' I still remember Clay looking dejected as we drove off."

"Did Clay witness to Mason?"

"I'm getting there. When I got back from the concert, Clay was in the hospital. Dad told me Clay had witnessed to Mason, and Mason had beat him so bad he broke some of Clay's ribs. Clay even almost lost an eye."

April gasped. "How awful."

"Dad chewed me out good."

"But Clay didn't lose his eye."

"No. When I saw Clay, he looked terrible, his eye all taped up. I thought he'd be mad. He wasn't. Said maybe he couldn't hit a home run in P.E., but he sure had belted it out of the park for Jesus Christ."

April wiped her eyes. "But Clay obviously recovered."

Tuck hunched over his plate. "Yeah. Through no help from me."

"We all make mistakes. And it sounds like Clay forgave you."

"He did, but that's just Clay. He'd forgive somebody if they ran over him with a steam roller." April's image blurred. "He could've gone blind in one eye."

"You were only a kid."

Tuck shook his head. "Dad taught us nothing excuses letting family down. That's why I can't let The Body take Clay."

April dipped her chin. "I understand." She ventured a troubled smile. "Other than you, has anyone else talked to him?"

"I tried to get Brother Eli to, but he said, 'no way.' Thinks Clay has his own free will and should make his own decisions. Also "

"Also what?"

"Clay hasn't thought this through." He gritted his teeth. "I've got to make him see Brother Moody as the phony he is."

"How?"

Tuck told April about his plans to ask Brother Moody

hard questions during tomorrow's presentation that would show what a fake the man was.

April shook her head and locked her hands. "That's taking a big chance. There's got to be another way." Her look brightened. "Has your mom talked to him?"

"Haven't told her yet. Anyway, I doubt Clay would listen to her." Tuck smiled. "Of course, he might listen to you."

April blushed. "Me?"

"He respects you."

"I respect him, too. But he seems to have a crush on me. It wouldn't be right to weaponize those feelings to change his mind."

"So, it would be better for Clay to wind up dead like Dad?"

April winced. "That's not fair."

As though he'd never heard a discouraging word, David Freeman strode up to their booth out of nowhere and saluted Tuck. "Hey, April, Tuck."

As usual, David looked as though he'd just stepped off the cover of *GQ*, his tailored suit form-fitting, his Windsor-knotted tie flawless—his cologne overpowering. With a flourish, David set iced tea before Tuck and April. "I saw when I came in you both needed refills. Thought I'd save the waitress some time."

"That's my David," April said, shaking Sweet 'N Low into her tea. "No one has more of a servant's heart."

"Also," David said, handing April a stack of napkins, "like we've talked about, please remember the body is the temple of the Holy Spirit. Therefore, please refrain from using sugar substitute in the future."

She arched an eyebrow.

David turned to Tuck. "I understand your brother Clay will join The Body soon. That should please you."

Tuck shrugged.

David smiled. "Perhaps soon you'll join us too. Perhaps soon, everyone will! Now, if you'll excuse me, I've got a

Good Sam prayer meeting in fifteen minutes." He pecked April on the cheek, gave Tuck a quick salute, and dashed from the premises.

Tuck shook his head. "Can you believe that guy? 'Perhaps soon you'll join us? Perhaps soon everyone will?' Sounds like a threat."

"Yeah, like 'Tomorrow Belongs to Me' from *Cabaret*."

"Another of your old movies?"

April nodded. "Released in 1972, nominated for Best Picture. Took place in 1930s Germany."

"Bad days."

"Yeah, but you can't compare Nazis to Good Sams."

"Can't you? Is David always this wacko anymore?"

April sighed. "I'm afraid so. He wasn't like this before."

Tuck wanted to reach across the table and take April's hand, but he knew it would be inappropriate.

His phone pinged. He read a text from Clay: "*See u in a week.*"

Tuck texted back: "*Where you going?*"

"*Can't tell u. Next time u see me I'll be a nu man.*"

"*The old man is fine.*"

"*U won't even know me.*"

"*Don't do this. I mean it.*"

Text silence for five seconds. Ten. More.

April's brow furrowed. "What is it, Tuck?"

Having lost his appetite, the leftover residue of David's cologne nauseating, Tuck rose. "It's Clay. Gotta run. I'll be in touch."

As he left, Tuck thought he heard April say, "Promise?"

Chapter 6

Tuck rushed from the Pizza Palace to Clay's first-floor apartment. Clay's car—gone. No surprise. Kenny Rhodes, Clay's shiftless roommate, might be home, and Kenny probably knew where Clay had bolted. Clay shared everything with Kenny.

Tuck knocked. "Kenny? You in there? This is Tuck Jameson."

No reply.

Tuck pounded on the door and yelled for Kenny to open up. Still no response.

A bald thirtysomething guy from the apartment next door stuck his head out. "Dude, hold it down! My kid's trying to sleep in here."

"Sorry," Tuck said. "You seen Kenny tonight?"

Bald Guy shook his head.

"How about Clay?"

"Left about fifteen minutes ago."

"He say where he was headed?"

"Didn't ask. But he seemed in a good mood. He was whistling."

"Thanks for your help. Sorry again about the racket."

"Yeah, yeah."

Tuck turned his back, and Bald Guy yelled. "Hey, dude," he said. "I forgot Kenny got a job with Aim yesterday."

"The one in Jonesburg?"

Bald Guy nodded.

Tuck climbed into his truck and sped to the interstate. Hard to believe Kenny had yet another job—at least six weeks had passed since his last one. Perhaps Clay had insisted on it? Nah, Clay was a Teddy Bear with slackers like Kenny. Though Tuck lectured Clay about being a soft-touch, his little bro's kindness was one of his most endearing traits. But kindness be cursed, Tuck would force Kenny to tell him where Clay had fled.

Aim's parking lot was, as usual, full. Not even Walmart could match their prices. Of course, the rumor was that founder and head T.J. LeMay was hiring mostly Perfs for his Arkansas stores. The Arkansas press op-eds had criticized him, but LeMay denied the accusations, bolstered by the testimonials of plenty of non-Body Aim employees. No one could find hard evidence. But Tuck had heard two major national TV networks were preparing pieces on LeMay and Aim's connection to The Body in Arkansas.

His stomach churning, Tuck took a deep breath and entered the store. Aim's maddening jingle assaulted him:

"At Aim, we aim to please.

Oh yes, indeed.

We're on our knees

To serve your needs."

An Aim greeter touched Tuck's arm. Smelling of lavender soap, she resembled a grandmother from an old movie. In fact, Tuck expected her to offer him a slice of apple pie.

"Good evening, good sir," she said, sincerity dripping from every word. "Beautiful weather we're having, isn't it?"

Tuck forced a smile. "The best."

"Can we help you find anything this fine December night?"

"Yes, ma'am, you can." Tuck explained he was looking for Kenny.

The greeter tapped her double chin. "Kenny Rhodes.

Hmm, name doesn't ring a bell. But sounds like a fine Arkansas gentleman." She touched Tuck's arm. "Let's call Mr. Draper up here, shall we?"

While she called, someone tapped Tuck's shoulder. He turned, and a gap-toothed male stocker with a clipboard greeted him. "How are you this glorious evening, good sir?"

"Fine."

He held the clipboard out to Tuck. "Care to sign our petition?"

"What's it for?"

Gap-Tooth recoiled. "For Aim associates like me to work longer hours with less pay, of course."

Tuck wanted to laugh, but he knew the guy—an obvious Perf if there ever was one—was serious as a graveside service. "Why would you want to work more for less money?"

"Because Mr. LeMay deserves our devotion." He grinned. "It's in the New Testament."

A stone sunk in Tuck's stomach. He wanted to grab the guy and shake some genuine Christianity into him. He'd read about Aim's Arkansas productivity soaring in the past couple of months—rumor had it Aim's Perf employees skipped breaks to work more. Now this. "Did Brother Moody put you up to this?"

Gap-tooth shook his head. "Of course not, sir. We love Elder Moody."

That was the saddest statement Tuck had heard in days.

"Will you sign my petition, sir?"

Tuck smiled. "Sorry. No."

"Fine and dandy. Have a wonderful evening, sir." The Perf stopped another customer and gave her the same spiel.

Mr. Draper finally appeared, sporting a full-toothed smile and a Johnny Cash Pompadour. His breath reeked of stale coffee. "I hear you're looking for Kenny Rhodes."

"That's right."

"Sorry, but he didn't clock in tonight."

Tuck sighed. "Why aren't I surprised?"

"This means we will have to let him go, I'm afraid. He who does not work will not eat." Mr. Draper crossed his arms. "He said he was one of us, but he isn't." The store manager's eyes gleamed. "You aren't either, are you, good sir?"

Tuck's arms tingled. "Thanks for your help."

Once back in his truck, Mr. Draper's eyes haunted Tuck—they were like Billy Wilson's eyes this morning. A chill shimmered across Tuck's shoulders. Maybe the sages were right. Perhaps there were worse things than death.

Tuck shook his head. No. Fear wouldn't conquer him. He had a job to do, perhaps the most important job of his life—find Clay. Imagining Clay morphing into a soulless Perf made him want to rail at the night.

Back on the interstate, Tuck recalled Clay saying Kenny often spent Thursday nights with relatives on Raven Mountain playing cards till dawn. But Tuck was no fool— Kenny and his clan probably gathered to smoke pot or, worse, abuse meth.

Tuck didn't know where on Raven Mountain Kenny's kin hung out. Also, Kenny only used tracfones, and Tuck didn't have Kenny's number. Looked as though he was out of luck. He could try the landline through the night, however.

He did, sleeping fitfully, and likewise continued to text Clay.

No luck.

Where might Clay have driven? Could be anywhere, maybe even The Body's Temple, a hundred miles away. But that would be too obvious.

Might be in a motel. But which one? Even if Tuck called every motel in a hundred-mile radius, Clay had probably given a fake name.

Clay might stay with a Perf, for in the past couple of months, they'd been springing up around Arkansas like opportunists after a weather disaster.

As five a.m. rolled around, Tuck yawned and hoped to get at least an hour's sleep before work.

He needed assistance to find Clay. But he wasn't ready to pray, although heaven help him, he might succumb to groveling again before this was over.

Chapter 7

At 7:30 a.m., Tuck shuffled into the Student Success suite of the Weaver Student Services Building, dreading what the day might bring.

Ms. Teas said, "Got something weird for you."

The envelope read *Mr. Jameson,* and someone had cut out and pasted each letter. A strip of Scotch tape sealed the envelope.

Tuck rubbed his sleep-crusted eyes. "This your idea of a joke, Ms. Teas?"

"No, sir. My idea of a joke is my monthly paycheck."

"Where'd this come from?"

"My paycheck or the envelope?"

"Very funny. The envelope."

Ms. Teas shrugged. "Don't know. It was on the counter when I got here."

Tuck ran his fingers over the envelope's letters, some glossy smooth, some newsprint rough. "Interesting."

"Aren't you going to open it?"

"Not out here."

Mrs. Teas nodded.

Once inside his office, Tuck noted no evidence of powder or oily substances on the envelope. That meant it probably didn't contain any toxic material. It had no postmark. He turned the envelope upside down and shook it. Nothing spilled from the partially Scotch-taped seal, which meant the letter's contents were neither anthrax nor drugs. The letter had likely come from someone on campus—it was probably safe. Plus, Tuck was in his office, away from other colleagues.

Tuck breathed in deeply and cut open the envelope. A folded sheet of paper fell out on which a hand-written scrawl read, *If you know what's good for you, don't attend Brother Moody's presentation tonight.* Tuck's hands iced over.

Somebody's idea of a sick joke? He willed his hands to warm up, a suggestion they ignored, and considered calling Dr. Pritchard. No. Given their last conversation, Tuck wasn't sure how the old warhorse might react.

Instead, Tuck called ARV Chief of Police Valerie Kwan, who arrived in minutes. Trim and fit, Chief Kwan looked custom-made for her police uniform, and though she was of average height, Tuck wouldn't want to tangle with her. Recently, she had flattened her male colleagues in a good-natured hand-to-hand combat tournament to benefit Angel Tree. Her presence reassured Tuck, an effect he'd noticed she had on most of his co-workers.

She donned gloves and examined the envelope and its letter. Tuck hoped she would declare it an obvious fraud, or recognize the childish scrawl and track down the perpetrator. Instead, she said, "Interesting." She looked at him hard. "First time you've gotten such a message?"

"Yes. Here on campus. Of course, I've received lots of emails wishing me the worst."

"How long has that been going on?"

"Two or three weeks." He sighed. "Guess I should have told you. I wasn't thinking."

"That happens when you don't get any sleep."

"Do I look that bad?"

"Worse."

Her grim face told Tuck she wasn't joking.

"You're a good man who's been under a lot of stress. That can impair judgment."

Tuck's contrition tightened its grip. "Chief Kwan, I sincerely apologize."

"No worries. But if you get another letter like this, please let me know ASAP. Okay?"

"Absolutely. I realize my prints are all over the envelope and letter, but could it be fingerprinted?"

"Yes. We'd need to fingerprint you to eliminate your prints, unless your prints are on file."

She was probably referring to the night he'd gotten drunk after Dad's death and had started a fight at Freeman's Sports Bar. "They did throw out the charges. Does that mean my prints won't be on record?"

"They should still be available." She frowned. "This letter could be a bad practical joke."

"Don't think so. Not even Ham would be clueless enough to pull something like this."

Chief Kwan tapped her chin. "Maybe not. But you and I both know Brother Moody's presentation tonight has stirred up controversy. I heard through the grapevine Dr. Pritchard doesn't want you to go."

Tuck's ears pricked up. "How do you know that?"

"Ms. Ayles told me."

Dr. Pritchard's administrative assistant? "How did she know?"

"She heard raised voices yesterday and put her ear to Dr. P's door. Says he threatened you."

"Are you implying this letter might be from Dr. Pritchard?"

Chief Kwan shook her head. "Doubtful. But I'm sure you're aware of the student newspaper's op-ed that Brother Moody is good for Arkansas. The article specifically criticized you."

"I know."

Chief Kwan's tone softened. "Everybody knows what happened to your father and how you feel about it. So, it's possible a student left the letter for you."

"But how did they get to Ms. Teas's desk before she got here?"

"Maybe one of your co-worker early birds unlocked the suite before Ms. Teas arrived."

"Yeah, maybe."

"Getting back to Dr. Pritchard, did you tell him about this letter?"

Defiance welled within Tuck despite his best efforts to push it down. "No."

"I know it's crazy, but it's his policy that any threat to Student Services staff should go through him before I enter the picture. I'm afraid I will have to report it to him."

"Should I tell him instead of you?"

Chief Kwan raised an eyebrow. "I'll assure Dr. Pritchard you were concerned for the students' and your coworkers' safety, and that's why you called me right away."

Tuck ratcheted his self-righteousness down a notch. "I'd appreciate that."

"Bottom line—I don't think you have anything to worry about tonight. Public Safety will be out in full force. Bags or purses will be barred from the coliseum."

"Thank you, Chief Kwan."

She rolled her eyes. "You're too button-down to do so, but like I've told you before, call me Val."

"I call you Chief because you're the best one we've ever had."

She smiled. "Thank you."

Though anxiety vexed him with frequent jabs, Tuck attacked the day's tasks with grit—offering guidance to a frustrated tutor; counseling a student trying to decide on a major; handling a faculty mentor's concern about a depressed student; sending Christmas cards to his twenty-five assigned mentees.

Then came the dreaded last two hours of the day—the monthly Student Services staff meeting. As Tuck sat at the large U-shaped table, his colleagues trickled in. Wet with perspiration, Tuck peeled off his sport coat and thought again about the hand-scrawled letter. Sweat stung his right eye.

Dr. Pritchard arrived, and everyone did a 180—Tuck's colleagues sat up straight and donned sober expressions, but one of them couldn't or wouldn't hide a sigh.

"Hey," Dr. Pritchard said, "no sighing allowed. Hold it for UCA when we clobber them at next week's game."

Polite laughter followed.

As Dr. Pritchard ambled through the agenda, Tuck fought a weightlessness rising in his stomach—could someone here have left him that letter? If so, who?

The agenda's last item was Brother Moody's presentation at Bailey Coliseum tonight. After telling everyone their designated duties, Dr. Pritchard turned to Tuck.

"Now," Dr. Pritchard said, "many of you may wonder why I haven't given Tuck any duties tonight. Out of consideration for his recent family tragedy, Tuck will not need to attend." Dr. Pritchard's eyes darted around the room, as though gaging any potential resentment. Perhaps to his surprise, Chief Kwan clapped, and her colleagues joined her.

As the applause died down, Dr. Pritchard returned his attention to Tuck. "Mr. Jameson, you won't be attending tonight's presentation, will you?"

All eyes turned Tuck's way, and his pulse thudded in his throat. "Dr. Pritchard, I appreciate your concern, but I feel duty-bound to attend."

Red spread across Dr. Pritchard's face, but his voice stayed flat. "I see. My stance, out of consideration for you, is that you'd be better off staying home."

"I understand, sir."

Dr. Pritchard dismissed the staff, and Tuck trekked to his office, relieved to be out of the sweltering conference room.

Despite Chief Kwan's doubts, Tuck wondered if Dr. Pritchard had left this morning's letter for him. The old warhorse could easily rationalize such a stunt. Because it had failed, he might try something worse.

Let him.

To wise Clay up about Brother Moody so he'd decide not to join The Body, Tuck had to confront Moody tonight—no turning the other cheek.

Chapter 8

From the stage, Brother Graham Moody beamed. Hundreds, mostly college students, filled Bailey Coliseum. Wonderful. The Body needed young people, not wizened geezers.

Thank you, Lord, for this opportunity to save dozens from eternal damnation.

Damp with sweat, Brother Moody shed his sport coat. The coliseum's toastiness reminded him of hell, where his father writhed right now. God, let it not be so. But he knew his plea was futile.

ARV professors, administrators, and staff milled in back. Good. More witnesses. Twelve Campus Public Safety officers in full uniform stood at critical points throughout the coliseum, observing the crowd. ARV Chief of Police Captain Valerie Kwan flanked the stage to the right, her professional demeanor impressive when she had shaken Moody's hand. He'd also met the less impressive Officer Donald Bates, who stood below the stage trying to suck in his gut, clearly a lost cause. Moody knew that either Captain Kwan or Patrolman Bates would sacrifice their lives for him. He thanked God for their courage and pleaded that he might win them over tonight, for the image of police officers twisting in hell troubled him.

Middle-aged townies, obvious by their cut-rate Walmart attire, sat together—some of them might stir things up. Let them. Moody prayed God would stomp them flat. They were like the board members who kicked Dad out of the church years ago, forcing him to hang himself.

Moody blotted the thought and focused on the crowd. The press, mostly young and fresh-faced, hovered in the aisles along with their camera people. Two tripod cameras set up in back were already filming, and some reporters had agreed to carry mics throughout the coliseum during the question-and-answer period. Andy Drewer, the anchorperson for Jonesburg's Fox station, sat on the front row and nodded Moody's way, a signal the clean-cut reporter would be following Moody's lead.

In addition, billionaire T.J. LeMay, a staunch Brother Moody supporter, and his stunning silver-haired wife Sofie, sat in the front row at the school's insistence, for the couple were ARV's biggest donors. LeMay didn't suffer fools gladly, and Moody knew the man planned to testify on The Body's behalf. No ARV official would dare challenge LeMay.

Student Services' Vice-President Dr. Van Pritchard—child's play to manipulate—took to the podium. "Ladies and gentlemen," he said, his voice booming through the coliseum as the audience chatter faded, "as you know, The Body of Jesus Christ on Earth, better known as The Body, has gained quite a reputation in Arkansas. Critics have unjustly maligned this new Christian denomination. So, Brother Graham Moody, The Body's founder and Chief Elder, will set the record straight tonight. Without further ado—academic types like me can go on till New Year's if you let me—I present to you, Brother Graham Moody."

Moody basked in the audience's applause. Adulation gave him a rush that rivaled the high of any controlled substance.

Thank you, Lord, for making me gifted above other men.

As the applause subsided, two young people booed, but nearby students shushed them. Some townies folded their arms and scowled. One of them chewed a clearly visible cud, despite the tobacco free campus policy, and spat in his Coke cup.

"Good evenin'," Moody said, putting on a red Razorback cap. "Thank you, Dr. Pritchard, for your kind words. Now we all know the mascot for ARV is the Pumas, who regularly play in this coliseum. We also know Arkansas is the home of the University of Arkansas' Razorbacks. I'd like to demonstrate how I feel about that." He pulled off his Razorback cap, tossed it to the podium, and donned a blue and gold ARV Puma cap in its place. "Take that, UofA!"

ARV students whooped and applauded.

"More seriously, humankind's best-laid and worst-laid plans to create a utopia are well-meaning, but fall far short of God's glory, for He will usher in a new heaven and earth when the time is right. Amen?

"In his introduction, Dr. Pritchard mentioned The Body has often been maligned. Now I don't mind constructive criticism, but I can't abide lies. You with me?"

Heads nodded, especially those of ARV students.

"First off, The Body is neither racist nor sexist. We welcome everyone with open arms. Yes, it's true Body members, or Good Sams as I affectionately call them, live by New Testament teachings. We do so without shame. The New Testament speaks of loving your neighbor, not judging him, and The Body aims to love everyone—Republican or Democrat, black or white, male or female, Razorback or Puma—equally.

"Also, the biggest misconception about The Body is that we brainwash our members. Nothing could be further from the truth! New members do undergo a rigorous orientation. But at any point, a prospective new church member can say, 'Hey, Brother Moody, this ain't for me,' and walk away with our blessing, no questions asked. You with me?"

A few students cheered, and a couple pumped fists.

"Now I could go on and on about the wonderful works

the members of my church are doing in Arkansas. As they say, a picture can paint a thousand words. A video can capture a thousand good deeds, so please look up at the big monitor; I want you to watch a video showing just who Good Sams really are, and what they do for this great state of Arkansas."

The monitor burst into life, crisp stereo filling the coliseum as a five-minute video highlighted The Body's community work in Arkansas. To a soundtrack of lightly swelling and ebbing music, Good Sams—all of whom looked like real people, paunches, thinning hair, and all—made their case for The Body. Although these Good Sams downplayed their accomplishments, the narrator extolled their compassion without reservation: building houses for the homeless; cleaning highways on weekends; helping at disaster sites to the point of exhaustion; sharing their homes with families who'd lost everything; visiting nursing home residents who had no relatives.

The off-screen narrator asked one red-haired Good Sam with a round, freckled face why she pushed herself to the limit to help others.

She smiled. "God's love. That's what it's all about. God loves me so much I have to share that love with the world." She threw up her hands and laughed. "I can't help myself!" She pointed into the camera. "Brother Moody, it's all your fault! No, just kidding. It's all God's love."

The video concluded with a tasteful montage of Good Sams helping others, accompanied by a moving praise song sung in a lilting tenor voice. The last scene displayed The Body's motto: "One Body, Many Hearts."

Moody smiled. If that video hadn't wowed them, nothing would. It provided stark evidence of why The Body was the only true church in Arkansas, and soon, the United States.

"That," Moody said, energy crackling through him like lightning, "is what The Body is all about! Like that woman said—and her name is Holly Jefferson, by the way—it all comes down to God's love. Our motto is 'One Body, Many Hearts.' And it's in that spirit of generosity we serve." Moody cocked his head. "In fact, I dare anybody to find fault with what we just saw. But I intended this presentation to be transparent, so I now open the floor to questions. Please limit your queries to two or three."

A line formed, and a tall ARV professor—Moody recognized him as journalism teacher Dr. Marv Gillespie, who'd repeatedly tried to interview him—stood at the head of the line. Fox anchor Andy Drewer handed Dr. Gillespie the mic.

"Brother Moody," Dr. Gillespie said, "are you here to recruit ARV's college students to join The Body?"

Moody smiled. "Not primarily, but of course, that's one of my goals."

"A handful of our students are seventeen. Are they ready to become Good Sams? And if so, what if their parent or parents object?"

"Currently, we only accept candidates eighteen or older. But we have considered allowing both the parents and their seventeen-year-olds to make the decision. In that sense, we are pro-choice."

"Isn't it true that college students at two of the state's major private four-year institutions have become Good Sams?"

"Yes. I'm glad you brought that up. We're as pleased as can be the Christian college students who've become Good Sams have excelled in every way. Their grades average a 3.8 GPA out of a possible 4.0. Their lifestyles are clean—no drugs, hooking up, any of that kind of thing. And no date rape. Male college students who are Good Sams respect women."

"Yes," Dr. Gillespie said, "so you claim. Isn't it also true that female Good Sams often become subservient to male Good Sams? Don't they order their girlfriends around, demanding they do the boys' laundry or clean up the boys' rooms, as though they were indentured servants?"

"That sort of thing never happens."

"Not according to a couple of interviews I've recently recorded, nor from video evidence that suggests the opposite."

Moody made a "go on" gesture. "You liberals always make mountains out of mole hills. Individual Good Sam heterosexual couples are free to conduct their own relationships as they see fit, and I'd figure liberals would be fine with that."

"What about students of color?" Dr. Gillespie said. "It doesn't appear The Body has done any recruiting of African Americans or Hispanics or Asians. Why?"

"I am not a racist, and neither is The Body. It just so happens that most Arkansas colleges have predominately white populations."

"Still, it seems you want to keep The Body as free from people of color as possible."

Moody fumed. "You know what? I've answered all I'm going to answer from you, Dr. Gillespie. You've already exceeded your allotment of three questions."

A tall ARV administrator was second in line—Moody recognized him as Tuck Jameson, a man who had given The Body its share of grief. But he welcomed the challenge of taking Jameson on in front of the great unwashed public.

Fox anchor Andy Drewer took charge. "Brother Moody, it looks as though you've got a second questioner."

"My name is Tuck Jameson, and I have three questions for Brother Moody."

Moody grinned. "Fire away, Mr. Jameson."

"You talk about the benevolence the Good Sams are doing. But what about the toll on their health? They push themselves so hard some of them have to be hospitalized. What about the toll on their families? Good Sams have reportedly ignored their loved ones in favor of the community. Good Sams have also been known to push their families into joining The Body."

"Mr. Jameson," Moody said, "these assertions sound more like hearsay than questions. Everything you've said is rumor. No Good Sam husband or wife pressures their spouse to join The Body. Of course, they try to talk them into joining, speaking the truth in love. But Good Sams don't use strong-arm tactics."

"I know of one case where a Good Sam who is engaged has told his fiancée if she doesn't join The Body, he won't marry her. Sounds like a strong-arm tactic to me."

"And who might this Good Sam be?"

"I can't tell you for reasons of confidentiality."

"In other words, your accusation cannot be verified."

"One thing that can be verified is the insensitivity of Good Sams to their loved ones. There are documented cases."

Moody laughed. "You make them sound like criminals. Nothing could be further from the truth. Yes, Good Sams are more honest than your average guy. For example, I admit to a case when a Good Sam's wife asked her husband if the outfit she was wearing made her look fat, and he said 'Yes.'" Laughter rippled through the audience. "But he meant no harm, even though he was in the doghouse for a week. In The Body, we teach it's okay to speak the truth in love, and in the long run, that's better for a marital relationship than disguised resentments."

"Then what about Good Sams who take their mission so far they kill themselves?"

"Mr. Jameson, no such cases have occurred. Suicide is an unforgivable sin, one none of our members has ever committed."

"Then what about the case of my father, Pastor Leonard Jameson?"

Moody shook his head. "With all due respect, Mr. Jameson, your father did not kill himself. He had a fatal heart attack while trying to dig a man out of a pile of tornado rubble. Your father gave his life to save another man's life. How can you not be proud of that?"

Jameson shot a finger at Moody. "Don't you dare lecture me about being proud of my father. He wasn't acting of his own free will—he'd been brainwashed. That's why he pushed himself over the limit."

"I feel sorry for you, Mr. Jameson. I have nothing but admiration for your father and your family. But the accusation of 'brainwashing' is a flat-out lie."

T.J. LeMay yanked the mic from reporter Andy Drewer and pointed at Jameson. "This man is a malcontent. My son-in-law joined The Body and became a new man. Before becoming a Good Sam, he'd been sleeping around on my precious daughter, and don't think I didn't consider taking a shotgun and blowing his head off. But he joined The Body. Now he is faithful to my daughter, treats her like a princess. That's what The Body does for a man. I say three cheers to Brother Moody."

Deafening applause erupted.

A middle-aged woman draped by an ankle-length coat, third in line to ask questions, waved her hands.

Moody nodded at T.J. LeMay, who handed the mic back to Andy Drewer. "Let the woman speak."

"Okay, preacher," she said. "What about my son? He became one of your precious Good Sams and chopped his hand off 'cause the Bible says to if it makes you sin."

"That sounds highly unlikely. We don't teach crazy things like that. Your son obviously struggles with mental illness—I suggest he get treatment. Send me the medical bills, and I will pay double the amount."

"You're a little late, preacher. Logan disappeared two months ago while I was at the Laundromat, and we ain't seen him since."

"Again, ma'am, my heart goes out to you. If I could help—"

"I ain't finished, preacher. My son disappeared under

what the cops call 'mysterious circumstances.' Mysterious, my foot. Your church kidnapped him."

"With all due respect, ma'am, that is a baseless accusation."

"Are you callin' me a liar?" The woman reached under her coat, pulled out a Smith & Wesson .38, and fired at the stage. Something punched Moody's right shoulder—he'd been shot.

The audience fled into the aisles.

Patrolman Bates grabbed the shooter's revolver barrel, twisted it high, and forced the gun from the woman's hand. He handcuffed her. Captain Kwan bolted to the stage. "Ladies and gentlemen," she said, "we have the shooter in custody. Don't panic. Hold up your arms as you leave the building so the law officers can see you are unarmed."

Most of the audience threw their arms into the air like Pentecostals praising God as they hurried from the coliseum—the campus police monitored the fleeing crowd. One elderly man lost his balance, and several people trampled over him, but a young Good Samaritan in an ARV cap helped him to his feet.

T.J. LeMay bolted to the stage and pressed his expensive sport coat over Moody's gunshot shoulder to staunch the blood. "Hang tight, preacher. An ambulance should be here any second."

"Thank you, T.J.," Moody said, "you are too kind."

Moody's shoulder burned, but his adrenaline drowned most of the pain. He had to fight back a smile, for such valuable PR had to have been signed, sealed, and delivered straight from above. Moody looked at the rafters and smiled. *Thank you, Lord.*

Chapter 9

Outside the coliseum, Tuck's smartphone squealed and flashed an on-campus alert. Two Winkdale police sedans, sirens whooping like banshees, let an ambulance through, then blocked the parking lot exits.

One of the fleeing patrons looked familiar—a middle-aged athletic guy who disappeared into the crowd. The man's gait. His bearing. Tuck knew him from somewhere.

A ping on his smartphone—a text from Dr. Pritchard: *"Meet me ASAP."*

Like a man welcoming the gallows, Tuck strode to Dr. Pritchard's office—let the VP do his worst.

Dr. Pritchard was talking on his cell. "Brother Moody's okay? Thank God. Give the 'All Clear' now? I don't know, President Green, I advise you not to rush this thing. We don't want parents thinking their kids are not our number one priority. Well, of course, I know they're our number one priority! What? I understand, sir. Call me if you need me."

Dr. Pritchard glowered at Tuck. "There are no words, Jameson. You almost got Brother Moody killed."

"Sir, I am deeply sorry for that. But I don't think I should be blamed for the shooter's actions."

"You don't think—you're blessed right, you don't think." His face red, the VP turned the air blue with curses and walked inches from Tuck, the reek of alcohol strong on his breath. "The press is going ballistic after that shooting, but fortunately, they're grilling President Green, not me. Chief Kwan is satisfied there was only one shooter—lucky for you there weren't more."

"My apologies, sir."

"T.J. LeMay is fit to be tied over what you said tonight. Word is many alumni feel the same."

"Sir, I had no intention of tarnishing the school's reputation. But family comes first."

His frown deepening, Dr. Pritchard stuck a finger in Tuck's face. After several seconds, his expression softened, the tension ebbing away. "I believe you, Jameson. Your devotion to your little brother blinds you to... I had a younger brother myself."

"I didn't know that, sir."

"Not many do."

Baffled, Tuck wondered where this derailed discussion was heading.

Dr. Pritchard's voice grew so soft Tuck had to strain to hear. "Hoppy—that's what I called him. Doesn't matter why. I was always daring him to do stupid things, boy things. Like climbing over a barbed wire fence. Like..." He stopped and appeared to be collecting himself.

Tuck wondered if his boss was cracking under the pressure.

Dr. Pritchard wiped his nose. "One day, in winter— Hoppy was nine, I was twelve—I dared him to skate across a frozen pond. He took the dare." Dr. Pritchard blinked. "It was the last dare he ever took."

Tuck felt as though the world had tilted on its axis—this unexpected tale of childhood tragedy cast the VP in a new light. "Sir, I'm so sorry."

Sighing, Dr. Pritchard shoved his hands in his pants pockets. "Tell you what, Jameson. If you issue a public apology about tonight, I will place you on unpaid administrative leave. It will be up to President Green and the board whether you stay or go."

Tuck recoiled. He had expected to storm into Dr. Pritchard's office, hear the VP fire him, and storm out. Now this. Tuck could apologize and keep his job, and if he did, he could still search for Clay. "Would it be enough to say 'I'm sorry for my tone to Brother Moody tonight'?"

Dr. Pritchard smoothed a hand over his hair. "That would be a start."

"A start?"

The VP smiled. "That's right. You would also have to apologize for claiming The Body brainwashed your father."

Tuck reared back his head. So, that was it. Complete capitulation. Still, Dr. Pritchard's heartfelt story about his brother tempted Tuck to relent. "Sir, I appreciate your offer." He locked eyes with Dr. Pritchard. "But I won't apologize for saying Dad was brainwashed."

Dr. Pritchard tapped his chin. "Afraid you'd say that. You give me no choice but to fire you."

"But, sir, what about the Student Awards Ceremony tomorrow night? The RAs in Stribling Hall expect me to be there."

Dr. Pritchard just stared. "I am banning you from tomorrow's awards ceremony. In fact, I am giving you twenty-four hours to pack up and get out of Dodge." The man's steely eyes glinted. "How dare you refuse my offer of mercy? Leave. Now."

Tuck trudged toward his truck. Had he done the right thing? Couldn't he have lied about being sorry he'd said Dad was brainwashed? No. Integrity demanded he fight the good fight. Dad would have wanted that if he had been in his right mind.

Amazing that when you were non-classified and on contract with the college, your superior could dismiss you on a whim. Tuck had seen it happen before, but never thought it would happen to him. The reality of having lost his job sank in with each step. He'd hoped to work at ARV for years to come—he had good friends here, fond memories, and he loved working with the students.

Was his getting canned predestined? Perhaps. Didn't matter. He hadn't just lost his job or his career, but his life's mission. His belly soured.

As he stepped into the parking lot, his phone shrieked— President Green and Chief Kwan had issued a campus-wide "All Clear." That should give Dr. Pritchard something else to fume about.

So what? The VP still had his job, but Tuck was finished. Gray clouds hid the stars, and Tuck felt that fate had likewise eclipsed his dreams. His chin dropped. How could he look any of his student mentees in the eye and tell them he was history? But in this age of social media, he probably wouldn't have to, a mixed blessing.

Would he be blacklisted? Have to sell his house? Dig into his Roth IRA while searching for a new job? Move from town, from the state, leave April behind?

Corporal Kale Maloney motioned Tuck to halt on the pavement across from Bailey Coliseum, then waved on a blue Toyota Celica. Few vehicles lingered in the parking lot, but public safety officers swarmed everywhere. President Green must have ordered all ARV police, both day-shifters and part-timers, to the campus.

Officer Maloney waved Tuck on.

"Quite a night, huh, Kale?" Tuck said.

"That's an understatement, sir. Supposed to be my night off, too."

"Tough break."

"Had a date all lined up. But hey, protecting the kids comes first."

He touched the officer's arm. "You're a good man, Corporal Maloney."

As Tuck's dress shoes clattered on the parking lot, the frizzy-haired woman shooting at Brother Moody flashed through his head. He didn't know her name, but he was sure everyone on social media knew by now. What that woman had done was wrong. But if what she said was true, if her son had amputated his right hand out of a misguided interpretation of Scripture championed by The Body, you couldn't blame her. Trouble was, no telling what would happen to her.

Should Tuck start a legal fund for the woman? No. He knew nothing about her. Maybe she had a history of taking potshots at people she didn't like. Besides, his priority was to wrest Clay from Brother Moody's clutches.

It was terrifying to picture Brother Moody manipulating his growing army of "Good Sams" against their will, but as Tuck slipped into his pickup, he knew that's what was happening.

Wait a minute—he always locked his truck doors.

A male voice from the back seat said, "Evening, Tuckster."

Only one person had ever called him "Tuckster," a man he'd never expected to see again.

Chapter 10

No worries," the man in Tuck's back seat said. "I'm unarmed."

The man's spicy breath—familiar. His lean, early to mid-fifties Asian face jogged Tuck's memory. Add fifty pounds, and this guy could be Tuck's high school mentor. "Coach?"

"Yes, Tuckster," Coach said. "It's me, former Assistant Principal Adam Shimura, at your service."

"But you're so—"

"Thin? Been on a diet."

"What the blazes are you doing here?"

Coach laughed. "Questions, questions. Same old Tuckster."

"I've got a right."

"Aye, lad, indeed you do." The headlights of a car leaving the parking lot passed over Coach's face like searchlights, revealing a web of crow's feet. "I know Clay plans to join The Body."

"You and everybody else in Winkdale."

"I stole into your truck because I wanted a private chat away from spying eyes." Coach smiled. "Good Sams are on the loose, dude."

Tuck fought off a chill that was becoming all too familiar. "Tell me about it."

"We've been watching The Body and Brother Moody for

some time now."

"We?"

"My employer. The government."

"Bull. You'll have to do better than that."

"Seriously, I'm black ops now. Remember how I used to hint my family was involved with a secret organization?"

"Yeah, but I never—"

"Believed it?" Coach chuckled. "Guess I can't blame you. I joshed with you too much back then."

"Like you're doing now."

"No. The less you know about my employer, the safer you and your loved ones will be."

"Loved ones?"

"Clay. Ham. April. Your Mom. Shall I go on?"

"No, I'm good." If he knew about Ham, he'd investigated Tuck's current life. Creepy. Tuck welcomed the goosebumps that shimmered across his arms.

Coach continued. "I know about Clay. He's on The Body's docket, waiting to be 'gloried' into Good Samhood. He's a special case, of course."

"Meaning?"

"If he becomes a Good Sam, it could have repercussions beyond Winkdale."

Tuck shifted in his seat. "If that's supposed to be a joke, it stinks."

Coach beamed, his eyes enigmatic. "Things have changed since high school, Tuckster. These days, I never joke about my work." He paused, as though for dramatic effect. "I want to keep Clay from becoming a Good Sam. So do you. Want to help me track him down?"

"If I don't?"

Coach shrugged. "Then we part with no hard feelings."

Tuck sucked in a deep breath. "If you're really black ops, why should I trust you?"

"Why shouldn't you?"

"Oh, because, among other things, you might have a

hidden agenda."

"I might."

"I could call the cops. Tell them you broke into my truck."

His old mentor grinned. "You won't. You're too curious about what I'm *not* telling you. Besides, you'd need a better reason than that to throw ole Coach under the bus." Coach ducked behind the front seat.

Tuck jumped when knuckles rapped against the window. But it was only Corporal Kale Maloney. He shone a flashlight into the truck, causing Tuck to squint. Maloney often overdid things.

As Tuck rolled down the window, the middle-aged officer frowned. "Everything okay, Mr. Jameson?"

"Couldn't be better."

Maloney's frown deepened. "You been sitting here several minutes. Thought maybe you was having car trouble."

"Just lost in thought."

Looking unconvinced, Maloney fiddled with his police cap. "After tonight's shooting, guess we all got a lot to think about."

"Guess so." Tuck's neck tensed. C'mon, c'mon, Maloney, get a move on.

Maloney nodded. Inhaling deeply, he smiled and tipped his cap. "Have a good evening, Mr. Jameson."

"You too, Kale."

After Officer Maloney had ambled from the truck, Tuck said, "Guess you heard all that, Coach."

"*Yuvol*. Which means ole Coach had better make tracks. If you would be so kind, drive me to Plenti-Burgers' parking lot, Jeeves."

Tuck drove to the decades-old hamburger hangout two blocks away. The Plenti-Burgers sign, still missing its "i," winked out as cars pulled from the lot. A beat-up Ford Taurus was parked by its lonesome. "That your ride,

Coach?"

"Indeed 'tis, laddie." He grinned. "I've come up in the world, wouldn't you say?"

"No comment."

"Before I take my leave, I've got something for you." He handed Tuck a sympathy card. Inside it read, *"Sorry about your old man, Tuckster. But the jerk never gave you a fair shake."*

Tuck said, "Thanks for the card. But you have no right to call my father a jerk."

Coach smiled. "The truth is the truth."

"How would you know? I haven't seen you in years. I saw Dad nearly every day."

"Your dear old Pop came to maybe two of your high school basketball games."

"No biggie. He had other fish to fry."

"He didn't give you an 'atta boy' for keeping a 4.0 GPA."

Tuck shrugged. "Not exactly a world-class tragedy."

"When you made 34 on the ACT—thirty rocking four!— he didn't brag on you. He lectured you about being proud, said you were working to please men rather than God."

"Your point?"

"Just wondered if he'd changed his ways since your high school years."

Tuck forced back emotion. "Some." He wanted to tell Coach to choke on it. "It got better when I became an adult."

"Good to hear."

"Dad loved me. That's the important thing."

"Aye, that's what they say. But if you'd been my son, it would have been a different ballgame."

Warmth welled in Tuck's chest, the way it had back in high school. "Yeah?"

"Oh, come on, lad." Coach squeezed Tuck's shoulder. "You know I looked on you like the son I never had. You even said you wished you'd had a different dad."

"I was only sixteen. I didn't mean it."

"Didn't you, now?"

Tuck balled his fists, and his nails bit into his palms. Who did Coach think he was to lecture him? "At least my real dad didn't run out on me."

Coach's voice lowered a notch. "No, he didn't." He sighed. "Got something else." He handed Tuck a business card.

Tuck snorted. "Come on, Coach. No black ops outfit would have its own business cards."

"They don't. This one I made just for you."

Tuck read the number on the card. "1-800-Weirder?"

"Hey, like the Veg-O-Matic, that number really, really works." He cocked an eyebrow. "Sure you don't want to help me hunt down Clay?"

Tuck hesitated. If Coach really was black ops, he might know how to find Clay. But could he trust Coach? He might be working for The Body. "Let me think it over."

"Whatever you say, Tuckster. But don't think too long. Time's a wasting."

"When do you need my answer?"

"Sooner than yesterday."

Tuck sighed. "Now what the heck is that supposed to—"

Coach wriggled his fingers. "Toodles."

As Coach pulled away in his Taurus, Tuck tapped his steering wheel. Should he tail Coach? Nah. If Coach really was black ops, might not be a good idea.

Instead, Tuck turned onto Highway 8 and headed home. He welcomed the familiar traffic signs and the billboard featuring lawyer Tommy Ray in a white cowboy hat. Good old Tommy. He was about as much a cowboy as Tuck was a tap dancer.

What a day. Clay had run off somewhere, some lady had shot Brother Moody, Tuck had lost his job, he'd probably lost April, and he'd met Coach for the first time in seventeen years. What next?

Why was Coach back after all these years? Sondra, Coach's wife, had divorced him during the last half of Tuck's senior year—she'd claimed infidelity, and Coach counter-claimed she'd slept with a high school sophomore. The students sided with Coach, but the School Board came down on Sondra's side. However, before they could fire him, Coach resigned and left town under cover of the night.

"Then his ex died," Tuck said to the green-lit dashboard, "under mysterious circumstances."

Why hadn't Tuck asked Coach about that? Probably because he didn't want to know the answer. Or maybe seeing him in the back of his truck after all these years seemed too weird.

Anyway, since Coach had fled, Tuck had received only two Christmas cards from the man, neither with a return address. Was Coach on the up and up? And black ops? No way he had gone the Fox Mulder *X-Files* route. Or had he?

Tuck tuned in to the local radio station. News anchor Fred Torreson said, "So, President Green, you're satisfied that Celia Garson, the alleged shooter, was acting alone?"

"Yes, Fred. Campus and local law enforcement assure me Mrs. Garson was a lone wolf. State police think so too."

"One mother of an ARV student living on campus says the school issued the 'All Clear' prematurely. What do you have to say to her and other concerned parents of ARV students?"

"The situation is well in hand. Although we're no longer officially on lockdown, we're maintaining a heavy law enforcement presence on campus tonight. They will stay on duty until tomorrow morning at the very—"

"Excuse me, President Green, we're switching to St. Andrew's where a spokesperson for Brother Moody is addressing the press."

A sanctimonious voice said, "Brother Moody is doing well and will be released in the morning. The surgeon said the bullet did no major damage, missing the subclavian artery and the brachial plexus, which controls the arm. The bullet was removed by arthroscopic surgery without incident."

A reporter said, "Do you agree with Good Sams who are claiming God spared Brother Moody from significant injury?"

Sanctimonious replied, "Well, a bullet to the shoulder can be dangerous, with serious consequences and surgical follow-ups. It's no coincidence Mrs. Garson's bullet caused no major damage."

Reporter: "Then you believe God directly intervened?"

Sanctimonious: "Of course."

Different reporter: "Does Brother Moody have anything to say about Mrs. Garson?"

Sanctimonious: "Only that he forgives her from his heart. He sees her as an obviously troubled woman in need of God's love."

Third reporter: "So, did Brother Moody say anything about Tuck Jameson, the ARV administrator who tonight blamed the minister for his father's death?"

Sanctimonious: "Brother Moody believes Mr. Jameson is a good but mixed-up man. His charge that Brother Moody caused the death of his father is baseless. Mr. Jameson's father died a hero. Brother Moody hopes Mr. Jameson will soon cherish his father's sacrifice as the act of courage it was."

Third reporter: "Then Brother Moody bears no ill will against Mr. Jameson?"

Sanctimonious: "Of course not. Brother Moody is all about tolerance and love of one's enemies. He sincerely hopes Mr. Jameson will—"

Tuck switched off the radio. His cheeks burned, and he gripped the steering wheel so hard his fingers ached. That holier-than-thou weasel Moody—Tuck was going to nail him if it was the last thing he did.

But first, he had to find Clay. Kenny had been fired from Aim, so he should be in Clay's apartment by now. Kenny might be a dead end, but what other options did Tuck have? A preposterous offer from Coach, who showed up after a zillion years?

Tuck turned onto Almanda Drive, glad to be free from the glare of the highway's headlights, but sighing at the road's potholes that jostled the car. He furrowed his brow when he saw a jet-black sedan parked in front of his house. MIB maybe? More black ops intrigue?

One way to find out.

Tuck parked as three men the size of night club bouncers eased out of the sedan—this crazy night was far from over.

Chapter 11

Tuck scrambled from his truck.

The three men from the sedan approached, U2's "With or Without You" humming from their car. Dressed in black with ski masks pulled over their faces, the middle one—Tuck dubbed him Bluto—stood a head taller than his two companions, making him around six foot seven.

They stopped.

Like an action movie hero, Tuck wanted to make a smart-aleck remark, but his mouth felt like cotton.

In a flash, Bluto's two companions grabbed Tuck's arms, and Bluto socked him in the gut. The air rushed from Tuck's lungs—like a comic book character, he said, "Oof!"

Bluto kicked Tuck in the belly, hard. A memory of getting winded from a lineman's tackle in high school pumped through Tuck's head. *Some fun, huh, kids?* he'd said when he'd recovered to the high fives of his teammates. But that lineman had nothing on Bluto.

The giant's fists plowed into Tuck's solar plexus. Agony fizzled Tuck's world into darkness. His gasps sounded like they were coming from beneath a swimming pool.

Another blow to the belly, and he gagged.

Another, and bile scalded his throat.

Another and Bluto's companions let Tuck collapse to the dead grass.

Heart thudding in his ears, Tuck's belly burned like fire.

Bluto's two associates forced him into a lawn chair, tied his hands behind his back, bound his ankles, and faced him towards his Ford 150 truck. Tuck's head wobbled.

Bluto, his voice a coarsened soprano, said, "I understand you're proud of your spotless truck, but that may change in the next five minutes." He gave his two companions a thumbs up, and they swung baseball bats at the windshield.

Tuck couldn't believe it—how stupid were these guys? Didn't they know about tempered glass?

But as the duo battered the windshield, the glass spider-webbed. With each wallop, a cloud of slivered glass sprinkled on the hood. The windshield eventually tore in two like cloth, the fragments falling inside the truck. The assailants hammered the hood, pounded the doors, smashed the sides. Soon the truck looked as though they had beaten it with a torrent of shot puts.

Abruptly, the two men stopped and slung their bats over their shoulders, looking for all the world like two jocks who'd just finished a satisfying game of baseball.

Tuck spit and said, "Batter up?" He congratulated himself on his wisecrack—James Bond would be proud.

Bluto tossed a baggy in Tuck's lap. Something small and white, like a pearl. No, more like a pebble. No, that wasn't it either. A tooth?

A shrill chortle escaped Bluto's lips. "What's inside the baggy belonged to your little brother. But don't worry. It's just a back molar he won't miss. We anesthetized him. Next time, we won't bother."

"You lousy—"

"Temper, temper."

"You guys couldn't possibly be Good Sams."

Bluto cocked his head. "Couldn't we, now?" He let loose a high-pitched chuckle and bent down so that the ski mask's eyeholes showed the whites of his eyes. "We could waste you, but your death, after your outburst at the presentation, might look suspicious."

"Ya think?"

"For Brother Moody, killing is a last resort. Consider this a warning. Next time, you won't be so lucky."

Tuck clenched his jaw.

"Forget about Clay. He's one of ours now."

Bluto waved his two cronies to the sedan, the trio a toxic version of *Newhart*'s Larry, Daryl, and Daryl. As they squeezed into the car, its stereo still played U2's *The Joshua Tree*, now up to the track "Running to Stand Still."

The sedan eased toward Highway 8, and Tuck realized Bluto's high, reedy voice must have been damaged. Maybe the man-mountain suffered from throat cancer, or maybe a fire had crisped his larynx. Whatever the eerie voice's origin, Tuck hoped he never heard it again.

As he stared at the baggy with Clay's tooth, he narrowed his eyes and bit back an oath. He fought against the cords that bound his hands, wrists chafing. Stupidly, he hadn't flexed his arms when they'd tied him. Then again, he'd been so dazed it amazed him he hadn't passed out.

Nausea gripped his belly, and he vomited. Tuck's stomach burned as though packed with hot coals—he hoped Bluto hadn't done any serious damage. Regardless, Tuck would do what he must to find and rescue his little brother.

The thought of those sadists yanking out Clay's tooth infuriated him, and he again chafed against his bonds. He didn't know Brother Moody would go this far. But then, Brother Moody didn't know how far Tuck would go, either. For that matter, neither did Tuck.

Chapter 12

Thi s is nuts," Tuck said as Ham untied him shortly after his three assailants had fled into the night. "The coincidence of you getting here so soon after those thugs left."

"It's God's will, bro," Ham said as he tossed the cords onto Tuck's front lawn.

"C'mon, Ham. You can't really believe the Holy Spirit led you here."

"Okay, I confess the Holy Spirit didn't lead me here. Coming back from Conway tonight, I heard what happened at Bailey Coliseum. Couldn't find you in town. Thought you might be home."

"Sounds reasonable."

Ham looked at Tuck and shook his head. "Dude, you look awful."

Tuck figured Ham was seeing a chalky face and a vomit-spattered chin. "I feel worse."

"Hard to believe." Ham motioned to the baggy containing Clay's tooth. "What's with the baggy?"

"Tell you on the way to the police station."

Ham's Toyota Celica was a mess as usual, and the big man tossed a handful of junk mail and a half-eaten donut into the back seat. "Sure you don't want to lie down in back?"

"I'm sure," Tuck said, dusting donut crumbs from the passenger seat. "Go by my house so I can change. I doubt the police station's duty officer wants to smell my puke."

Ham wrinkled his nose. "That makes two of us."

At home, Tuck washed his face and changed shirts. As he and Ham were on their way to Winkdale, met by occasional headlights, Tuck told Ham what had happened since Dr. Pritchard had fired him. While talking, Tuck sent Clay a barrage of texts, all unanswered.

Ham pulled into the Winkdale Police Department's dimly lit parking lot. Two squad cruisers were parked in front, and a couple of cops in uniform loitered beside one of the cars, laughing. Tuck envied them—he wished he felt like laughing.

Ham said, "You okay, bro?"

"As okay as I can be after getting beat to a pulp and being given my brother's tooth."

"You sure we should tell the cops about Clay?"

"This tooth is proof of assault."

"But didn't you say this Bluto guy said to lay off?"

"Yeah. So?"

"So, maybe you should lay off. Just sayin'. I don't want Clay to get hurt."

"He's already been hurt."

"Well, I mean, more hurt than he's already been."

Tuck shook his head. "Sometimes I don't believe you, big guy."

"I'm just thinking about you and Clay."

"I appreciate your concern, misguided as it is."

"Maybe we can find Clay ourselves."

"We're not pros—the cops are."

"What if they won't help?"

"I'll cross that bridge when I come to it."

His belly smarting, Tuck hobbled into the police station. The décor was as Spartan as he remembered—a handful of visitor chairs, a table loaded with dog-eared copies of *Field & Stream*, a wooden counter whose top could use refinishing. Ham sat in a chair splitting at the seams, his lineman's bulk the last thing it needed.

Just as Tuck was about to call someone to the desk, Sergeant Dabney Wakeman appeared, his posture stiffer than a straight edge. Tuck's hopes sank like a torpedoed sub, and Wakeman's eyes narrowed.

Wakeman had arrested Tuck the only night in his life he'd gotten drunk and disorderly, but the Chief of Police had thrown out the charges. That had rankled by-the-book Wakeman.

"Good evening, Mr. Jameson," Wakeman said with exaggerated cordiality. "How may I help you, sir?"

Tuck told the officer about his beating, the tooth in the baggy, his fears for Clay's safety.

"Mr. Jameson," Wakeman said, "with all due respect, you don't have a case."

"No?" Tuck held up the baggy. "What about this?"

Wakeman shrugged. "Could be anybody's."

"Well, what about doing DNA analysis on it?"

"You watch too much TV. Can you prove the tooth belongs to Clay?"

"Not exactly."

"Not at all."

"Officer, it's evidence of a crime."

"So you say. Sounds like a scam to me."

"I want to speak to Chief Colson."

His eyes gleaming, Wakeman grinned. "He won't back you up this time, Mr. Jameson. He thinks you should be arrested for starting a riot in Bailey Coliseum tonight."

Tuck's cheeks burned. "Officer, I did not start a riot."

"Chief says Mrs. Garson probably shot Brother Moody 'cause you stirred her up."

"I didn't stir anybody up. She already had the gun."

"Besides, the chief has a policy for us not to wake him unless it's important."

"Are you saying my brother isn't important?"

"I'm not saying anything, Mr. Jameson. Sir. Just telling

it like it is."

Tuck imagined how righteous it would feel to pop Wakeman in the nose—fury almost eclipsed his stinging belly. But a familiar worry told Tuck he was living in denial because, much as he hated to admit it, Sgt. Wakeman had been right to arrest him for starting a fight at Olson's Bar & Grill.

"Sgt. Wakeman, I understand why you're sore. But see, my dad had just died the night you arrested me, and—look, I know Chief Colson shouldn't have thrown out the charges. I apologize for being a jerk."

The officer rose an eyebrow. "That makes it all okay?"

"No. But please don't let your resentment of me blind you to the fact my brother is in danger."

"Since you last saw him, has he texted you?"

"Yes."

"May I see those texts?"

Tuck handed his smartphone to Wakeman, who read the texts with apparent interest. "Problem here, Mr. Jameson, is your brother seems to be just fine. The fact he doesn't want to tell you where he is doesn't violate any law."

"What about the frigging tooth?"

"I only have your say that some goons beat you up and gave you this tooth."

Tuck pulled up his shirt, showing the black and purple bruises on his abdomen. "You think I did this to myself?"

"Frankly, Mr. Jameson, I don't know what to think. I know you hate Brother Moody and want to see him go down. You made that obvious at Bailey Coliseum tonight."

"I don't hate the man. I just think he's dangerous."

Wakeman shook his head. "I wouldn't put it past you to make up a story about getting beat up. Maybe Ham worked you over so you could come in here to tell your tall tale about three men in black."

"—it's no tall tale—"

"And really, three men in black? Not very original." A

smug smile spread across Sgt. Wakeman's face. "Bottom line: The Body is not doing anything illegal, and your brother Clay has every right to join any denomination he darn well pleases."

Tuck sighed. "This is the best I'm going to get, isn't it, Sergeant Wakeman?"

The officer's smile hardened. "I'm afraid so, Mr. Jameson."

Still hobbled over, Tuck motioned to Ham. Once they were back in Ham's Toyota, Tuck said, "We're not licked yet. There's always Sheriff Harrington."

Ham fired up the ignition. "Bad idea, bro."

"Why?"

The light from a parking lamp slid over Ham's face as the big man pulled onto Boulder Avenue. "Because Molly told me Sheriff Harrington has become a Perfect."

Tuck recoiled. "Can't be. What about turning the other cheek? Harrington couldn't do that and still be sheriff."

"Don't know how that would work, either. Molly said Harrington's wife became a Perfect a month ago, and she pressured him into joining last week."

"So, he's only been a Perf a few days?"

"Yeah. Maybe he hasn't had to fight anybody since then."

"Since his brainwashing, you mean?"

"Yeah."

"There is," Tuck said, "the Scripture in the New Testament about an authority not wielding the sword for nothing. That could explain how a Perf could be a sheriff. Or a soldier." All under the command of Brother Moody. What a nightmare.

Abruptly, Ham braked at a red light. Tuck jerked forward, wincing as the seatbelt cut into his belly. "Ow!"

"Sorry. My bad."

"You know, Ham, you're going to have to stop speeding."

Ham looked skyward. "Please, Lord, not another lecture."

"You need to drive the speed limit. Getting a ticket wouldn't look good for the dean of campus discipline. But now there's a more important reason."

"Which is?"

"We don't want any cops pulling us over from here on out."

"What do you mean, 'from here on out?'"

"I mean," Tuck said, crossing his fingers, "are you with me in the hunt for Clay?"

With his free hand, Ham gave Tuck a thumbs up. "You know it, amigo."

Tuck touched Ham's shoulder. "Thanks." A squad car passed in the opposite lane. "We need to keep a low profile. Starting now."

Ham sighed. "Okay. Driving the speed limit is about as much fun as liver and onion ice cream, but okay."

"Head over to Clay's."

"But you said Clay is gone."

"He is, but Kenny might be there."

"You think Kenny knows something?"

"I'm sure of it."

Chapter 13

Kenny itched his scruffy goatee. "I would say, 'Make yourself at home,' but I'd be lyin'."

The guy's bedroom made Tuck want to lecture the high school dropout to get his act together. You couldn't step in here without crunching a candy wrapper or squashing a fast-food sack, and the gallon jar of Kenny's snuff juice still set beside his nightstand. The stink turned Tuck's stomach, but he'd never let Kenny know that. Ham, meanwhile, had no problem waving his paw of a hand in the air and saying, "P.U."

Kenny spat snuff juice into a cup and, grinning, offered it to Ham. "Care for a swig?"

Ham shook his head. "No thanks. I'm a bat urine man myself."

Tuck frowned—there was no time for this. "Kenny, have you seen Clay tonight?"

Kenny's expression sobered. "Can't say that I have."

"Any idea where he might be?"

"Can't say that I do."

"Has he texted you tonight?"

Kenny shook his head and spat another stream of snuff juice into his cup.

"Well, he texted me. I guess you know he plans to become a Perf."

Kenny looked offended. "You mean a Good Sam. Sure,

I know. What's it to you?"

"Did Clay say where he was?"

"Told you he ain't texted me."

"Do you know where he's hiding until his Good Sam initiation?"

Kenny grinned. "What if I do?"

"Tell me."

"What's in it for me?"

"Name your price."

Kenny smiled, showing off both rows of crooked teeth in all their tobacco-stained glory. "You cain't go that high."

"Don't mess with me, Kenny. Clay's my only brother, and if you know where he is—"

"Honest, dude. Ain't got a clue."

"You wouldn't tell me if you did know."

Kenny spat another stream of snuff juice. "You don't like me much, do you, Tuck?"

"Why should I? You've mooched off Clay for over a year. He's too good-hearted to kick you out."

Kenny recoiled. "I do not mooch off Clay. He's my friend."

"So, when was the last time you helped with the rent?"

"I can't help it if I keep getting fired."

"It couldn't be because you never show up to work on time, could it?"

"Bosses don't like me, that's all. I ain't never got a square deal from any of 'em."

"Not even Brother Eli? He told me he hired you to mow the grass last summer, and you didn't show up once."

"Couldn't. Rained all summer."

"You have an answer for everything, don't you, Kenny? Except Clay's whereabouts."

"If Clay wants to be a Good Sam, that's his business, not yours or nobody else's."

Tuck held up the baggy with Clay's tooth. "This is what being a Good Sam did for Clay."

Kenny shook his head. "You're lying. That ain't my friend's tooth."

"I'm not lying."

"Bull." He shook a finger at Tuck. "I got you figured out. You think Clay needs more schooling. Well, he don't. He's fine the way he is."

"Don't lecture me about my own brother. Of course, he's fine the way he is. I've never said different."

Kenny grimaced, his eyes contemptuous. "You lie like a dog."

"We both want the best for Clay. If you know where he is, for the love of God, tell me."

Kenny's face twisted into a defiant mask. "Not a chance. Clay's my only friend in this rotten world, and a man don't snitch on his friends."

Tuck grabbed Kenny's T-shirt by the neckline and jerked him close. His breath stank of tobacco. "Clay's life may be at stake, you little—"

Ham pulled Tuck away. "Ease off, beanpole."

Tuck's face steamed. Fear swam in Kenny's eyes, and Tuck relented. "I'm sorry."

Defiance washed over Kenny's face. "No, you ain't."

Tuck swallowed the words but still thought them: *No, I ain't.* He buttoned up his coat and left Clay's apartment, followed by Ham, whose boots clomped on the driveway. As Tuck and Ham got into the Toyota, Ham cocked an eyebrow. "What just happened in there, bro?"

"Loyalty," Tuck replied, fastening his seat belt as gently as possible against his tender abdomen.

"Loyalty?" Ham said, starting the car and firing up the heater.

"Kenny is loyal to Clay. Kenny had a rotten upbringing—his parents abused him. Used to punish him when he was a kid by chaining him to a post in the basement and shutting out all the lights till morning."

"Man, that's cold," Ham said as he entered Main Street's

traffic flow.

"At school, kids called him Ratface. Clay took up for him as far back as sixth grade." Tuck sighed and regretted having yanked Kenny by his T-shirt. "Guess I should be more like Clay."

"If you were more like Clay, you'd be a stranger. Anyways, where to now, beanpole?"

"David Freeman's."

"But Tuck, he's a Perfect."

"That's right. Perfs can't lie. So, if I ask where Clay is hiding, and he knows, he has to tell me."

"Hmm," Ham said, his face scrunching. "Don't think it's gonna be that easy."

"I have to try." And if David didn't pan out, duty demanded Tuck call 1-800-Weirder.

Chapter 14

"Everyone should join The Body," David Freeman said as he handed hot chocolate to Tuck and Ham. "It's God's church the way it always should have been."

The Southern Baptist quartet on the radio, the *Good Housekeeping* living room, and David's toothpaste commercial smile combined to create a retro atmosphere.

"David," Tuck said, "Ham and I are interested in joining The Body."

"Praise God in the highest!" David said. He high-fived Tuck and Ham. "The angels are rejoicing in heaven. Especially since you're the sinner who slandered Brother Moody tonight."

"Yes." Tuck hoped he sounded convincing. "The Lord has convicted me of my wrongdoing."

"Wonderful. Like the Lord's grace, Brother Moody's forgiveness is a blessing in this world and the next. Ham, you also need to repent."

"Right," Ham replied, fidgeting in his seat.

"Tuck, it would be fantastic if you could convince April to join The Body, too. You're both friends, and she respects you."

"Before we go there, you hear all kinds of things about The Body—is it true Good Sams can't lie?"

"Yes," David said. "Lying causes so much sin in our world. As Brother Moody says, if you tell the truth, you don't have to remember anything."

Tuck yearned to inform David this truism came from Mark Twain, not Brother Moody. "What about initiation? What's that like?"

David's smile froze. "I, I can't say for sure. I only know it's a life-changing experience."

"You don't remember your own initiation?"

David's eyes went blank. "No."

Tuck hadn't expected this. "How do you account for not remembering?"

David's smile resumed its male model perfection. "Brother Moody had that memory wiped."

Tuck did a double take. Had David gone nuts? "You're saying Brother Moody can erase memories?"

"You know I can't lie."

"But how could he do that?"

David shrugged, his voice monotone. "There must be ways."

"Why would he do that?"

David's face went rigid. "Brother Moody is The Body's Chief Elder. You don't question the Elder of the flock. Hebrews 13:7 tells us to obey our elders and submit to them."

"But David, I Peter chapter 5:1-4 says elders should have compassion on their flock and shouldn't lord it over them."

"Brother Moody doesn't lord it over anyone. You don't question the decisions of the Chief Elder. You obey them, just as Hebrews 13:7 commands."

David was repeating himself as though on a computer loop, but Tuck pressed on. "Tell me, if you don't remember your initiation, do you remember where it was held?"

"If I can't remember having it, how could I remember its location?"

"Do you know where most initiations take place?"

"No." David's eyes narrowed. "What difference does it make? What counts is becoming a Good Sam, a believer whose servant's heart leads him in all his ways."

The gig was up. "Problem is, Brother Moody doesn't have a servant's heart."

David regarded Tuck warily. "Watch yourself, my friend. It's not wise to criticize a prophet. Look to the Old Testament to see the fate of scoffers."

"You really consider Brother Moody a prophet?"

David looked at Tuck as though he were a simpleton. "He's more than a prophet. Second only to the Trinity."

Dad had said the same thing, and the memory drove a spear into Tuck's soul. "David, I know you're being straight with us, so I'm going to be straight with you. I want to know where Clay's gone."

David sneered. "So, this was all a deception."

Tuck rose from the couch, and Ham followed his lead. "I apologize for lying. But Clay is family."

"Clay will be fine. It is you who are in danger of Outer Darkness, my friend. Remember what Scripture says about the days being evil."

Tuck's scalp tingled.

"It's only a matter of time," David said as Tuck and Ham stepped into the night. "One day, both of you will become Good Sams. Or else."

"Or else what?" Ham said.

"You will die."

Tuck shivered against both the cold and David's last comment. He and Ham traipsed to the big man's Toyota, and once inside, Ham said, "What have you gotten us into?"

Rubbing his hands together to warm his icy fingers, Tuck replied, "You want out?"

Ham made a face as he pulled from the driveway. "You know better than that. But Outer Darkness? One day you'll both be Good Sams? This dude's scarier than Michael Myers."

"Well, at least he doesn't carry a butcher knife."

"No," Ham said, turning the car's heater to full blast,

"but he may give me nightmares. Where to?"

Tuck shrugged. "Not sure. Let me think."

The car heater warmed Tuck's legs but couldn't touch the cold spot within his soul. How had it come to this? In days, his little bro might become a stranger, lost like Dad. One day Clay might even order Tuck to become a Good Sam, "or else," as David had threatened. Would Clay demand Mom's conversion as well? What would Clay's transformation into a Perf do to Mom?

If only Moody could be dispatched like Dracula—Tuck would gladly drive a stake through the charlatan's heart or take a stake through his own heart if it would free Clay. But the real world offered few options. God, of course, offered none.

"You okay?" Ham said, glancing from the driver's seat. "Been awful quiet."

Tuck pulled out Coach's business card. "Think it's time to make a phone call."

"Oh, no," Ham said, braking at a four-way stop. "I've got a feeling I'm not gonna like this."

"You won't."

Ham glanced at the business card and sighed. "1-800-Weirder, huh? Now I've heard everything."

"Everything?" A draft coursed through Tuck's soul. "If only."

.

Chapter 15

The number 1-800-Weirder worked, and Tuck arranged to meet Coach at Pizza Palace—because of ARV's finals, this week it remained open until 2 a.m.

In record time, Ham pulled into the restaurant, its crown-shaped neon sign a beacon to late-night pizza fans. Minutes later, Coach's Taurus cruised in, and Tuck, Ham, and Coach secured a booth.

Tuck got down to business. "Coach, what do you know about Clay?"

Coach held up his hand. "Hold on, Tuckster. Clay is safe. Will be for the next few days."

"What are we waiting for?"

"The green light from my higher ups. Everything's cool. But we need to talk."

Mostly pacified, Tuck nodded—Coach had always been a man of his word.

"So," Coach said to Ham, "how long have you known Tuckster?"

"Too long," Ham replied.

Coach chuckled. "I heard that. I was Tuck's high school assistant principal. Tuckster was a big shot in high school."

"Yeah?"

"Straight-A student, basketball star, student body

president—oh, and did I mention unpredictable? As a junior he told the beauty queen if she wouldn't go with him to the prom, he'd break his little finger. She called his bluff. True to his word, he broke his little finger."

"Yeah," Tuck said, recoiling at the memory. "Worst part was, she still wouldn't go to the prom with me."

Ham made a scrunched expression. "Ouch."

Coach's face sobered, a look that had always signaled playtime was over. "Guys, I thought I was going to be talking to Tuck solo." He turned to Ham. "I can drive him home."

Ham looked at Tuck. "This okay with you?"

Beneath the booth table, Tuck twisted his hands. "Let's do things Coach's way."

Ham nodded and rose. "Need to get home, anyway." He squeezed Tuck's shoulder. "Don't worry. We'll find Clay."

Once Ham had left, Coach unzipped his leather jacket and stretched his arms over the back of the booth. "Tuckster, you should know this is a job interview."

Tuck cocked his head. "You're kidding, right?"

"Wrong. My higher ups don't like the idea of me taking you under my wing. Course, I assured them you could help me find Clay." He compressed his lips. "Bring me up to speed."

Tuck did so, Coach nodding at appropriate points, and he showed Coach the baggy with Clay's tooth.

Observing the baggy as though it contained a radioactive isotope, Coach said, "Doesn't surprise me Moody would go this far. Or that the authorities won't help you."

A skinny waitress with a nose ring brought their tea. Once she was out of earshot, Coach continued.

"Gonna tell you some things you probably don't know. The Body is scarier than you think. Brother Moody—familiar with his background?"

Tuck shrugged. "A little. His dad had an affair and killed himself."

"Well, there's more, grasshopper, much more. Moody believes suicide is an unforgivable sin. Couldn't stand the thought of his dad burning in hell for eternity. So, Moody created The Body. According to Body doctrine, as long as every sin is confessed at the time of death, you enter the pearly gates. And if not." Coach made a *shhhtk* sound that accompanied a slicing motion across his throat.

Tuck sipped his tea. Too bitter. "Moody probably uses a combination of hypnosis and drugs and who knows what to brainwash Perfs."

"You're close to the truth. You probably know Brother Moody pulled a man out of a burning car ten years ago."

"Sure, everyone's heard that story."

"Well, the entire incident was staged. The man in the car was one of Moody's followers. But it didn't go as planned— that's why Moody suffered serious burns."

"You don't say."

"Moody parlayed his public heroism to gain financial support for his ministry. Also, Moody brags he's celibate and has remained unmarried because he's committed everything to God. Actually, he was born impotent. Oh, he's rich enough to have surgery to make himself virile, but he refuses because he considers his impotence the thorn in his side—and yes, he equates himself with the Apostle Paul."

"So, he's driven by egotism," Tuck said, dumping a packet of sugar into his tea.

"Not entirely. He really wants to save people from going to hell. He's decided the only way to do that is to make sure people confess their sins as soon as possible after they've converted. His goal is to make people more righteous, so they sin less. He also wanted a way to make believers confess shortly after they have sinned."

Tuck took another swallow of tea and smiled—the packet of sugar had given it just the right sweetness. "And Brother Moody has devised a way to do this."

"Yes. Or to be more precise, his scientists have. Dr.

Albert Sloan—heard of him?"

Tuck shook his head.

"He's a top research scientist who's been working for Moody for two years now. We believe Moody is blackmailing him. Sloan's twelve-year-old daughter disappeared two years ago, and the FBI hasn't been able to find her. We suspect one of Moody's acolytes has her stashed somewhere, that Moody is forcing Sloan to do research to keep his daughter safe."

"Moody would do something like that?"

"In a heartbeat. Remember, to him, he has a noble goal, to turn everyone into a Good Sam so they'll go to heaven."

"Wait a minute—you said Moody's acolytes had her stashed somewhere. You mean as in the devil's acolytes?"

"Not according to Moody. But yes, he uses disgruntled former military men and cops to enforce his will. Of course, they don't become Good Sams."

"Then the three guys that beat me up were acolytes?"

"Sure as shootin'."

"That explains a lot of things."

"The one you call 'Bluto' goes by the nickname Mace. He's Moody's chief enforcer."

"Could acolytes wipe a Good Sam's memory?"

"With the right stuff, sure."

"Tonight, David Freeman said his orientation memories had been wiped. Does Moody do that to all Good Sams?"

"No. He must've been afraid you would ask David where initiation takes place, so had him injected."

"With what?"

"Nanobots. As in nanotechnology. We believe Dr. Sloan has developed nanobots so Moody can control his followers. Probably started six months ago when Good Sams began popping up in Arkansas and got the nickname 'Perfects.'"

"Nanobots? Sounds like *Star Trek*."

"I wish. The nanobots set up housekeeping in your head, rewiring the brain to follow a predetermined script, one that compels the recipient to live out New Testament teachings. That's why Good Sams can work themselves to the brink of exhaustion. Or, as in the sad case of your father, death. Good Sams get a rush of dopamine the more they sacrifice.

"Still, the technology is not perfect. Some Good Sams continue to sin. When they do, if they don't confess within sixty seconds, nanobots release chemicals that cause nausea and anxiety. This continues until the Good Sam confesses, a decision that of course happens in the brain, which then shuts off the nausea and anxiety."

"I see a problem," Tuck said. "Sometimes we deny sins we have committed, so we honestly don't believe we have sinned."

"That is supposedly taken care of during The Purge, during which a variety of means—chemical, psychological, spiritual—are used to force the prospective Good Sam to confess every sin he's aware of before he gets the nanobot treatment. This satisfied Moody. I think he's full of hot air."

"I'm with you. Moody may be rich, but how can he afford this stuff?"

"Friends with deep pockets. Mostly, T.J. LeMay, Aim's mastermind."

"Mmm," Tuck said, stirring his tea, "why aren't I surprised?"

"Sounds like you know LeMay is mostly hiring Perfs for his Aim stores in Arkansas."

"But what keeps them from working 24/7 and putting their survival needs aside?" *Like Dad had.*

"Aim managers, from the top down, give the Aim Perfs their marching orders. Part of that is ordering them to sleep at least six hours out of every twenty-four hours, and to eat three times a day. Aim's Perfs are given designer nans so to them, the managers are biblical elders ministering under Brother Moody. We speculate Moody knew this arrangement would be necessary to satisfy LeMay. Soon, we think Lemay will give the green light for Aims stores across

America to start quietly hiring Perfs only."

"But that's illegal. He'd never get away with it."

"He's getting away with it in Arkansas. Yeah, there've been a couple of lawsuits, but they quietly went away." Coach smirked. "Moody's ultimate goal is to make everybody in the United States a Good Sam."

"But he can't do that now, 'cause if he could, you and I wouldn't be having this conversation."

"Point taken. But he hopes one day to develop airborne nanobots that will turn everyone in the world into Good Sams."

"Holy moly. That's not possible, is it?"

Coach shrugged. "Not now. But in five years, ten, fifteen, who can say?"

Tuck and Coach shared a moment of silence. Three college students in baseball caps goofed off in a booth across the restaurant. Tuck envied them. "The woman who shot Moody and said her son cut his hand off. Did that really happen?"

"Yes. He was only one of many Good Sam failures."

Despite the well-heated restaurant, goose bumps broke out on Tuck's arms. "What kind of failures?"

"I'd rather not say."

"What's the failure rate?"

"Low." Coach smiled. "Worried Clay may be a failure? Not likely."

Tuck found little comfort in Coach's cryptic words but dropped the subject. "A lot of Christians are against nanotechnology. There's some futurist guy I've read about, can't think of his name, but he says nanobots in our brain will make us god-like, that we'll become 'techno sapiens.' Isn't that what Moody is trying to do by making Good Sams sinless? What about free will? Doesn't God want us to choose to follow him, not be forced to?"

"I agree God prizes free will. But Moody would say, isn't it better to go to heaven against your will than go to hell because of your free will?"

"Hell is a messy subject, all right. It keeps some good people from considering Christianity."

Coach leaned back in his booth. "You know the argument that we send ourselves to hell by refusing God's offer of salvation?"

"I bought into that once. Now, I don't know. I guess Moody and I would agree on one thing—hell is a problem."

"Speaking of problems, there's something you haven't asked me, and I'm surprised," Coach said. "Aren't you curious about my organization's interest in Clay?"

Tuck frowned, a sinking feeling in his stomach. "Guess I didn't want to ask." He couldn't read Coach's face, a bad sign. "You're not going to tell me something I don't want to hear, are you?"

Coach leaned forward and lowered his voice. "You can take it."

What could Coach know about Clay that Tuck didn't? The fluttering in his stomach belied his would-be assurance.

Coach raised a brow. "If Moody wins, Clay will not be an ordinary Good Sam. Moody knows about your brother's exceptional faith. Once Clay becomes a Good Sam, Moody hopes to use Clay's faith to—and so help me, I'm not lying—usher in a new heaven and earth."

Tuck shook his head. "That's nuts. Clay is a better man than I'll ever be, but he's no prophet."

"Moody thinks he is. For example, he knows Clay's prayers brought Gollum back to life."

Tuck frowned, recalling the deceased feline rising from the dead twenty-five years ago, but convinced it had been a coincidence. "It didn't happen that way."

"Didn't it? Moody believes it did. He had a vision where Clay was his right-hand man."

The thought of Clay uniting with Dad's murderer turned Tuck's stomach, and tea burped into his throat. "Clay would never go along with Moody."

"Maybe he won't have a choice."

"If he could, what do you think Moody would make Clay do?"

Coach smiled grimly. "We don't know. But we want to find out."

Tuck said, "In sci-fi films, when aliens or whatever take over people, they can't be changed back." Tuck wanted to stop himself but couldn't. "If we find Clay and nanobots have scrambled his brain, can the damage be undone?"

"Probably not. Experimental Prophet-nans were given to ordinary Good Sams to see if they would obey Moody if he ordered them to do something contrary to the Sermon on the Mount. The results were disastrous. Several of the Good Sams went blank, like their brains had short-circuited. Ever seen the old 1950s sci-fi movie *Forbidden Planet*?"

"Nah. Not much into old movies."

"Too bad. In the film, Robby the Robot follows a programmed directive never to harm a human being. But somebody gives Robby the order to use its blaster on a human being. This order runs counter to Robby's directive to never harm people, and the robot shuts down, paralyzed. That's what happened to some of the Good Sams given the Prophet-nans."

Tuck lowered his gaze. "So, Moody is going to give Clay this stuff?"

"Possibly."

Tuck frowned as the assistant manager ran a vacuum cleaner between the booths, its whine grating.

"However, Clay will first undergo The Purge. That buys us at least three days, a good thing because my higher ups have to approve you. That won't happen until tomorrow at the earliest."

Tuck's warm-hearted feelings for Coach wavered, and he wondered if he'd ever known the man. "Maybe I can find Clay on my own." Tuck sat up straight and puffed out his chest. "Ham can help. I've got some leads."

"You've got squat." Coach offered a mirthless smile, his gaze reptilian. "I mentored you for three years. I know when you're trying to pull the wool over ole Coach's eyes."

Tuck held his rigid posture, despite the doubt swirling in his chest. "What happens if your higher ups give me a thumbs down?"

"Then you'll be on your own. But I have a pipeline to someone who can help us find Clay."

"Who?"

Coach shook his head. "Can't tell you now." His tense expression relaxed, and the warmth returned to his smile. "But where's that old optimism? I'm sure my boss will give you a thumbs up. This time tomorrow, we'll probably be hot on Clay's trail."

"What am I supposed to do until then?"

Coach patted Tuck's shoulder. "You might start by getting some sleep."

Once they reached Tuck's house, Coach promised he would give Tuck a call as soon as he knew anything.

His stomach sore, Tuck crashed on his bed, his brain buzzing with Coach's commentary. Clay, a prophet of God? Could Brother Moody make Clay accept such hogwash? A chill rippled across Tuck's shoulders. What if it wasn't hogwash? What if things were worse than Tuck imagined, or could imagine?

Slowly, the quicksand of sleep sucked him under, deep.

A black fog cleared. Clay stood atop the First Baptist Church, his face a warped caricature. The demons he summoned stole into fleeing Winkdale residents, whose possessed bodies twisted like bedsheets in a hurricane. Among the last to succumb, Ham and April shrieked, their bodies contorting as diseased spirits consumed their souls. His eyes wide, Clay turned to Tuck, pointed, and said, "Your turn."

Tuck bolted upright in bed. Soaked in sweat, he thought he saw a shadow flit across the ceiling. But no, that couldn't be—must have been his imagination.

He was still assuring himself he hadn't seen anything when, an hour later, he fell into a troubled slumber.

Chapter 16

As if her righteousness could shame him, Mrs. Moody glared at Mace, all six foot seven of him. She struggled to draw strength from her surroundings—the divan's Bible, the hassock's books, the piano's picture of her late husband—but she longed for a drink. Hard to believe Grahmmie had no qualms about using an acolyte to discipline his own mother.

Mace held out the burner phone and said in his high-pitched rasp, "Take it."

"It's after midnight. Too late to call."

"I said, take it."

"And if I don't?"

Although a ski mask covered Mace's head, she imagined him grinning. "You know your son won't let me seriously injure you. But there are ways to cause pain that leave no marks."

Mrs. Moody stood her ground. "I have a few tricks of my own, you know."

Mace laughed, a falsetto tittering. "Do you now?"

"Yes," she said, cursing the tremor in her voice.

"So, are you a good witch, or a bad witch?"

"My prophecies are from God and God alone. The Holy Spirit has deemed me worthy to dream dreams and see—"

"Well, your son has deemed me worthy to enforce his will, so call Mournful's wife and recant."

"His name isn't Mournful. It's Derek Chambers."

"A Lep is still a Lep by any other name. Call."

What was she going to tell Mrs. Chambers? That it was a case of mistaken identity? That Derek never wanted to speak to her again? That he was dead?

Mrs. Moody called.

Mrs. Chambers said, "We talked this afternoon, didn't we?"

"Yes."

"Please tell me anything else you know. Oh, it would be so good to have Derek home again."

"I'm sure it would be." Please, God, burst my heart.

"You don't know how many nights I've prayed for this. We have a prayer circle at church, and we've been praying Derek would show up."

"Prayer does a soul good." She didn't want to keep stalling but couldn't help herself.

"I've been so worried he was kidnapped, or worse, murdered. But now—"

"Yes, well, Mrs. Chambers, I'm afraid there's a problem."

"Oh?"

"The man I thought was Derek Chambers—he is someone else."

Silence over the air. "But you said this afternoon you'd seen him, that he was safe, that you were going to tell me more—"

"I'm afraid there's nothing more to tell."

"You must be—"

"Mistaken? I only wish I were. I apologize ever so deeply. But I'm sure he's all right, wherever he is."

"How dare you! Is this a prank? What sort of person gets a wife's hopes up and then—"

Mrs. Moody hung up, her eyes stinging. "Satisfied?" she

said to Mace, wiping her face.

"Yes, you could say that, Wicked Witch of the West. I thought you were going to tell Mrs. Chambers her husband was dead."

"That would be too cruel."

"But claiming a case of mistaken identity wasn't?"

Wishing looks could kill, Mrs. Moody glared at Mace. "I hate you more than words can say."

"Glad to hear it. I'd rather you hate me more than words can say than love me more than words can say. You're not my type." He patted her shoulder. "Then again, you're not anyone's type, are you? No wonder your husband killed himself."

Mrs. Moody shook her fists at him. "You're enjoying this, aren't you?"

"No more than I enjoyed hearing my grandmother call me Lava Cheeks. You've never seen me without the ski mask, have you?"

Mrs. Moody shook her head. A sick feeling stirred in her stomach, and she worried if Mace's countenance was as awful as Grahmmie claimed.

Mace fingered his ski mask. Hesitated. Dropped his hand. "Don't worry, I won't make you look. I have some mercy in my soul." He paused. "Still, it'd be a hoot if someone dropped a house on you." Shaking with laughter, he left.

Mrs. Moody collapsed on the divan. What a horrible thing she'd told Derek's wife. How awful to inflate the woman's hopes this afternoon, then puncture them after midnight. Separating the Leps from their loved ones was wrong, and it seared Mrs. Moody's conscience that she was complicit in Grahmmie's godless scheme. Even worse, she was legally culpable as an accomplice to kidnapping—or as Mace called it, Perfnapping.

She needed a drink.

No.

She had to be strong. She hadn't had a drink for two days. Two days! "God, I've held out for you. Please give me the strength." Yes—tomorrow would be sober day number three.

Since her husband's death, God didn't seem to answer her prayers about drinking. How many times had she sought His strength? Dozens? Hundreds? Thousands? The weight of her sin overwhelmed her, and her desperation deepened.

Before her husband's suicide, she had abstained for years. But after he took his life because of his affair with that harlot, she needed something to dull the pain. To her shame, prayer and Bible study hadn't done the trick. Now here she was, debating whether to medicate herself again.

Whom could she call for help?

Not AA. Grahmmie had long ago banned her from using them, calling them apostates.

And not her former followers. Grahmmie had made her disband her group of disciples and give up writing books and maintaining blogs. He said she needed to be humbled, that it wasn't a woman's place to teach other women.

Maybe she could call or text Tuck Jameson. But Grahmmie had said contacting Mr. Jameson could mean trouble not only for her but also the Leps. And they had suffered so much already.

As though in the thrall of an invisible guide, she staggered into the kitchen and poured herself a drink. It burned as it slid down her throat, and she poured herself another. She had the disconnected sense of watching herself in a dream. In no time, warmth baptized her insides. Before long, she wasn't sure how many drinks she had tossed back. Didn't matter. In the background she heard a still, small voice. Determined to drown it, she took another drink and passed out.

Chapter 17

Wrenched from sleep, Tuck grabbed his phone, surprised to hear Mom.

He sat up and tried to shrug off his nightmares. "Mom. What's wrong?" He wished she were here instead of Little Rock.

"Nothing."

"It's five in the morning—obviously, something's wrong."

Her voice sounded small. "Well, it is…and isn't."

"Please. No riddles."

"You okay, son? Really okay?"

"Couldn't be better."

"Liar. Ham called and said you suffered quite a beating last night."

Tuck reminded himself to punch Ham in the nose. "Really, Mom, I'm good."

"Don't patronize me, son. Have you gone to the ER?"

"Of course not. Okay, a couple of thugs roughed me up last night. Don't know why. I'm a little bruised but otherwise no worse for wear."

"Do the police know?"

"Yes."

"And?"

"They're on it, Mom."

"That's not what Ham says. He says they told you to

jump in a lake."

Tuck ran a hand through his sweat-slicked hair. "What else did Ham tell you?"

"That Clay is going to join that awful cult that took Larry's life." She sobbed.

"Mom, Ham was exaggerating, as usual. Clay is only *thinking* about joining The Body. He's not necessarily going to."

"You're lying again. Ham said Clay definitely wants to join. And it wasn't a couple of thugs who beat you up last night—according to Ham, it was three of Brother Moody's acolytes."

"Mom, are you at Aunt Dolly's?"

"Where else would I be?"

"Still taking your antidepressants?"

Silence.

"I asked if you're still taking your antidepressants."

"Don't badger me. I'm barely hanging on as is."

"I assure you I've got things under control."

"Oh, if only I could believe you, son."

"You can."

Her voice grew tearful. "Do you have any idea how close to the edge I am? How awful it is to live without Larry?"

"Mom, I am so sorry. That's why I need to know if you're taking your antidepressants. You need them to get through this thing."

"What thing? Larry's death? Clay's becoming a Good Sam? You getting beaten half to death?" Her voice grew hushed. "I don't think I can bear losing you and Clay."

"You're not going to lose us."

"If I did, there'd be no reason to go on living."

Tuck wished he could change the subject. "Are you saying you've considered killing yourself?"

"Just the thought stages. No plans. But if God takes my whole family, suicide may be my only choice."

"You're wrong." He pictured her shivering, the way she

had the day of Dad's death. He recalled her tears wetting his suit lapel after Dad's burial. It had taken all Tuck's strength to keep from weeping himself. "I can't imagine the depths of your pain, but please think about my pain and Clay's pain if you committed suicide."

"That isn't fair, Tuck."

"I'm sorry, Mom. But we're your sons." His sinuses stung. "We've already lost Dad."

"I know. You're hurting too, and I'm sorry for that. But I can't make any promises."

Wishing he could drive straight to Little Rock, but knowing he couldn't, Tuck struggled to find the right words. "Mom, at least make me one promise. I may be out of touch the next few days. Promise me you'll talk to Aunt Dolly any time you feel the bad thoughts coming on."

Sniffling over the line.

"Mom, promise. Please."

"All right, I promise."

"Thank you."

Another voice started talking to Mom—Aunt Dolly. Apparently, Aunt Dolly had counted Mom's remaining number of antidepressants, and Mom hadn't taken the pills she was supposed to have taken at midnight. Aunt Dolly coaxed Mom into swallowing them, along with a prescription sleeping aid.

"Tuck?" Mom said. "I took my pills." More sniffling. "Just wanted to say I love you before I go to bed."

"Love you too, Mom."

Aunt Dolly took over the phone. "Don't worry, buckaroo," she said, her childhood nickname for Tuck she used when feeling stressed. "Ole Aunt Dolly has things under control."

"Did you know Mom's thinking about suicide?"

"Yes. I've already rallied the troops. Each of the ladies in my Sunday school class will take a shift in your mom's bedroom. We'll be watching her like a hawk 24/7. When she's awake during the day, one of us will stick like glue."

The tightness in Tuck's neck relaxed a notch. "Good to hear, Aunt Dolly."

"Tuck, we're out of your mother's earshot now. I heard her promise you she'd talk to me if she has suicidal feelings. Her word is as good as gold. She never reneges on a promise."

"I'm counting on that."

"Did I ever tell you about the time she promised to take the blame for my first fender bender, and—"

"No offense, Aunt Dolly, but yes, you have told me that story."

She laughed. "Probably only a hundred times, right? Well, you know how us old folks are. I heard you say you might be incommunicado the next few days."

"That's right. A friend and I hope to talk Clay out of becoming a Good Sam."

"What if he doesn't listen?"

"He will." He had to. Tuck's neck tensed.

"Just like your dad, you have the old Jameson confidence. Or arrogance, depending on which day it is." She punctuated the barb with a laugh.

Tuck chuckled. "Thank you for taking care of Mom, Aunt Dolly."

"Don't mention it. And Godspeed to you. You won't say so, but I know you'll be in danger the next few days."

If she only knew the half of it. "Maybe."

"Maybe, my eye. Just know me and my Sunday school class will be praying for you day and night."

"Thanks." Like that would do a lick of good.

After disconnecting, Tuck winced.

He couldn't lose Mom, too. But how would she take it if Clay became a Perf? Or if Tuck should die trying to save Clay? After his beating, Tuck realized Brother Moody meant business, and next time, murder wasn't out of the question. But if Clay and Tuck were taken out, Mom would be left alone, and there was only so long Aunt Dolly and her friends could watch her.

His throat thick, Tuck clenched his fists. Why was this happening? Wasn't Dad's suicide enough? Before Dad had become a Perf, he and Tuck had, for the first time, really started talking. Their last weekend camping trip had been golden, just the two of them, at Dad's request. They'd caught a mess of fish and sated themselves on fried crappie. Tuck had forgotten most of their conversation, but one moment he would never forget—after he and Dad had talked politics before the campfire, Dad squeezed Tuck's shoulder and said, "Son, you may back Senator Jefferson, but you're still all right in my book." Perhaps this was only a crumb under the table, but Tuck savored the memory as though it were a six-course meal.

Then Dad joined The Body. Hadn't even discussed it with Tuck, but Clay had known. Dad became a stranger to Mom, and a cipher to Tuck. He no longer cared about camping trips, only that Tuck join The Body or suffer eternal damnation. When Tuck refused to become a Perf and declared The Body heretical, Dad had disowned him.

If only, somehow, he and Dad could see each other again.

If you're really there, Lord in heaven, answer my prayer.

But the silence grew deafening, and Tuck lamented having resorted to God talk.

Speaking of talk, what bee had gotten under Ham's undershirt to make him tell Mom about the rotten time Tuck had been having? Impulsively, he called his best friend.

Ham answered the phone with a yawn. "It's five-thirty in the morning."

"Glad you can tell time, big guy. Why'd you tell Mom about Clay deciding to become a Perf?"

"She has the right to know. Didn't figure you'd tell her."

"You got that right." Tuck's neck muscles flexed. "Do you realize you've scared her half to death?"

"I didn't mean to."

"She started crying over the phone."

Ham sighed. "Oh, man. I'm sorry."

"If you're referring to your character, we're in total agreement." Tuck's voice rose. "Mom was already having a hard time dealing with Dad's death. I can't believe you'd do something like this."

"Tuck, I said I was sorry. I think she had the right to know."

"She's a troubled woman, barely making it without Dad. Last week she said it felt like half her soul had been torn off."

"That's awful. Beanpole, tell you what. I'll call her and say I didn't know what I was talking about."

Tuck shook his head. "Mom's not an idiot. She'd see through you in a heartbeat."

"So, punch me in the nose next time you see me. I mean it."

Love to take you up on that, big guy. "Don't be a moron."

"Look, if I'd known how depressed she was, I wouldn't have called. How can I make this right?"

Tuck sighed. "You can't. Still meeting me at McDonalds this morning?"

"Of course."

"Don't be late."

Tuck ground his teeth. Ham could be such a dipstick. This was worse than usual, though, because it concerned *Mom*. True, Ham hadn't known how depressed she was—Tuck had hidden that from everybody in Winkdale—and the big guy had meant well.

Also, when things got hairy, Ham had your back, and Tuck had a hunch that things were going to get hairier than a barbershop floor at closing time.

Chapter 18

Over breakfast at the Winkdale Restaurant, April rallied her nerve and told Mom and Dad she might break off her engagement with David.

Mom's fork clattered to her plate. "April, I can't believe my ears."

"Yeah," Dad said, chewing. "You campaigning to be next year's Miss Runaway Bride?"

April inhaled slowly. "I hoped we could talk this over like adults. I'm not a little girl anymore."

Dad said, "Sunshine, you'll always be our little girl."

April smiled, warmed by memories of Dad as her childhood hero.

"No, no, no," Mom said, spoiling the moment. "If April wants to talk this over like adults, fine. Muffin, what do you think the school board will do if you break off another engagement?"

"I don't plan to leave David in the lurch. I know what I did to Mel stunk, but he forgave me. Can't you do the same?"

"April, when you jilted Mel—a doctor, for heaven's sake!—you cast shame on the Showers' family name. This isn't just about you. It's about our family's reputation."

Family's reputation. For Mom, family rarely came first. "Mom, you know I wouldn't want to hurt you or Dad."

"You already have." She sniffled. Restaurant customers turned to watch.

Dad gulped another bite. "April, if you break up with David and get fired, don't come crying to your mother and me."

"Look, I haven't broken off the engagement. I'm just thinking about it."

Mom squinted. "This isn't like you. Who put this crazy idea into your head?"

"Nobody."

"You mean to tell me you haven't talked to anybody about this?"

"Well, I have talked to Tuck."

Mom crumpled her napkin and tossed it on the table. "Him! I never understood what you saw in him. Such a know-it-all."

"He's a good friend."

She and her parents grew quiet, tinkling glasses and clinking silverware filling the void. "Just so you know the whole situation, I have feelings for Tuck."

"What?" Mom yelled. April sensed all eyes had turned to the Showers' table.

Dad whispered to Mom, "Rosie, keep your voice down. People are starting to stare."

"Hmph. Let them." She glared at April. "You can't be serious about Tuck."

"Why not?"

"Muffin, he's damaged goods. The Bible says if you marry a divorced person, you'll be committing adultery."

Dad gestured to Mom and nodded. "What she said."

April replied, "Tuck's wife had an affair. Several. Everybody knows that."

"Muffin," Mom said, "how many times have I told you not to gossip?"

"Oh, about as many times as you've told me the mayor is sleeping with Deacon Johnson's wife."

Dad frowned. "April! How dare you talk to your mother like that?"

Mom pleaded. "I don't understand why you don't want to marry David. He's got a bright future ahead of him—he'll be bank president one day, and he treats you like a princess."

Score two for Mom—April couldn't argue either point.

Mom continued. "Has he ever mistreated you?"

"No."

"That's a real rarity. Not that your father has ever raised a hand to me."

Dad said, "If I ever did, you'd clobber me with one of my golf clubs."

April was contemplating a comeback when David, dapper as always, strode to their table. Leola, the veteran waitress with the white streak running through the middle of her dark hair, hurried over to take David's order, which was a stack of four pancakes, no butter or syrup.

"Now, David," Leola said, "I can't believe anybody could eat pancakes without butter and syrup."

"Don't need 'em," David replied. "This establishment makes the best pancakes on the planet. And, of course, has the best waitress on the planet as well."

Leola blushed. "Oh, how you go on." She poured fresh coffee into Mom and Dad's cups, the aroma tantalizing, but April begged off.

"Thank you for your excellent service," David said to Leola, and she blushed again before scurrying toward the kitchen. April had to admit David was kind to compliment Leola lavishly, and since having become a Good Sam, he also gave generous tips.

Mom said, "David, if you can believe it, April is thinking of breaking off your engagement."

David's shoulders drooped. "Is that true, April?"

She refused to look David in the eye, pretending she didn't notice the heat that had to be turning her cheeks crimson. "Yes." She looked at him, her throat tightening at the concern in his eyes. "I'm sorry. I just don't think marriage might be right for us."

David frowned and tapped his chin, as though trying to solve a math problem. "Is it something I've said or done?"

April knew the answer was "yes," but he'd never understand.

Mom said, "David, I told her you treat her like royalty. I don't understand why that wouldn't be good enough for any woman."

"Frankly," David said, "neither do I. April, I'm doing my best to live out the Lord's commands. If we marry, I promise I will uphold Ephesians 5:25-33. I'm trying to live it out right now. Is there some way I haven't put you on a pedestal?"

"No, David. But I don't want to be put on a pedestal. I want to be treated like a normal human being, one who makes mistakes and has dreams and hopes of her own."

David arched an eyebrow. "Sounds selfish."

"Yes," Mom said, "it certainly does."

April said, "Well, not to me. Everyone needs dreams and hopes of their own."

"Hmm," Dad said, "Have to admit I agree with her."

"David, I'll bet you wouldn't want me to teach Sunday school, would you?"

David looked puzzled. "Of course not. You know what Paul says about that in 1 Timothy 2:12."

"But what about Priscilla? Acts 18:26 tells us she taught a man about the gospel."

"Priscilla taught under her husband Aquila's headship."

"The Bible doesn't say that."

"Man is to exercise authority over women but not vice versa. That's clear throughout Scripture."

"Bet you wouldn't even want me to teach Sunday school to women and children, would you?"

"No. Brother Moody says no woman should teach the Gospel to anyone because the serpent deceived the woman, not the man."

"Adam and Eve were *both* deceived."

David's frown deepened. "Did you bring this up because

you want to teach Sunday school?"

"No. I brought it up because we don't see eye to eye on a lot of things. Would you insist our children be raised as Good Sams?"

"Of course."

"And what if I choose not to become a Good Sam?"

David looked dumbfounded. "You have to. You must. It's the only way to be sure you are following the Lord with all your heart, mind, soul, and strength, the only path to heaven."

"So, what have Christians done for 2,000 years before The Body existed? Is The Body the only true Church on earth?"

"Of course. So-called believers who aren't part of The Body are backsliders in danger of hell."

"Am I in danger of hell?"

"Yes. But if you go through The Body's purge process, you can be sure of your salvation."

April's cheeks burned, and she gestured to Mom and Dad. "What about my parents? Are they in danger of hell too?"

David shrugged. "Of course."

Dad said, "Now hold on just a minute there. We are just as Christian as you."

"No," David said, "you are not. You don't belong to The Body, so if you died this morning, you would both be cast into hell."

"Well!" Mom said, picking up her crumpled napkin so she could toss it to the table again. "David, here I thought you were such a nice young man."

David furrowed his brow. "Ma'am, I am a born-again Good Sam. I am the only true Christian in this restaurant. If you want to be assured of your salvation, you must join The Body."

April trembled. "You never answered my question, David. What if I refuse to be a Good Sam?"

"Then the marriage is off. I will not be unequally yoked to a sinning daughter of Eve."

April bolted to her feet. "Mom, Dad, I hope you have a wonderful day. And David… I don't know what I hope for you."

She dashed to the parking lot and sped all the way home, cops be hanged. Plopping in her recliner, she blew out a rush of air. Mandy, her cat, hopped in her lap and meowed.

"Hi, Mandy," she said, scratching the cat's head. "Wish I had the hard life you have. Must be grueling getting all those naps in every day."

She knew it was ridiculous, but as she'd done in the past, she told Mandy her troubles. Should she break off the engagement? Had David given her any other choice?

Before having become a Good Sam, David wasn't the best communicator, but he had made her laugh. Not anymore. Also, they used to watch old movies, and she loved old movies, but now David refused, claiming movies were, at best, a waste of time and, at worst, the work of godless humanists. He didn't even hang out with his old fishing buddies anymore, primarily spending time with other Good Sams, lockstep believers all. They seemed not only to be of one mind, but of one personality.

She pictured herself as a Good Sam wife with a plastered-on smile and shuddered.

But if she broke off the engagement, she might lose her job and have to leave town to find another, assuring her separation from Tuck. Then again, since Tuck had lost his job last night, he'd probably leave town himself. April's chin trembled at the thought of never seeing him again. Even though they'd broken up years ago, he still owned a piece of her heart.

"Mandy," she said, petting the cat, "what would you do?"

When she'd called Tuck early this morning, she hadn't been able to gauge his mood. She also hadn't said a word about her feelings for him. Did he have feelings for her? She thought he did. But would he act on them?

Tuck would be cleaning out his ARV office around noon, and he said he didn't need any help.

Fat chance.

After lunch, she would show up at ARV to help—in fact, she'd text Tuck to set up an appointment.

"Thanks, Mandy," April said, stroking her cat. "You're better than Dr. Phil was."

The cat purred loudly enough to wake a sleeping baby in China.

Chapter 19

Ham smiled over a sip of coffee. "Shouldn't be long."

Tuck squirmed in the McDonalds' booth. "What shouldn't be long?"

"Molly."

Uh-oh. Tuck took a bite from his sausage biscuit—lukewarm and greasy. He was glad the few customers present sat several booths away. "You two on the outs again?"

"A little."

Tuck raised an eyebrow. "A little?"

"Okay, a lot. But I know how to make things right." He winked. "A present for her and Jake."

"She know you're here?"

"I left a note."

Outside, Molly pulled up in her Buick Century, helped Jake out of the back seat, and slammed the door.

"Speak of the devil," Tuck said.

Ham frowned. "That's not a happy face."

As Molly and Jake moved toward Tuck and Ham's booth, the contrast between mother and son couldn't have been sharper. Molly's jaw was set as though she was ready to chew iron, while Jake's energetic smile suggested impending cartwheels.

Jake ran toward Ham. "Daddy! Daddy!"

Ham scooped up his five-year-old son. "Hey, little man."

"Thanks for the tickets, Daddy!"

"Tickets? What tickets are you talking about, awesome little dude?"

"The ones—"

Molly broke in. "The ones that came in the mail this morning. Three tickets to Disney World in January. The ones you hadn't bothered to tell me about."

"Oh," Ham said, "those tickets."

"Daddy, put me down," Jake said, squirming.

Ham obliged.

Jake looked up at Molly. "May I be excused, Mommy?"

"That depends. You going somewhere?"

"Gotta take a dump."

"Now Jake, I've told you we don't talk that way."

"Mommy's right," Ham said. "You can say, 'Gotta poop,' 'Gotta pass dung,' or 'Gotta doo-doo bad-bad.' But never say 'Gotta take a dump.'"

Jake laughed. Tuck couldn't help but smile himself.

Molly excused Jake to the bathroom, crossed her arms, and glared at Ham.

Tuck shook his head. When was his best friend going to learn?

Molly said, "I suppose you thought that was funny."

"Well, Jake did laugh."

"Sometimes, I don't believe you, Ham."

Tuck fidgeted in his seat. Watching other couples fight reminded him of his final row with June before the divorce. "Uh, look, I can step out for a while if—"

"No," Molly said, her voice softening. "Please stay, Tuck. I want you to hear this."

Tuck nodded and hoped they wouldn't draw knives.

Molly faced Ham. "So. You decide to get tickets for you and Jake, and I suppose me, to go to Disney World in January. How thoughtful."

"I wanted it to be a surprise."

"Oh, it's a surprise, all right. And in the meantime, did it ever occur to you I will need to ask time off to go anywhere in January?"

"Well, sure, but I don't think Professor Johnson will have any problems with—"

"Letting me take time off? How would you know?"

"I admit I didn't think—"

Molly planted fists on hips. "Well, there's a first. You admitting you didn't think. You and 99 percent of the other men in this godforsaken world." She looked Tuck's way. "No offense."

"None taken," Tuck said, crossing his arms. Why couldn't a fire alarm go off?

Ham sighed. "I didn't mean any harm, Molly."

"Was getting the tickets your way of making a down payment on Jake's love?"

Ham's expression hardened. "What's that supposed to mean?"

"You know. I'm sure you've told Tuck, so I don't mind spilling the beans. If we separate, you probably think you'll get custody of Jake."

Tuck lowered his head—he really didn't want to be hearing this.

"Molly, I thought we were past talking about separation."

"Maybe we are, and maybe we aren't. Did you think getting tickets for Jake would make him love you more?"

"That's a terrible thing to say."

"And that third ticket. For me, I presume? Or have you gone on the prowl again?"

Knowing about Ham's previous two extramarital affairs, Tuck hoped he wasn't about to hear of a third.

Ham wagged his head. "For heaven's sakes, no, I haven't gone on the prowl again."

"You've lied about it before."

"Yeah, I did. But I confessed. I apologized."

"All it will take is one more affair." She held up her index finger in front of his face. "Just one more."

"Before what?"

Her eyes narrowed. "You know, Ham hock."

Tuck winced—*Ham hock* was Ham's least favorite nickname.

"Molly, how many times do I have to tell you, there won't be any more affairs."

Molly sighed and looked at the ceiling. "If only you'd asked me about a trip to Disney World before getting the tickets."

"If I knew you'd take it this way, I would have."

Molly's expression softened, and her green eyes became deep pools. "Oh, Ham. We just don't talk any more. Maybe we never did."

Gently, Ham took her arms. "Molly, I thought getting the Disney World tickets would make us all happy. Just the three of us, a family, going somewhere to have fun."

Molly sighed and shook her head. "I wish it was that easy, Ham."

Tuck rested his chin on his hands. Ham and Molly were more civil than he and June had been toward the end—recalling June's parting words, a knife twisted in Tuck's stomach.

Jake rejoined them, his smile plunging into a frown as he looked from Molly to Ham. He turned to Tuck and cleared his throat. "Ms. Jameson, are Mommy and Daddy still mad at each other?"

"Don't know," Tuck said. "Guess you'll have to ask them."

Smiling, Ham kneeled down and ruffled Jake's hair. "Mommy and me aren't mad at each other, Jake."

"Promise?"

"Promise."

Jake stared at Ham for several seconds. He turned towards Molly. "Do you promise too, Mommy?"

A smile flit across Molly's face. "Jake, we need to run."

Jake leaned into Ham. "Do we have to?"

"Yes," Molly said, sniffling, "I'm afraid so, sweetie."

"Okay." Jake looked down as Molly took his hand.

"Remember, Jake," Ham said, "Mommy knows best."

"And Daddy knows second best, right?"

Ham smiled. "You know it, partner." He and Jake bumped fists. But as Jake left with Molly, he hung his head.

Ham sighed. "Oh, man, oh man, oh man. Hate you had to hear all that, good buddy."

"No worries," Tuck said, though he wished he'd been anywhere else on earth the last ten minutes.

Ham sipped his coffee and made a face. "Ugh. Cold."

"Sure you shouldn't go after them?"

Ham shook his head. "Wouldn't do any good. Might make things worse." He frowned. "Can't believe she got so mad about those Disney World tickets."

"Would've been a good idea to clear it with her first."

"I suppose so. But dang it all, I can't believe she thinks I might be catting around again." He locked eyes with Tuck. "Beanpole, it's taken all the willpower I have sometimes to ignore it when a babe looks at me like she's interested. Know what I mean?"

"Sure," Tuck said, guilty at the number of times he'd been tempted himself.

Ham crumpled his coffee cup. "If only she knew how hard I've been trying."

"I hear you, big guy. But remember, you have slept around on her, but she's never slept around on you."

Ham looked as though he'd been skewered. "I know, I know. Dumbest thing I ever did."

"Here's my recommendation. After you help me move out of my office, take Molly and Jake to lunch, just the three of you. Or better yet, text her that you have no intentions of ever taking Jake away from her."

Malice laced Ham's smile. "Oh, no. I'm not gonna go crawling to her. If push comes to shove, there's no way

Molly will ever take Jake away from me."

Tuck and Ham exited McDonald's. Only five feet from the door, Ham lit a cigarette and inhaled as though it were a life-giving tonic.

Tuck wrinkled his nose at the acrid odor. "That's not going to help, big guy."

"Well, you won't let me smoke in your house."

"If it was up to me, I wouldn't let you smoke anywhere."

"You're such a spoilsport."

As Ham continued to drag on his cancer stick, Tuck wondered if Ham's resolve to stiff-arm Molly would coarsen. Should Tuck try to set him straight? No. Ham was trying to hide it, but his deep draws on his cigarette were a sure sign he was ticked. Better to let Ham simmer a while, then try to straighten him out. Course, Tuck had already told Ham what he should do.

As Ham snuffed out his cigarette, Tuck inwardly sighed—if only people would listen to him.

Chapter 20

His bruised stomach burning, Tuck swore as he stuffed office diplomas, books, and knickknacks into two computer boxes. He snatched the ARV baseball cap from his desk and shoved it over unwashed hair. Ham teased him about being a neat freak, but after last night's beating, this morning's conversation with Mom, and the blowup between Ham and Molly an hour ago, Tuck didn't care how he looked.

So what if Dr. Pritchard would be meeting him in fifteen minutes? He'd already fired Tuck. What more could the warhorse do?

Tuck packed sacred family pictures, mostly of Mom, Dad, and Clay. There was also the one of just him and Dad from Tuck's college graduation—Tuck still thought their big grins looked ridiculous. Half an hour after that picture had been taken, Dad had treated Tuck to a pricey dinner at the fanciest steak house in Fort Lincoln. Now Dad was gone, Mom had fled to Little Rock, and Clay was fixing to become a Good Sam. Could things get worse?

He tried to stifle his fears and focus instead on a photo almost as important to him as his family's—him with the Resident Director and Resident Assistants of Stribling Hall, the all-male residence hall he'd mentored the last three years. The guys had all autographed the photo. Who knew it would so quickly become a memento?

The last thing Tuck packed meant more than all the rest—a hand-written thank you note from Clay: "Of all the big brothers in the world, I thank God daily He blessed me with the finest of them all. May the Lord grant you the hopes of your heart." The words blurred, as they always did, and Tuck gently placed this treasure in a clear plastic bag, which he taped shut with the greatest of care.

Tuck couldn't wait any longer. He called Coach.

"Tuckster, I told you I'd call when I got clearance."

"I keep thinking about Clay's tooth."

"That was just a scare tactic. Moody won't seriously hurt Clay—he needs him too bad, just like you need me to find Clay."

"Maybe I could go to The Body's Temple by myself."

"They won't hold Clay there. Even if Moody is at The Temple, armed guards patrol the place. How do you propose getting in?"

"You're the black ops guy. Don't you have any ideas?"

"Plenty. But we want to be smart about this. It takes three days for a new Perf to go through the Purge. That buys us time. Back at Winkdale High, did I ever let you down?"

"No."

"So do you trust ole Coach now?"

"I want to."

"That the best you can do?"

"Yep."

"Sport, without me, you don't stand a chance of finding Clay. With me, you have a good shot."

Tuck frowned. "All right, I'll wait." *For now.*

"I'm on your side, Tuck."

"Yeah." Tuck punched off the phone. His cheeks burned—Coach's tone had changed. Last night he'd talked about how he needed Tuck's help, but now his slant was that Tuck needed *his* help. And hang it all if Coach wasn't right.

A wheel squeaked from the hall, and Ham pushed a lopsided dolly into Tuck's office. "One tire is flat," he said, "but it'll do. Sorry it took me so long."

"No worries."

Ham frowned at the two filled boxes. "What's up with that? I told you to wait to pack till I got back."

Tuck waved the concern aside, though actually, his stomach throbbed. "I'm fine."

"Yeah, right," Ham said, "about as fine as your trashed truck."

Ham insisted on loading the boxes on the dolly. Tuck wasn't helpless and thought about dressing down his friend, but realized he was having a case of AMS—acute macho syndrome. He chuckled inside.

Scanning the now featureless walls, Ham whistled. "Man. Just not gonna be the same here without you."

"Well," Tuck said, "what's done is done and can't be undone. I'm sure going to miss this place. In fact…" Tuck stopped before he became emotional.

As though rescuing Tuck from the awkward moment, Dr. Pritchard stepped in. Ham acknowledged Dr. Pritchard, but Tuck just stared.

"Glad you're on time, Jameson," Dr. Pritchard said.

"Thank you, sir."

"A few things. Don't even think about suing me or the school. I can have you blacklisted. Don't make me do that. Just get out of town peaceably."

Tuck frowned. "You may have the right to fire me, Dr. Pritchard, but you can't tell me where to live."

"Just some friendly advice, Jameson. Take it or leave it." He pointed at Tuck. "One last thing. The Stribling Hall RAs? Better call them off or I'll expel their insolent behinds."

"Don't know what you're talking about."

Dr. Pritchard smirked. "In case you really don't know, I'm talking about the posts they've plastered on social media. Shut it down, or else."

The VP pivoted and marched from the office.

On his smartphone, Tuck went to Facebook. The

Stribling Hall post read, "For speaking his mind, for criticizing Brother Moody and The Body, Mr. J has been fired, but Mr. J has the right to free speech like any other citizen in this country, and Dr. Pritchard had no right to fire him. If you agree, share this page. Tell your friends—skip class on Monday and meet at Stribling Hall at 8 a.m. We are going to organize a protest vigil outside President Green's office."

Ham was looking at his own phone. "Looks bad. The Stribling RAs could get expelled."

"Yeah," Tuck said, "but ARV would face potential lawsuits if they kick them out."

"I doubt Dr. Pritchard cares."

"I'm sure he doesn't."

Tuck texted Farris and asked the Resident Director and his RAs to meet him ASAP in front of the Student Services building. Farris texted back, *Will do, Mr. J. Need to see u anyways. Got something for u.*

Tuck said, "Hope I can talk some sense into their stubborn heads."

Ham snickered. "You, the dean of bullheadedness, are calling them stubborn? Now I've heard everything." Ham's expression sobered. "What if they won't listen to you?"

"I'll cross that bridge when I come to it."

"Well, you may be crossing to it pretty darn quick."

Chapter 21

The Rolling Stones' song "The Last Time" played in Tuck's head as he greeted Stribling Hall's Residence Director and four Residence Assistants on the Student Services plaza:

Hunter Tomkins, white, sporting his Ducks Unlimited cap;

Manny Rodriguez, Hispanic, campus heartthrob, about which he received endless teasing from his fellow RAs;

Drew McCoy, white, self-proclaimed uber-Geek.

Jerome Sims, African American, wearing his "Mr. ARV" windbreaker;

And Farris Steel, their Resident Director, white, a Who's Who recipient destined for great things. Farris held something, and Tuck hoped he didn't get emotional when he received it.

"Mr. J," Farris said, his thin hair tufted by a cold December breeze, "we heard you've been banned from the Leadership Banquet tonight. That stinks."

"Amen to that," Jerome said. "We all know you're getting a raw deal."

His fellow RAs echoed Jerome's sentiments.

"And," Hunter said, "come Monday, we ain't going to class."

Shouting agreement, the guys pumped their fists.

"Mr. J," Drew said, "you've always been there for us."

"Yeah," Jerome added. "Brought more food pantry donations than all the other halls put together."

Farris: "Got pizza for the whole res hall every Super Bowl."

Manny: "Got in the dunk tank for Res Hall Olympics every year."

Hunter: "For an old dude ready for the nursing home, you're all right!"

The gang laughed.

Overwhelmed, Tuck's throat tightened. "Guys, I appreciate it. But I didn't get a raw deal."

The RAs' responses overlapped: "We ain't havin' that, Mr. J." "No way." "No freaking way." "We see how it is."

Tuck held up his hands. "No, really, guys, I'm okay. Dr. Pritchard is the boss, and he's totally within his rights to fire my behind."

The RAs murmured disagreement.

Tuck ignored them. "Would you guys do me a favor?"

"Sure, Mr. J.," Farris said. "Anything."

"Go to class Monday. Tell everyone else in Stribling Hall to attend class Monday. Take down your social media posts about me getting a raw deal."

The RAs shook their heads.

"Mr. J, I don't know," Drew said. "That would be letting you down."

"No," Tuck said. "I assure you, if you guys really respect me, you'll do what I ask. ARV is a great school, and I don't want it to get a black eye on my account. Get me?"

Farris turned to his four RAs. "What do you say, guys?"

Heads hung low, all four nodded.

"Mr. J," Farris said, "we had intended to give this to you tonight at the Leadership Banquet, but since you won't be attending, we want to give it to you now."

Tuck took the plaque, cherry wood with a high-gloss finish and a gold faceplate engraved with the words: "To Mr. Tuck Jameson, Mentor of the Year, With Heartfelt

Appreciation and Gratitude from the Resident Director and Resident Assistants of Stribling Hall."

"Mr. J," Farris said, "you also need to know it isn't just us hoodlums who think you're an okay dude. I surveyed your colleagues about who the best res hall mentor was, and sixty percent chose you."

Tuck hadn't expected that, and his nose stung, but he had to stay in control—these guys deserved an inspiring send-off.

"Thank you, gentlemen," Tuck said. "You're all fine young men, and it's been a privilege working with you. I wish all of you the best. Even you, Hunter."

That provoked a ripple of laughter.

"Now gentlemen, I hate to cut this short, but I happen to have a date at 12:30."

Farris and the RAs grinned and winked at each other. "Whoa, Mr. J's got a date." " Way to go, Mr. J." "Don't keep her out too late, Mr. J."

After they were done joshing, Tuck shook hands with each of them. Beaming at the ragtag group as though they were his own children headed for a distant land, Tuck gave them a thumbs up. "Make me proud, men."

"You know it, Mr. J." "Have a great life, Mr. J." "Take care."

Drew stayed after the others had trooped off, the wind stirring his thick hair.

"Mr. J," Drew said, "I'll make doubly sure the social media stuff comes down."

"Thank you, Drew."

The young man hung his head. "Something I have to tell you."

"What is it?"

Still looking down, Drew said, "That letter you got in Student Services saying you better not go to Brother Moody's presentation?"

"How did you know about—"

"I wrote it."

Tuck felt as though he was in a roller coaster car that had leaped from its tracks. "You wrote it?"

"Yes, sir." He looked up. "I plan to become a Good Sam."

Alarm stabbed Tuck's chest. This couldn't be. "Drew, no."

"You're wrong about Brother Moody. Dead wrong." Drew offered a faint smile. "I'll be praying you will see the light."

As Drew walked off, the wind buffeting leaves across the sidewalk, Tuck couldn't believe what he'd just heard. How could someone as smart and decent as Drew fall for Brother Moody's lies?

God, if you're listening, please rescue Drew.

Tuck recoiled. What had happened to his newfound deist status? But even if God had heard his prayer, didn't matter. When you needed God, He was off healing lepers somewhere two thousand years ago.

Chapter 22

With his phone to his ear in front of the Weaver Student Services Building, Tuck squeezed his eyes shut. "So, you'll do it?"

"Yes," Marv said. "What you've told me about this Adam Shimura—"

"Coach."

"Yes, Coach, sounds fascinating. Should be an intriguing topic of investigation."

After Tuck thanked Marv, he bit his lower lip—he hated having Coach investigated, but he had questions. Why had Coach gone into black ops? The reason was no doubt important, though Tuck dreaded finding out what it might be.

April arrived at 12:30 p.m. on the dot, and Tuck shivered, but not from the cold.

"So," April said, sitting beside him on a bench, "where's Ham?"

Her subtle perfume could win a man over with ease. "Working in his office. He's my wheels today."

"Well, I could have been."

"Didn't want to bother you."

She smiled impishly. "That so? Or did you think all the packing and heavy lifting should be left to macho men like you and Ham?"

"You know better than that."

"Maybe I do, maybe I don't."

"You do."

She asked about his beating from the previous night, and Tuck considered showing her his black and blue belly but thought better of it.

"I can tell you this," Tuck said. "My stomach is more tender than an Elvis Presley love song."

She rolled her eyes. "You and your golden oldies."

"They beat the new stuff hands down."

"So you say." The mischief in her eyes changed to concern. "Still no idea who roughed you up last night?"

"No." He wouldn't get April mixed up in this.

"Even if you did know, I don't think you'd tell me."

"Maybe I would, maybe I wouldn't."

"Don't be flip, Tuck. Those guys could've killed you. If anything had happened to you…"

Tuck displayed indifference, but her unfinished sentence sent tingles down his spine. Was her concern as a friend, or something more? The chilled drizzle that grazed his cheeks offered no answers. Overhead, the gray clouds thickened, blotting out the sun the same way Tuck's uncertainty blotted out his hopes.

April pushed back her hair. "Talked to Mom and Dad this morning."

"Oh? What new gossip did your mom share?"

April swiped Tuck's arm. "That's a terrible thing to say."

"That's a true thing to say."

"You're awful!"

After the teasing, she shared that she'd told her parents and David she might break off her engagement.

"How did David take it?"

"Badly. I stormed out of the restaurant after he told me and Mom and Dad we were all going to hell."

"Well, that could definitely be a conversation killer." He hoped that might merit a chuckle, but it didn't. "What do your parents think about you breaking it off with David?"

"Mom doesn't get it. I think Dad does, but he's afraid to say anything." April studied her hands. "Mom's worried I might get fired."

"Mm. I'd hate to see you lose your job."

April's face went sour, as though she'd swallowed a grapefruit whole. "You said it would be best for me to break off with David."

"I know. But if you lost your job, what would you do?"

April cocked an eyebrow. "I imagine I'd find another one."

"Might not be that easy."

"Meaning what?"

"Meaning education jobs are hard to come by."

She shook her head. "I don't believe you."

"What?" Tuck's face flushed.

"I guess you think I'd have to move home with Mom and Dad until Prince Charming came along to sweep me off my feet."

"I don't mean that at all."

"A prize catch, no doubt, with a six-figure income and a vacation home in Bermuda."

"Come on, April, that's not fair—"

"And besides all that, what about us?"

The outburst left Tuck speechless. Slowly, he examined April's face. In her eyes he saw hurt and hope. The years melted away, and he pictured himself stupidly breaking up with her because he'd fallen for June, who'd used all her considerable sexual allure to nab him. "Us?"

April frowned. "Look, I know you're hoping I cancel my engagement with David. You're just too polite to say so."

Tuck wanted to touch her, but didn't, couldn't. "April… there can't be any us."

"What do you mean? I thought—"

"You thought wrong."

"That's a lie."

"April, I'm sorry. I'm unemployed now. I may get

blacklisted." He spread his hands. "I have no security to offer."

"If I break up with David, we'll both be out of work." She smiled, her eyes misting. "So what? We'll set up housekeeping in a charming cardboard box under a highway overpass."

Tuck shook his head. "No, April. It's more than that. Don't you see? I'm no good. For you. For anybody."

She sighed and raised a hand into the air. "The divorce thing again? You had biblical grounds for divorce."

"But if I had been a real man, I wouldn't have… it wouldn't have…"

April furrowed her brow.

Tuck ached to take her in his arms, like old times. "Us. It just wouldn't be right." He was proud to have said his piece, but part of him needed April to balk.

She tapped her chin, her hair growing damp as the drizzle became a steady sprinkle. "Maybe you're right."

Tuck hadn't expected that and didn't like hearing it. She was supposed to disagree vehemently. "I'm glad you're seeing reason."

"Yeah," she said, running a hand through her long honey blond hair, now wet. "You're probably right. It would never work between us."

He wanted to say, *why not?* But instead, he said, "You need someone better than me. Somebody who can offer you more."

"Yes," she said. "I do deserve someone better."

She might as well have slammed him in the head with a hammer.

She smiled. "Funny. I never saw you as a loser."

Tuck's chest turned cold. *Loser*—that's what June had called him as her parting shot. That couldn't be April's last word to him, too.

As though having been released from a great burden, April strolled to her Camry.

The sprinkle burst into a downpour, and Tuck watched April pull from the parking lot. His head tingled as though dozens of needles lanced his scalp, and he hoped April would turn just once to look his way. But she didn't, her gaze apparently trained on a future without Tuck Jameson.

A police cruiser eased up to the curb of the Weaver Student Services Building, and Tuck shook his head, cold rain dripping from his soaked hair. What now?

Chapter 23

Two suits left the squad car and introduced themselves to Tuck—the short one with a neatly trimmed mustache was Detective Sam Kowalczyk, his tall partner, Detective Dusty Munoz. Both appeared oblivious to the rain.

"Mr. Jameson," Red Mustache (what was his name again?) said, "we'd like you to come to the station and answer a few questions."

Tuck smoothed back his wet hair. "Am I under arrest?"

Red Mustache smiled. "Not at all, Mr. Jameson. But if you would, please follow us to the station. It won't take long."

Tuck called Ham, and the duo followed the police sedan in Ham's Toyota.

Ham said, "What's going on, beanpole?"

"You tell me."

"How'd they know where to find you?"

"Don't know. Dr. Pritchard maybe. Anonymous tip. Lots of folks knew I was moving out of my office today."

"Yeah, guess so."

Ham tailed the cop cruiser to the old brick police station on 3rd and Jackson next to Hardy's Pawn Shop, its porch festooned as always with a tattered American flag.

Ham waited in the car, and the two detectives took Tuck

to a small room with a plain desk and three chairs. A strong disinfectant odor clawed into Tuck's nostrils.

"Sorry about the smell," Red Mustache said, draping his rain-dampened suit coat over the back of one of two chairs that faced Tuck. "A guy puked in here. You know how it is."

Tuck figured Red Mustache's affable tone was intended to relax him, but the detective's words had the opposite effect. Why would someone vomit in here? Sick to their stomach, or a reaction to intense interrogation? Or had Tuck watched too many reruns of *Law & Order*?

"Mr. Jameson," the tall detective said in a deep voice that fit his lean looks and severe crewcut, "we appreciate you coming down here. Like my partner said, we just want to ask a few questions."

"Sure."

"But we would like to Mirandize you first."

Uh-oh. "Read me my rights? Am I a suspect?"

"Mr. James, an acquaintance of yours, David Freeman, was found murdered inside his home this morning."

Tuck's scalp prickled. "I can't believe it." Dread seized his heart in an icy embrace. "You don't think I have anything to do with it, do you?"

"We have to cover all our bases, Mr. Jameson. Right now, we don't know who murdered Mr. Freeman. So, we have to cast a wide net. That's why we want to read you your rights."

Tuck took a deep breath. Maybe if he went along with them, they'd realize he was innocent. No reason to antagonize them. "Okay, you can read me my rights."

Crew Cut did so while Red Mustache punched on a digital voice recorder. Both detectives sat and assumed relaxed postures.

Red Mustache said, "Did you know Mr. Freeman well?"

Tuck shrugged. "Not really. We're only acquaintances."

Crewcut said, "Ever see him socially?"

"Occasionally. We don't—didn't have a lot in common."

"Where were you this morning around 11 a.m.?"

"Home. I'd had breakfast with a friend, and he took me home while he ran a couple of errands. He was my wheels because my truck got trashed last night."

"Yeah," Red Mustache said. "Vandalism is becoming a plague in small town America."

Tuck considered telling the detective what had really happened to his truck but decided that might be a bad idea.

Crewcut crossed his arms. "Can anyone verify you were at home around 11 a.m. today?"

Sweat sprouted across Tuck's forehead, and he couldn't will it away. "Not exactly. April Showers called me around then. Ask her. Check our phone records."

"No worries," Red Mustache said. "Own any firearms, Mr. Jameson?"

"Yes."

"Used any of them lately?"

"No." Sweat stung his eye. "Look, I haven't killed anyone. But I've got to leave town this afternoon." Tuck chastised himself—what the blazes was wrong with him?

"Urgent business?" Red Mustache said.

"You could say that. But I'm not running away 'cause I killed David."

"Mr. Jameson," Red Mustache said, leaning forward, "you mentioned earlier you and April Showers had a phone conversation this morning. How would you characterize your relationship with Ms. Showers?"

"We're friends."

Crewcut arched an eyebrow. "Nothing more?"

"No."

"She's not married, so if the two of you are intimately involved, you're not committing adultery. We're not going to spread it around town."

"We are not involved."

"What about April and David? How would you characterize their relationship?"

"Well, they're engaged. They get—got along okay."

"No recent fights?"

Tuck wiped his forehead—they apparently suspected April. "I hear they had a tiff this morning."

"What about?"

Tuck's mouth dried. Like it or not, he had to tell the truth. "About maybe ending the engagement."

Red Mustache nodded. "Sounds serious."

"You don't really think April could have shot David?"

Crewcut shrugged. "Who said he got shot?"

"You asked me if I had a weapon and if I'd used it lately. That implied David had been shot."

Red Mustache said, "Sure does, Mr. Jameson. But we're not accusing anyone of anything. We're just trying to get as much information as we can."

"My partner's right," Crewcut added. "We know you're a solid citizen, but we have to check all leads."

Red Mustache rose, followed by his partner. Tuck also stood.

"Mr. Jameson," Red Mustache said, "thank you for taking the time to speak with us. We know your time is valuable. We won't hold you any longer."

"But," Red Mustache said, "we may need you for further questioning."

"Also," Crewcut said, "we'll be checking your and April Showers' phone records."

After Tuck got in Ham's Toyota, he told his friend about this new development.

Ham whistled. "Wow. I can't believe David is dead. We were just talking to him last night."

"Yeah," Tuck said. "Hard to wrap your head around."

Ham raised his hands. "How can somebody be here one minute and gone the next? Who would want to kill David?"

"Search me," Tuck said, heart beating in his throat.

"When was the last time we even had a homicide in Winkdale?"

A year ago on Thanksgiving. But Tuck just shrugged—might seem incriminating if he said it. He ran a hand through his hair. Man, he couldn't believe he was thinking this stuff.

"Hey," Ham said, looking at him funny, "you okay?"

Tuck nodded. "Sure. Just thinking about David's parents and friends… and April." Tuck had never cottoned to David, but he had seemed like a decent enough guy. He meant well, despite having become a Perf. Plus, April was probably still in love with him. And now this. "Gotta admit I feel guilty after being in his house last night."

"The cops think you or April did it?"

"Looks that way."

"Why would April kill David?"

Tuck considered sharing April and David's falling out but decided against it. "I'm sure she wouldn't."

"Then who would?"

"Can't say." Tuck scratched his nose. "Maybe Brother Moody is involved."

"You think he'd go that far?"

"I wouldn't put it past him."

"But what would be the point?"

"Not sure. But there's a lot I don't know about Moody." And a lot he needed to find out.

Ham pulled onto 3rd street. "You say anything about Clay?"

"After Sergeant Wakeman's reaction last night? Not on your life."

Ham punched on an oldies station and briefly sang along with Bryan Adams' "Summer of '69." "So, what's next?"

"Wait for Coach's call, then peel out to find Clay."

"After what the cops just told you?"

"I'm not under arrest."

"But they said they might need you for further questioning. If you run, they might slap you with an arrest warrant, haul your behind to jail. You wouldn't be able to help Clay then." Ham braked at a four-way stop at the same time as an opposing Dodge Ram, and he waved the pickup on.

"Are you suggesting," Tuck said, "that I let Moody brainwash Clay? 'Cause once it's done…" Tuck knew he shouldn't have let that slip.

"Once what's done?"

Tuck had entrusted Ham with a wealth of sensitive information during the last seven years—but Coach's revelations about Moody, The Body, and Clay?

"Look," Tuck said, "I have reason to believe once it's done, it can't be reversed."

"Who told you that? That guy you call Coach?"

"I can't answer that."

"You don't have to. Here I thought you trusted me with everything."

The accusation stung, even though Tuck had good reason to keep a lid on Coach's information. Still, withholding it from Ham seemed disloyal.

Ham and Tuck rode the rest of the way to Tuck's house in silence, Tuck wondering if he should clue Ham in on just how ominous Moody's plans were. If Coach called today— and when was he going to call anyway?—and said his higher ups had nixed the idea of bringing Tuck on board, he would be on his own. In that case, Ham would make an ironclad ally.

Considering his next move, Tuck asked Ham into his house.

"So," Ham said, motioning to Tuck's demolished Ford pickup as he and Tuck walked to the door. "You just gonna leave that smashed truck in the drive?"

Tuck shrugged. "I'll worry about it later." Much later.

Once inside, Ham plopped into a recliner in the living room, and Tuck paced. "Ham, Coach told me some things last night, some incredible things, about Brother Moody and The Body. And worst of all, about Clay."

Ham leaned forward. "I'm listening."

"You have Molly and Jake to consider. Because when you hear what I've got to say, it's going to scare you spitless." He paused for intentional dramatic effect. "If you help me find Clay, your life may be in jeopardy."

An eyebrow shot up. "You serious?"

"As a heart attack. If you help me, you need to understand what you'd be getting into."

Ham's face grew solemn, as though he were a pallbearer at a funeral. "Tuck, you're my friend. A man doesn't have many friends in life. If this is as serious as you say, you're gonna need help."

"You need to know the stakes before I tell you more. And I hope I'm dead wrong about how far Moody will go."

"Doesn't matter. I don't wimp out on my pals. Consider me on board."

"But what about Molly? Jake?"

"I don't want Jake to have the kind of daddy who turns his back on his friends. If I don't help you find Clay, I could never look Jake in the eye without knowing his old man was a coward. Like I said, I'm in whether you like it or not."

Tuck smiled, struggling to keep his stoic façade intact. "Thanks, big guy."

Tuck told Ham almost everything, his friend astonished at each new revelation, but Tuck didn't tell him about the cult's use of nanotechnology. That was Coach's most explosive secret, one Tuck chose to keep under wraps. Instead, Tuck just told Ham that Good Sams had been brainwashed and left it at that.

Tuck was taking a risk—what would Coach think?—but if Coach refused to let Ham accompany them on their quest to find Clay, at least Ham would know most of the truth so he could hold down the fort in Winkdale. Or could he?

Chapter 24

Torture on his mind, Brother Moody entered the trailer home at dusk, and its floor squeaked.

OG&E had shut off the power a year ago, but a Coleman gas lantern lit the room, casting thick shadows behind Mace and the workbench to which Mace had strapped Kenny. Moody sidestepped mouse droppings whose stench stained the air. A cockroach scuttled across Kenny's shoulder, and the disobedient acolyte yelped.

This trailer's coarseness recalled European torture dungeons. Moody had once disdained such medieval practices, but the closer he got to God, the more he realized how wrong he had been.

As always, Mace looked like a professional wrestler from hell clad in black, including his perennial ski mask. Few knew he wore the mask to hide his face, the flesh of which resembled blowtorched plastic. Kids teased him during grade school, so as a teenager, Mace had taken up bodybuilding and pummeled his former bullies into submission. Such began his skirmishes with the law—a perfect acolyte.

Stripped to his boxer shorts, Kenny lay chest down across a workbench, leather straps binding his hands, arms, and legs. Mace had bound Kenny's ankles so that the soles of his feet faced the ceiling. The acolyte whimpered as Moody crossed his arms.

"Chief Elder," Kenny said, his face sweat-slicked, "I swear to God I was just trying to help."

"Don't swear, Kenny," Moody said, as though rebuking an unruly child. "It's not fitting for an acolyte of the Church of the Body of Jesus Christ to swear. By shooting David Freeman, you've put all Good Sams at risk. Killing is the last resort, never the first."

"But I framed Tuck Jameson for it! I used a gun like his and left it there, and-and I told the cops I saw Tuck coming out of David's house this morning."

Moody shook his head. "If you left your gun, the police will probably find your fingerprints on it."

"But, but I wiped 'em off like I seen on TV."

"Did you use gloves when you broke into David's house?"

"Didn't need to. David done left the door unlocked."

"I don't like to repeat myself. Gloves? Did you wear them?"

Kenny lowered his eyes. "N-no, sir."

"Then you probably left fingerprints. You have a simple mind, Kenny. Did blood get on any of your clothes?"

"No, sir. At least, I d-don't think so."

"What about your goatee? A whisker might have fallen off. Someone might have seen you go in or out of David's house."

Kenny looked mortified. "I, I didn't think about that, Chief Elder. But I don't think no one saw me."

Moody ignored him. "Tuck Jameson is a problem, yes, but Mace had already taken care of him."

"But," Kenny said, "I did it so's Tuck can't find Clay and ruin everything."

Moody replied, "You killed David Freeman without submitting to the Chief Elder's authority."

Tears spilled down Kenny's cheeks. "Please, Chief

Elder, I didn't mean no harm."

"Even worse," Moody continued, his voice deepening, "David Freeman was a Good Sam, one of us, and you murdered him."

Kenny looked in Mace's direction. The acolyte clutched a large cane. "Please don't let Mace hurt me, Chief Elder."

"Mace won't kill you, Kenny. You'll survive, and we'll provide medical aid if necessary."

Panic crawled into Kenny's eyes. "Medical aid?"

Moody's resolve hardened. "A torture known as foot whipping has existed for centuries, both in the East and the West. It goes by many names—bastinado, foot caning. The Nazis used it in their concentration camps."

Kenny's voice became a whispered croak. "Is that, is that what Mace is gonna do to me?"

"The purpose is to inflict punishment without leaving any marks. Mace will use the cane to strike the soles of your feet, particularly the arches. Many nerve endings are clustered there, and a typical caning results in agonizing pain."

"Please, Chief Elder…"

"Hebrews 12:17 teaches that God is not moved by unrighteous tears. He ignored Esau's tears. I will ignore yours." He turned to Mace. "Proceed."

Mace did so, and Kenny's screams filled the trailer—it was over a mile from the nearest neighbor, so no one would hear.

A minute later, Moody considered stopping Mace. But with each slap of cane against flesh, he realized the rightness of Kenny's punishment. After all, Hebrews 12:7 declared that God disciplined his sons, so could Moody do any less to his servants?

The trailer floor squeaked fiercely with each of Mace's blows, and Moody worried Mace might cause serious injury—caning that was too vigorous could break bones. But perhaps that's what Kenny deserved.

Praying for Kenny's soul, Moody left, content that Mace was doing the Lord's work. He had to remember to reward the acolyte with his favorite meal.

Chapter 25

In her living room, April had started half a dozen texts to Tuck, ranging from "Sorry I called you a loser" to "Snap out of it, wimp!" She'd erased them all.

Mandy purred as April and the cat snuggled in the recliner, Mandy warm against April's belly. "Mandy, can you believe I called him a loser?"

If this were a Hallmark Channel movie, she would have accidentally sent the "loser" text, a series of misunderstandings would occur, and two hours later, just when it looked as if they were going to part for good, they would bond, romantic soulmates for eternity.

"Why can't it be that way in real life, Mandy? Grandma always said, 'God will come to the rescue.' I used to believe that. Until today."

Made for each other—that's what classmates had said about her and Tuck during high school. She and Tuck joked about it when they played tennis. He claimed she won their first match because of beginner's luck, but she told him it was beginner's superiority. They both laughed.

So many memories. The richness of his cologne, the warmth of his hands, the tenderness in his eyes. Almost going too far that one night—and swearing they would never do so again, a vow they'd kept. But she'd never seen the breakup coming. And she'd never have guessed he had fallen for her temperamental and spoiled doubles partner June.

April made a face, imagining, as she often did, June falling into the bad place.

But April would pray for June's soul if God would just let her have Tuck back.

Mandy shifted as April started another text to Tuck. She erased it when inspiration hit—instead of Tuck, she'd text Clay.

True, she rarely texted Clay, and he probably had romantic feelings for her. But after seeing how The Body had changed David, April knew Clay wouldn't be the same person they had known and loved all these years if he became a Good Sam. In Tuckspeak, Clay would have become a brainwashed Perf.

Scratching behind her cat's ears, April sighed. "Mandy, here goes nothing."

She sent Clay a simple text: *"Clay, ur brother is worried about u. U K?"*

In seconds, she received a response: *"I'm OK. How is Tuck?"*

"Concerned about u joining The Body. Says u haven't answered his texts."

"He means well. Wrong about The Body."

"Why not text him?"

"I am not texting anyone in Winkdale except you."

April raised an eyebrow—why only her? Because he had a crush on her? Something more serious?

April texted: *"I don't suppose u'll tell me where u are?"*

"No. You'd tell Tuck. I know he's sweet on you. And you on him."

April frowned. *"Clay, I'm engaged to David."*

"I know. People in love don't always wind up together. Life isn't a Hallmark movie."

She smiled at his ironic remark, given her musings minutes earlier—could this be God trying to tell her something? *"Clay, please text Tuck. U know he'd die for u."*

Seconds passed, and April wondered if her text had been

too strong. Then: *"Tuck doesn't need to die for me. Jesus Christ has already. I need to die to myself. If I do, I'll be free to serve the Lord 24/7."*

"Clay, Tuck is ur brother."

"All men are my brothers." A pause. *"Brother Moody says I can't text you again."*

April texted back: *"Clay, don't shut us out. We care about u."*

Two minutes later, April set her smartphone aside. Cults like The Body discouraged communication with family and friends. So many prominent Arkansans—politicians, lawyers, business leaders—gave Brother Moody and his church a thumbs up. What if those same Arkansans changed like David? What if Clay became like David? She shuddered at the thought.

Her phone buzzed—Mom calling. April rolled her eyes. "Guess I should take this, huh, Mandy?" In response, the cat licked its paw.

April answered, surprised to find Mom hysterical. "Muffin! I'm so, so sorry."

"About what?"

"You don't know?" Mom's words devolved into sobs.

"April"—Dad must have taken the phone from Mom—"you'll have to excuse your mother. Are you all right, pumpkin?"

"All right about what?"

"You mean, you haven't heard? David... David was murdered today."

The breath caught in her throat. She couldn't have heard right. "What?"

"I'm afraid so, April. It's on the news. Terrible."

Shock chilled April's chest. "I can't believe it. How? Who killed him?"

"They don't know yet, sweetheart."

Mother's voice came back on the line. "Muffin, we know you didn't mean the mean things you said to David at breakfast. But those are the last words you said to him. I'm sure you're sorry." April felt as though Mom had slapped her in the face. Of all the things Mom could have said, she'd chosen some of the cruelest words possible. Subtlety—and sensitivity—had never been her strong suits.

Mom relapsed into raucous sobs, and Dad chastised her for her last remark. "April, your mother shouldn't have— you know she doesn't always realize what she's saying."

"I know, Daddy."

"Would you like us to come over?"

"No. I've got Dr. Mandy to talk to."

Dad chuckled. "You and that cat."

The shock had given way to a sinking emptiness. "Really, Daddy, I'm okay. Promise."

Headlights swept through the front window curtains, and April wondered who might be driving up this time of night— she wasn't expecting anyone. It was only fifteen after nine, but still…

"Daddy, somebody just drove up."

"Who?"

"Not sure. I'll call you back."

It surprised April to see two men in business suits at the door, one tall and thin, the other short and stocky. After introductions, April said, "Is this about David?"

"Yes," the one who'd identified himself as Detective Kowalczyk said. "I'm afraid so."

April held back tears. "I just heard the news."

"We're very sorry for your loss, ma'am."

She inhaled deeply. "Do David's parents know?"

"Yes. We've spoken with them. We hate to intrude at a time like this, but the more information we can gather, the quicker we can find the perpetrator of this crime."

Feeling as though she were in a bad dream, April invited the two officers in. They sat on the divan, and she served them coffee. The odor was rich—and disturbing. David had often told April that freshly brewed coffee was his favorite smell, and coffee had been the one vice he'd clung to as a Good Sam. April's throat tightened.

"Ms. Showers," Detective Kowalczyk said, "would you mind if we Mirandize you?"

Adrenaline shot through her body. "Am I a suspect?"

Detective Munoz said, "Reading you your rights is basically a formality. But it's necessary in order for us to ask you questions."

April fidgeted in her chair. His pleasant voice sounded reassuring. And she'd rather answer questions than have them think she was hiding something. She gave them permission to Mirandize her. Afterwards, with a nervous smile, she said, "Fire away."

Detective Kowalczyk said, "Ms. Showers, where were you this morning around 11 a.m.?"

As she answered the detectives' questions, she moved to the edge of the recliner. If she said one wrong thing, she might go from being a person of interest to a person behind bars. She wished Mandy could speak on her behalf, but the cat seemed more interested in curling up next to Detective Kowalczyk and taking a nap.

"So," Detective Munoz said, "we understand you and Mr. Freeman had a fight this morning."

April swallowed. "Yes, that's true."

"What about?"

How much should she tell? "Our upcoming wedding."

"Would you characterize the argument as serious?" Detective Kowalczyk said.

"Yes. You could say it was serious."

"Were you considering breaking off the engagement?"

"Yes."

"How did Mr. Freeman feel about that?"

April's forehead felt damp, her hands clammy. "He wasn't happy."

Detective Munoz said, "We've also heard rumors about a relationship between you and Tuck Jameson. Any truth to those rumors?"

"No. We're just friends." April winced inside.

"So, you don't have any feelings for Mr. Jameson?"

April struggled to stay calm. "No."

Detective Kowalczyk cut in. "You sure?"

"No, I'm not sure. Okay, yes, I do have feelings for Tuck. But that has nothing to do with my argument with David."

"You may not have mentioned it to Mr. Freeman, Ms. Showers, but are you certain your feelings for Mr. Jameson might not have contributed to your doubts about marrying Mr. Freeman?"

She fidgeted. "Yes. I'm certain." She prayed her body language hadn't given her away.

After a few more questions, the two detectives thanked April for her time and left.

April held her forehead and looked at Mandy, who had moved where Detective Kowalczyk had just been sitting. "Can you believe the third degree they gave me, Mandy? Thank God that's over."

Or was it? A flood of feelings drowned April's short-lived relief. She couldn't believe David was dead, that someone had murdered him. Despite their differences since David had become a Good Sam, April cared for him deeply, and now he was gone. Hot tears boiled down her cheeks.

How dare those detectives suggest her feelings for Tuck might have led her to kill David? Or did the detectives think Tuck and April had partnered to murder David, like a femme fatale and her lover in an old 1940s' film noir movie— *Double Indemnity*, anyone?

"Maybe," she said to Mandy, "they were just doing their job."

But who had murdered David? Could it have something to do with The Body? She'd known since David's transformation that something wasn't on the up-and-up about Brother Moody and his cult. Did they control the town? Were the detectives who grilled her secretly under his power? Did Moody want her imprisoned?

And who would care for Mandy if she went to jail?

The thought made her laugh, briefly, before she buried her face in her hands and sobbed.

Chapter 26

Ordering his pulse to slow down, Tuck said, "What's the verdict?"

Coach stretched his arms across the back of Tuck's living room sofa—a classic Coach pose—and smiled. "You're in like Flynn."

Relief washed over Tuck. Thank God. But God had nothing to do with it, did He?

Coach cocked his head. "Afraid I was going to say 'no'?"

"Frankly, yes."

"And I know just what you would have done."

"Enlighten me."

"Try to find Clay on your own, with Ham's help."

Coach had him pegged right on that one. "So, you think you've got me nailed?"

Coach's grin widened. "I know I do."

"Speaking of Ham, he's on his way over."

"Oh?"

"He and Molly had a fight. A bad one."

"In other words, she's thrown him out again."

Tuck blinked in surprise. "Well, yeah."

"They fight all the time. He's crashed on your couch before."

"Guess you know all my secrets."

"And then some." Coach donned his smug look, the one that had gotten him into trouble at school board meetings.

"So, what are we going to do about Ham?"

Tuck recoiled at Coach's tone. "I hope we're going to take him with us."

"Even though he hasn't been vetted?"

"Coach, I'd trust him with my life."

"But would I?" Coach arched an eyebrow. "No worries. I'm a known maverick. The agency keeps me because I'm so darn good." He winked. "Ham can join our posse."

Tuck had expected an argument. "Just like that?"

"I would have taken you with me even without my superior's approval. But I needed to see if you were still a straight arrow. Besides, sweating it out can be good for the soul."

Heat flooded Tuck's cheeks. Of all the lousy… "You're really something, Coach. I can't believe you made me wait when it wasn't necessary."

Coach waved his hand. "Cool your jets. The Purge takes at least three days. Moody likes the symbolism of three days mirroring the Trinity."

"But if today counts as one of those days, that only leaves two."

"Tomorrow is Sunday. That's the traditional day Moody begins the week's Purges. That gives us three days."

"Why should we wait that long?"

Coach leaned forward. "Because you need to meet someone."

"Who?"

"Wild horses couldn't drag it out of me."

"Then tell me when and where we're meeting them."

Coach smiled. "You'll find out. Or not."

"What's that supposed to mean?"

"All I can tell you for now."

"You're hiding something."

"Obviously. That's what black ops agents do." The smugness vanished from Coach's face, replaced with an earnest set of his jaw. "Trust me."

Tuck wanted to, but in his gut, something didn't feel right. Still, what choice did he have? Coach was his best bet to rescue Clay—unless Coach turned out to be a double agent for Brother Moody. Not likely. But possible. Meaning Tuck would have to keep his eyes pried open.

Five minutes later, a Chevy Silverado roared into the drive. A Luke Bryan anthem blared from its cab, and one of Ham's friends dropped him at Tuck's doorstep. Ham carried a suitcase and reintroduced himself to Coach, who wasted no time letting Ham know he was on board for the mission. Likewise, Tuck wasted no time letting Ham know he disapproved of the nicotine stink that clung to his friend's clothes.

"Give it a rest," Ham said, collapsing in the rocking chair Tuck had inherited from his grandmother.

"Big guy, if I've told you once, I've told you a thousand times. Cigarettes aren't called cancer sticks for nothing."

Ham closed his eyes and sighed. "Not in the mood, beanpole. Molly wants a separation. Thinks I'm having an affair."

"Are you?" Tuck regretted the words after they'd left his mouth.

Ham looked at Tuck as though he'd been ambushed. "Thanks for the vote of confidence."

"Sorry. Didn't mean it the way it sounded."

"How did you mean it?"

"I think," Coach said, "he means you've slept around on Molly before."

Ham fumed, his chair squeaking as he rocked. "I've been behaving myself."

"Maybe," Coach said, "but once you've broken a woman's trust, it's hard to get it back."

Ham stopped rocking and glared at Coach. But in seconds, his angry expression melted into regret, and he hung his head. "That's true. I've let Molly down twice before. She's got a right to believe the worst."

Tuck touched Ham's arm. "Look, big guy. She'll come around. Show her you're a changed man."

"What do you think I've been trying to do?"

"I know, I know." But Tuck had his doubts—his husky friend flirted at the drop of a come-on. He didn't know when to leave well enough alone.

Ham stared at the floor. "Molly said if we divorce, she'll make sure I never see Jake again."

Tuck's chest tightened. Jake was Ham's pride and joy, and the six-year-old revered his daddy more than his beloved Captain America.

Still, Tuck could see Molly's side. Ham needed more discipline, less impulsiveness. But how could Tuck ever get that into his bud's thick head? Why wouldn't people realize what was best for them?

"Well," Coach said, "time to make tracks."

"Not so fast," Ham said, his words lowering a decibel.

Tuck cocked his head. That was Ham's caution voice— what was up?

"Mr. Shimura," Ham said. "I did me a little checking. Found out why you left Winkdale."

Coach appeared unfazed. "Oh?"

"Found out your ex-wife died under mysterious circumstances. Some townies think you were involved."

Coach shook his head. "Townies think a lot of things."

"Were you?"

"Involved?" Coach snorted. "What do you think?"

"Don't know."

Anxiety clenched the back of Tuck's neck—where was Ham going with this? Maybe he should derail this train. "Look, Ham, we have to find Clay. Of course, Coach had nothing to do with his ex-wife's death."

"Then what about his grandfather's ties to Unit 731?"

Tuck frowned. "How do you know about that?"

"C'mon, Tuck. It's on the Internet. Two of the bigwigs on the school board when Coach here's ex-wife died did a little digging. Found out his grandfather was one of the doctors for Japan's Unit 731 during World War II."

Tuck didn't want to hear this. He knew all about Unit 731—the live vivisections of POWs without anesthesia, the medical experimentation on Chinese civilians, the injection of plague into prisoners. "Coach had nothing to do with that. You can't blame him for what his grandfather did."

"As Pop used to say, the apple doesn't fall far from the tree."

Coach rose and put hands behind his back, his diplomatic pose. "I can understand why you might think that, Ham. But I had nothing to do with Sondra's death."

Ham cocked his head. "No? Or the disappearance of her body from the morgue?"

"No," Coach said. "I hate what happened to Sondra. I was as shocked as anybody else. I wish it had been me instead of her."

Ham's expression softened a degree. Coach's sincere tone seemed to be winning him over. "You're saying it's a coincidence?"

"That's what I'm saying."

Tuck said, "Ham, you've experienced guilt by association. If a Razorback got busted, a lot of folks tarnished you and your teammates with the same broad brush."

Ham nodded. "True."

Coach said, "Ham, Tuck's telling the truth. My question to you—are you with us?" He extended a hand.

After hesitating, Ham shook Coach's hand and held the grip for several seconds. "I'm with you."

Coach smiled. "Glad to have you on board."

"Thanks, Mr. Shimura."

"Call me Coach."

"Okay. Coach." Ham's mellow expression indicated he was probably settled on the matter. For now, anyway.

In a light tone, Coach said, "As my old man used to say,

tomorrow is a big day. Let's load up and head out."

"Where to?" Tuck said.

"A rental house in Jonesburg. Everything we need for our mission is there." Coach smiled enigmatically. "You will be amazed at what you see and hear tomorrow afternoon."

In minutes, the trio was zipping down I-40 headed northwest, Tuck riding shotgun, Ham in back. In the car's close confines, the nicotine stink on Ham's clothes thickened, but Tuck resolved to keep quiet. Coach didn't seem to mind the stench, or if he did, chose to say nothing, maybe a bid to further win Ham over.

As the night deepened, red taillights dotted the interstate's westbound lanes. A state police sedan zoomed past them, light bar flashing but no siren sounding. Tuck exhaled slowly. Last thing they needed was state police on their tail.

"Coach," Tuck said as the Ford Taurus's speedometer climbed from 75 to 82, "you think it's a good idea to break the speed limit?"

From the back, Ham said, "Don't listen to Tuck, Coach. He's always been a grandma on the highway."

Tuck ignored his friend's barb and said to Coach, "Surely, we don't want the police to pull us over."

"We've got nothing to hide," Coach said, "and don't call me Shirley."

Tuck and his high school mentor laughed.

"*Airplane*, right?" Tuck said.

"You got it," Coach replied.

"Airplane?" Ham said, apparently unaware of the 1980 movie or its famous pun. "What does an airplane have to do with the 'don't call me Shirley' remark?"

Tuck and Coach exchanged looks.

"Culturally deprived," Tuck said with mock solemnity. "Sad."

"Yeah," Coach agreed, touching a fist to his heart. "Gets you right here."

Ham shook his head. "Whatever, cheddar."

Anxiety shoved Tuck's merriment aside. "Coach, I may not be under arrest, but I think the cops wanted me to stay in Winkdale. And I think we could all agree I have definitely fled the premises."

"Copy that," Coach said. He eased the Taurus to 70 and stayed in the slow lane. "But you can't be anything more than a person of interest, or you'd already be in jail."

"Yeah," Ham said, "but old Tuck here hasn't had the best luck lately. Still hate that Dr. Pritchard canned you."

Tuck shrugged and donned his poker face, unable to quiet the tremors in his belly. "It is what it is."

Ham continued. "The Winkdale PD may decide you killed David. That's nuts, but I imagine they feel pressure to pin it on somebody. And your story—you were at home waiting for me—isn't exactly airtight. In fact, I'd say it was alibi-challenged."

"But it's the truth."

"You know that, and I know that, but the men in blue don't."

"They can do whatever they want with me after we rescue Clay."

"Just one thing. What if Clay doesn't want to be rescued?"

Tuck had only dimly considered the possibility, and he didn't appreciate Ham shining a spotlight on it. "I'll talk him into it."

"What if that doesn't work?"

Tuck watched a semi speed past them in the fast lane. "It will."

"But if it doesn't?"

"Then kidnapping may not be out of the question." Tuck couldn't believe he had said those words, hearing them as though they had come from a man he didn't know. But he wouldn't take them back, even if he could. Clay's soul was at stake.

"Gents," Coach said in a carefree voice, apparently intended to lighten the mood, "what say we play a little music to cheer us up while we're headed down the path to perdition?"

"Oldies 105.8!" Ham said. "My favorite station."

Moments later, Bruce Springsteen's "Glory Days" blared.

Ham pumped a fist. "Pop's favorite song!"

He rocked out big time, bellowing the lyrics. Ham's technique may have been questionable, but his pleasure was infectious, and Tuck joined in. Coach came in on the third verse, and the trio belted out the song like a tone-deaf boy band.

Next, the radio blared U2's "I Still Haven't Found What I'm Looking For," and this time it was Tuck's turn to rock out—U2 was his favorite group. His voice broke as he strained to hit Bono's high notes, and Ham howled. But as Tuck warbled his best, the song's lyrics of unfulfilled longing hit too close to home, searing his joy into ashes.

"Heads up, dudes," Coach shouted over the music as he took the Jonesburg exit onto Highway 74. "Going to be changing vehicles soon."

Ten miles from the exit, Coach cut off the radio and pulled onto a dirt road beside which a wooden sign read "No Trespassing."

"Don't worry," Coach said, "the sign is one of ours."

Like many unpaved roads in rural Arkansas, thick trees, mostly oaks, towered over both sides of the road, their branches interlocking overhead as though forming a hand to screen out the stars. Despite its bumpiness, the ride was smoother than the jaunts in the sticks Tuck had taken with his teenage buddies back in the day.

Tuck read his smartphone texts, something he hadn't done since Dr. Pritchard had canned him. Multiple ARV colleagues deemed Tuck's dismissal unjust. A couple threatened to go to President Green.

Marv Gillespie's text expressed condolences over Tuck's firing and also asked when Tuck could meet for an interview, noting "*You don't have the excuse of employment to put me off any longer.*" If someone else had written that, Tuck might have taken offense, but Marv's peculiar remark resonated with the professor's offbeat humor. There was more: "*Found some interesting information about your Coach. Will share later.*" Tuck hoped "interesting" didn't mean "nefarious." He'd had second thoughts about just how much he wanted to know about Coach's past. But integrity demanded he hear the truth.

While he was grateful to have heard from Marv, Tuck hadn't gotten a text from the one person he'd most hoped to hear from—April.

Five miles later, Coach braked beside a Buick Century.

"Okay, guys," Coach said, "leave your smartphones in the Taurus."

"Can't do that," Ham said. "That's my lifeline to civilization."

"It's also an easy way for Moody's acolytes to find us. We leave our smartphones here so we can't be tracked to the safe house."

Ham looked troubled. "No cell phones at all?"

"We'll use burner phones," Coach said. "I've got one for each of us at the safe house. They can't be tracked, and we dispose of 'em after we use 'em."

"Man," Ham said as they boarded the Buick Century, "I didn't realize this was going to be all James Bond."

"Coach," Tuck said, "time for a quick text to April?"

Coach frowned. "Hurry it up. Tell her you're headed to Little Rock."

"To throw off The Body if it's monitoring the conversation?"

"Bingo."

Tuck texted: "*April, I will be gone to Little Rock for a while. Sorry about our last convo. Also, no matter what anybody says, I didn't kill David."* "Can I wait for a reply?"

Coach glowered. "Five minutes. No more."

Seconds later, Tuck's phone pinged. April's text read, *"Sorry about our convo 2. I know u didn't kill David. Talk is eyewitness saw u leave his house."*

Tuck: *"Not true."*

April: *"Could be arrest warrant for u soon. Gotta go."*

Tuck: *"Don't leave me hanging like this."*

But she did.

Chapter 27

Coach planted hands on hips. "Get the lead out, Tuckster!"

Reluctantly, Tuck tossed the smartphone into the Ford Taurus and boarded the Buick Century.

Coach tore back to Highway 74 and turned right. "Moody's goons have had plenty of time to scope out the Taurus, 'cause I've been driving it three days. They won't be expecting this Buick. Nobody tailed us off the interstate, so we should be good to go."

Twenty minutes later, they arrived at the safe house on the outskirts of Jonesburg. Unlike a snazzy high-tech hideaway in a 007 movie, it was just an ordinary ranch home—single story, low-pitch roofline, rectangular design, mixed exterior of stucco and brick. But of course, Tuck figured black ops agents like Coach had to keep a modest profile, and houses didn't get more commonplace than this.

Once inside, Coach set a laptop on the kitchen table and clutched another. "Gents, I'm taking my laptop to the bedroom. Don't want to give you the willies, but I have to look at some sensitive sites meant for my eyes only."

Tuck nodded. "We understand."

Coach continued. "While I'm in the bedroom, go to Brother Moody's The Body site. There's new stuff on it— some of it about you, Tuckster—as well as the usual rah-rah anecdotes about what a holy man Moody is. It's good material to look at to prepare for the surprise I have in store for you tomorrow."

Tuck went to The Body site, and Ham sat beside him at the kitchen table.

"You know, beanpole," Ham said, "I don't think you're going to find anything important."

"What makes you so sure?"

"This is just a wild goose chase while Coach is looking at who knows what in the bedroom."

"I can't see it will do any harm."

"I can't see it will do any good."

Tuck regarded Ham with mixed curiosity and worry. "What have you got against Coach? Besides his grandfather, I mean?"

"Just a feeling," Ham said. "I don't think we should trust the guy."

Tuck wasn't about to tell Ham he shared his friend's misgivings. "Well, he can help us find and rescue Clay. As a black ops operative, he's got resources we can't touch."

"I hear you, beanpole. You're saying we have no choice but to trust him."

"Basically, yes."

On the laptop, The Body's attractive homepage displayed the cult's motto "One Body, Many Hearts." Beneath it was a photo of the gun-shot Brother Moody in the hospital, smiling, flanked by two Good Sams. The headline read, "Brother Moody hits another home run for Christ! You can't keep a good saint down!"

From the menu, Tuck clicked to "Ten Most In Need of Prayer," only to find his picture—an unflattering shot of his ranting during Brother Moody's Bailey Coliseum presentation—set at the top. The text called Tuck a lost soul for whom a prayer chain had been organized, and proclaimed Good Sams should treat him with compassion and grace.

A photo of the woman who had shot Moody at the conference set just beneath Tuck's.

"Wow," Ham said, "they think you're even badder than the lady who plugged Moody."

"Big surprise," Tuck replied. He moved to the "Endorsement" section, less than amazed to find T. J. LeMay and other Arkansas luminaries showcased there, praising Moody as though he were God's right-hand man.

Under "Testimonials" was the usual. Beneath a beaming Good Sam female—she looked like the same one in The Body promotional video—the headline read, "My husband used to beat me, but since he became a Good Sam, he puts me on a pedestal!"

Tuck navigated to "Sticks and Stones," a laundry list of The Body's public naysayers. The website designer had prominently posted the ACLU there, with the text declaring the organization was an avowed enemy of The Body. Other foes included a libertarian-leaning state senator who denounced The Body's authoritarian hold over its members. About these adversaries, the site read, "We make enemies on both sides of the political fence, just as Christ would have if he were walking the earth today."

The true thorn in The Body's side, small in numbers but big in outrage, was The Anti-Bodies, headed by Maurice Holcomb, listed dead last on the "Sticks and Stones" section as though they were an irritation rather than a serious threat. Word on the street said the Anti-Bodies had produced a TV ad filled with testimonials about The Body's abuses and excesses, but because of its controversial nature, no Arkansas TV channel would air it.

"Wish I owned a TV station," Tuck said. "I'd sure as all that's holy air it."

"Yeah," Ham replied, "but that ad would make some bigwigs in Arkansas unhappy campers."

"Not just bigwigs in Arkansas," Coach said behind them, having seemingly appeared from nowhere. "The Body is aiming at the top—the beltway. In the future, of course."

"So," Tuck said, "we have to wait until tomorrow

afternoon to meet this mystery person who can shed some light on Clay's location. Any chance we could do this in the morning?"

Coach's face went slack, his demeanor aloof. "No."

The way he said it—as though it were a warning—unnerved Tuck, and he was glad Ham didn't respond with a smart-aleck comeback. He wondered just what lay in store tomorrow.

Coach's expression returned to its usual affable bearing. "You guys ready to hit the sack?"

"Not sure," Ham said, stretching.

"Yeah," Tuck said. "I had nightmares last night." The vision of Clay siccing demons on Winkdale sent a shudder down his spine. "Don't know if I can sleep anyway, thinking about tomorrow."

"Well," Coach said, "if we're going to be up anyhow, might as well hear some of Ham's war stories from his UofA Razorback days."

Ham smiled. "You a Razorback fan?"

"Born and bred."

As though they were tailgating, Coach opened a bag of cool ranch Doritos, unsealed cheese dip, and handed Tuck and Ham chilled Cokes. They retired to the living room, where Tuck scarfed the refreshments, savoring the salty flavor. He figured he might suffer an acid reflux attack in the morning, but so what? His two companions likewise indulged themselves.

As the chips, dip, and pop disappeared, passionate onetime offensive lineman Ham answered Coach's questions about specific Arkansas Razorback games, strategies, rumors, coaches, players, you name it. Tuck had heard it all before, but it was nice seeing Ham bask in his element. Still, Tuck's mind returned to Clay every few seconds—where was his little bro? And if they did have to wind up kidnapping him, what happened next? If only Clay had listened to Tuck instead of tuning him out, as always.

But with any luck, in the next three days, they would wrest Clay from Brother Moody. And if not? Tuck would cross that bridge when he came to it.

Chapter 28

Brother Moody smiled—so far, so good. Still, the most important questions awaited.

The White Room's walls, floor, ceiling, and chairs glowed in spotless purity. Clay lay on an altar. In a bleached robe, he looked born for this chamber. Other prospective Good Sams clashed with the décor, the rot of their souls an offense to the cell. The gravity of their sins made some candidates vomit, whimper, or beg—the nantruth pills prevented them from consciously lying, and the torrent of transgressions that poured forth had become, after dozens of similar confessionals, tedious. So, Moody had entrusted assistant elders to perform the task while he only spot-checked the results.

But Clay was different. Only Moody deserved to lead him through the ordeal.

Freshly scrubbed, Clay smelled of scented soap, a fitting exterior for the interior cleansing that awaited.

"Clay," Moody said, "we've discussed your civic, educational, and professional life. Now we must delve into your personal life."

"I understand," Clay said, his inflection flat.

"When did you start feeling attraction toward women?"

"When I was twelve."

"Did you date during your junior high school years?"

"No."

"Did you date during your high school years?"

"Once."

"With or without an adult chaperone?"

"Without."

"Did anything come of it?"

"I asked if I could kiss her, and she said no. I felt stupid and embarrassed."

"I see. When you turned eighteen, your father made you a camp counselor at Cove Lake. Correct?"

"Yes."

"And you were entrusted with high school age boys?"

"Yes."

"But there were girls in an adjoining church camp. True?"

"True."

"Did you meet any of the female counselors of the girls' church camp?"

"Yes. One of them."

"Was her name Rosie Thornton?"

"How did you know?"

Hard to believe that wasn't obvious. "The Holy Spirit shows many truths to me." Clay's trusting expression revealed he'd bought it. "Tell me, did you and Rosie become friends?"

"Yes."

"More than friends?"

"Yes."

Moody warmed to the subject. "What happened?"

Clay told Moody the two of them found a private place in the woods. There, Clay confessed to Rosie he didn't know how to kiss a girl. She showed him. Both of them being sexually naïve, before long they went too far. Moody longed to hear clinical details about the couple's lovemaking but restrained himself. "Did you tell the church camp superintendent?"

"No."

"To the best of your knowledge, did Rosie tell anyone?"

"No."

"Did she get pregnant?"

"No."

"You and Rosie lived on opposite sides of the state. Did the two of you keep in contact following church camp?"

"Only through emails and phone calls. Once we were sure she wasn't pregnant, we thanked God and again asked His forgiveness. After a couple more phone calls, we never spoke again. I pray for her sometimes."

Moody pondered his response. "Did you tell your father?"

"Yes."

"How did he react?"

"He was disappointed. Told me I could never again be a church camp counselor, that for the next twelve months, I couldn't teach Sunday school."

"Was he angry with you?" As if Moody didn't know.

"Yes."

"Did he forgive you?"

"Yes. But he told me I needed to learn that though sins are forgiven, they have consequences. That's why he wouldn't let me teach Sunday school—he knew it was my favorite ministry."

"And you taught an adult Sunday school class, correct, even though you were only eighteen?"

"Yes."

"Why did you tell them you would not be teaching anymore?"

"I didn't. Dad told them he'd decided I was too immature to teach adults, that God had other duties for me."

"Did you consider that a lie?"

Clay wrinkled his nose. "Sometimes. Sometimes I rationalized it. Dad was a great guy. But everyone falls short of the glory of the Lord."

"Amen. Since that time with Rosie, have you ever again

slept with anyone?"

"No."

"We live in a highly sexualized culture. As a single Christian, how have you handled your sex drive in the eighteen years since you slept with Rosie?"

"Self-stimulation. I don't plan to do it. Weeks pass, and I think I've become strong enough in the Lord to give it up. Even thank Him for his deliverance. Then I relapse." He frowned. "I always feel terrible afterwards."

Don't we all. "Some Christians say the practice is a sin. What do you say?"

"I say it's better to err on the side of caution and not do it than to wind up burning in hell."

Smart boy. "Have you told anyone but me about this struggle?"

His tone became plaintive. "No. It's my secret sin. My secret shame."

"When was the last time you did it?"

"Six weeks ago. But I'm done, Brother Moody. That's one reason I want to join The Body, so I can live a holy life free of sin."

Moody could barely hide a smile. "How far would you go to show the Lord you will now remain celibate?"

"As far as necessary."

"Would you have a chemical castration for the Lord?"
"Yes."

"Would you have a physical castration for the Lord?"
Clay paused. "Yes."

"Would you be castrated if I asked you to?"

This time, Clay waited several seconds before responding. "If I felt the Lord was leading me to, yes."

"Good answer. Do nothing you don't believe the Lord leads you to do. Would you marry if you had the chance?"

"No."

"Why not?"

"Because I want to be fully devoted to the Lord. And I'm

afraid I wouldn't be a good father."

"Why do you say that?"

"Because I'm not a regular guy. I don't hunt, I'm not into sports. I'm afraid any son I had would be ashamed of me."

"You think rural culture would mean more to your son than having a nonconformist father who loves him?"

"Yes. Most guys in church are regular guys. My brother Tuck is."

"Speaking of Tuck, do you have feelings of resentment towards him?"

"Yes."

"Only sometimes, or 24/7?"

"Both."

"Do you typically pretend you don't have these hostile feelings?"

"Yes."

"Do you bury and deny these hostile feelings?"

"Yes."

"Would you like to kill him?"

"No."

"Hurt him?"

"Maybe."

Maybe? Under the influence of the nantruth pills, Clay shouldn't be able to deceive—but perhaps he felt conflicted about his feelings for his older brother. Moody chose a different   route.

"Clay, are you certain God is leading you to become a Good Sam?"

"Absolutely."

"If you become a Good Sam, people will say you are brainwashed. Will you be able to handle that?"

Clay's voice rang with passion. "Chief Elder, I want to be free from sin. I don't want to keep going back to my own vomit. I want to love the Lord with all my heart, mind, soul, and strength, and if it takes brainwashing to make that happen, I welcome it."

"Just how far would you go to please the Lord?"

"As far as necessary."

"Would you disown friends for the Lord?"

"Yes."

"Coworkers?"

"Yes."

"Family?"

A hesitation. "Yes."

"Would you disown Tuck for the Lord?"

"Not sure what you mean."

"Would you shun him for the Lord?"

"Yes."

"Never see him again for the Lord?

A pause. "Yes."

"Would you kill him for the Lord?"

Clay looked puzzled, as though two sets of wheels in his head were spinning in opposite directions.

Moody said, "God told Abraham to kill his son."

"But it was just a test. God intervened and spared his son's life."

"But God did not spare his own Son. Would you spare your brother if the Lord told you to do otherwise?"

Clay's voice thickened. "Scripture tells us not to murder. Would a loving God command a believer to murder his own flesh and blood?"

"Doesn't Scripture teach you must place God above even your own family?"

"Yes."

"Then I ask again—if the Lord asked you to kill Tuck, would you?"

"Yes." Clay shut his eyes tight, and tears seeped between his eyelids. Moody's soon-to-be Prophet appeared conflicted. Not surprising, since most Good Sam candidates vacillated about loving God more than their wife, husband, child, sibling, or parent. But only five had said they would slay a relative for the Lord.

Moody affected a fatherly tone. "The Lord's demands can be hard, Clay, but He wants the best for you. Submit yourself to him fully, and he will give you the desires of your heart." He clasped Clay on the neck. "Now you are free to get up and eat. Self-flagellation comes next, and I know you will hold out longer than any previous Good Sam candidate."

Clay slipped off the altar. "I'm sure that won't be the case, Chief Elder."

"But I am sure you're wrong. Your sin quota is lower than anyone's who has undergone The Purge."

Clay looked embarrassed. "I can't believe that."

"You *can* believe that. It's gospel. And if anyone knows gospel, it's your ole Brother Moody." He clapped Clay on the back, and the humble sinner smiled.

As Clay left to eat a lunch of fruit, whole grain bread, and honey, Moody assured himself what he'd just told Clay was a useful lie. No, Clay didn't have the lowest sin quota of any previous candidate, but his was lower than all but three, clear evidence of Clay's special status.

He wondered if he should reveal to Clay his destiny as The Body's Prophet. The Holy Spirit hadn't moved Moody to speak with Clay, but Clay's forthcoming mission had worldwide implications. Better to hold off, perhaps until Clay met Dr. Sloan and went through the usual nanbless briefing.

After all, for Clay, after self-flagellation came the twenty-four-hour fast and prayer vigil. Next, indoctrination of the ways and history of The Body, which, of course meant the history of all Christianity, since no sect since the first century A.D. had come close to The Body's level of sainthood.

Moody could hardly wait for the new heaven and earth, and with Clay as his obedient Prophet, it could happen soon. As for the thousands who would die during the transformation, didn't they say you had to break a few eggs to make an omelet?

Chapter 29

The next afternoon Tuck, Ham, and Coach sped off for Haven, their destination's codename. Tuck wished Ham could read his mind: *Don't say it again.*

But Ham did say it again: "Are the blindfolds really necessary?"

"Yes," Coach replied from the driver's seat, "for the third time, they're necessary. Unless you'd prefer I put your eyes out with a red-hot poker."

A bump in the road jolted Tuck, and he wanted to rip off his rubber blindfold—how did blind people manage? He strove to memorize the car's twists and turns for future reference, but it seemed futile.

Coach said, "The mystery person you'll meet at Haven is Brother Moody's mother, Mary Moody."

"Moody's Mom?" Ham said. "What's she going to do? Bake us cookies?"

Coach replied, "She's going to scare you silly is what she's going to do."

Silence settled over the car, and Tuck assumed Coach's pause was for dramatic effect. If so, it worked.

After they hit another bump on what had to be an unpaved rural road, Coach continued. "Brother Moody keeps his relationship with his mom low key. She's an integral, though unwilling, part of The Body. She's also a government double agent."

Coach summarized what he apparently assumed Ham didn't know, that Moody's dad had been the president of a prestigious Baptist college in Arkansas but had been caught in an affair with a local beauty queen. After being fired and shunned, he killed himself.

"And," Coach said, "there's more. Following her husband's suicide, Mary Moody spiraled into a deep depression. Since she couldn't kick the blues, her church kicked her out. The bottle became her new religion. Alcoholism runs in the family."

"Hey," Ham said, "I know how that goes."

"But I'll bet you don't know the rest of the story. Mary survived on the meager savings her husband left her. She claimed she had prophecies. Started writing books, developed a following. Moody at first wrote her off as a kook. Then he noticed many of her prophecies were coming true.

"For example, in a dream, she saw one elder in Moody's church roasted alive. Two days later, the elder's car flipped over on the interstate, trapping him inside. The vehicle exploded, and he burned to death. Moody put his Mommie Dearest on the payroll, but only on the condition she kept a low profile. She gave up writing, took down her website, disbanded the cult that had grown around her."

"So," Tuck said, "how does she connect with what Moody's doing now?"

Coach said, "I'm getting there. You never did have much patience, Tuckster. Moody brought Mary back to Arkansas and set her up in a house in the sticks. She kept having prophecies, one of them about Christians who avoided hell because they had become sinless. That got Moody's attention, for his church said his dad had gone to hell because he couldn't repent for suicide once he was dead.

"Moody wanted to spare other Christians the anguish of fearing a loved one was burning in Outer Darkness. Given his mom's prophecy about sinless believers, Moody looked into the possibility that nanotechnology might make believers sinless."

"Nanotechnology?" Ham said.

"That's right, you don't know." Coach summarized how Moody was using nanobots to turn people into Good Sams. As Tuck heard the story again, he relived the truth that as a nanobot-programmed Good Sam, Dad had no choice but to die trying to save the guy buried beneath tornado debris. If it had been Dad's decision, fine—but it hadn't been, and Tuck seethed that Moody had turned Dad into a robot. He fisted his hands, and nails dug into his palms.

"Gents," Coach said, "Mary Moody helps Moody with the Good Sam movement by taking care of the, shall we say, rejects."

"Rejects?" Tuck and Ham said it simultaneously, a coincidence Tuck might have found comical under other circumstances.

"That's right," Coach said, "rejects. Another thing. She's only sixty-five but looks a hundred."

The vehicle lurched to a stop, and Tuck winced as his seatbelt cut into his still tender belly.

Coach first opened the padlock to Tuck's rubber blindfold, then Ham's. Tuck rubbed his eyes.

With a flourish, Coach said, "Welcome to Haven."

"After all the mystery, not much to see," Ham said.

Tuck agreed. Surrounded by thick woods, before them set a medium-sized, one-story farmhouse, white clapboard, with a roof over the porch, from which hung two flowerpots. The porch swing creaked as its lone occupant, an elderly woman who had to be Mary Moody, swayed. The tang of wood smoke wafted through the air, but Tuck didn't see a chimney—perhaps it was from a neighbor a mile or more away.

Coach handled the introductions, and he was right. Mrs. Moody might have only been sixty-five, but she looked older than a California redwood. Sporting an angular chin and a hooked nose, except for the fact she wasn't green, she could have been the twin of the Wicked Witch of the West in 1939's *The Wizard of Oz*. Only Mrs. Moody was that same witch after the years had clawed furrows across her face.

She led Tuck, Ham, and Coach into her house, at once a revelation and a surprise. Chin-level stacks of magazines, books, Bibles, and boxes took up three-fourths of the living room, and Tuck and his two companions followed Mrs. Moody into the kitchen through a crooked corridor flanked by piles stacked six feet high. Tuck figured she'd be a shoo-in for the reality show *Hoarders*.

Happily, the kitchen had no stacks, but mildew made Tuck sneeze.

"Bless you," Mrs. Moody said. "Wouldn't it be wonderful if we could send the spirits packing with just a little ole sneeze?"

"Spirits, ma'am?" Ham said.

"Demons. Diseased Ones. Don't you know the ancient history behind the custom of saying 'Bless you' when someone sneezes?"

"'Fraid not."

Coach said, "Some say Gregory the Great started the custom, Mrs. Moody, as a protection against the plague."

Mrs. Moody harrumphed. "You have your history, I have mine." She squinted at Ham. "As for you, Mr. Crouch, I'm not surprised you wouldn't know. Our education system is so inadequate these days. Where did you go to college?"

"The University of Arkansas in Fayetteville."

"Really? What was your major? Science? English? Philosophy?"

"Criminal Justice, ma'am. I also played for the Razorbacks."

Tuck figured Ham assumed the latter fact would impress Mrs. Moody, as it did most Arkansans, but instead of asking what position he played, she looked him over with more than a hint of disapproval and said, "Oh. A jock. That explains a lot of things."

"Mrs. Moody," Coach said, "we don't have much time. Please tell Tuck and Ham your vision. Tuck is Clay's older brother."

Mrs. Moody's eyes brightened, as though she'd received a surprise Christmas gift. "Clay's brother? Oh, my, my, my. Do I have news to tell you about your little brother!" She frowned. "That is, if Mr. Shimura hasn't already spilled the beans."

Coach said, "I wanted Tuck to hear it from you. And also to see what he's up against."

Mary's bright eyes dimmed, and her voice grew hushed. "Ah, yes. The Leps. Clay's brother needs to see the Leps."

Tuck didn't ask who "the Leps" were, though he assumed the moniker was shorthand for lepers. Probably figurative, which made them more mysterious.

Mrs. Moody led Tuck, Ham, and Coach to a cinder block building behind her house. Shivering, Tuck sized up the place—the size of a small medical clinic, the dwelling appeared unfinished, like a nursing home awaiting the final touches, yet it strangely lacked windows.

Mrs. Moody said, "You are about to see the Leps, unwilling test subjects given experimental Prophet-nans that didn't work but instead turned them into… well, you'll see."

Inside, six beds set on each side of a large room on which men and women in bedclothes lay, most moaning or weeping. Tuck welcomed the room's warmth, but not its dim light or the sting of its disinfectant tang.

A young, dark-haired woman in sunglasses shuffled to Tuck. Slowly, she removed the shades. Her eyes were gone—black holes darker than midnight gaped where eyes should have been, and the empty sockets seemed to absorb what little light shone in the room.

"'And if thine eye offend thee,'" Mrs. Moody said as though the girl wasn't there, "'pluck it out.' I'm afraid that in Krystal's case, she subjected both eyes to this literal interpretation of Scripture."

As though sharing a private joke, Krystal clutched a hand to her mouth and giggled.

A chill fanned out across Tuck's shoulders.

Mrs. Moody led Tuck, Ham, and Coach from bed to bed, as though she were a medical doctor conducting a tour of hopeless cases.

"Gerald Garson," she said, gesturing in his direction, "like Krystal, also took a Scripture to enter hell without his whole body quite literally." A stump in place of his right hand left no doubt which Bible verse Gerald had employed. Tuck recognized the man's last name—this was the son of the woman who had shot Brother Moody. Gerald scowled at them.

"These next three," Mrs. Moody said, "are inexplicable."

A white-bearded man said the first line of the Lord's Prayer, the hairless man in the next bed said the second line, the long-haired man in the successive bed the third line, and then the prayer in the round returned to White Beard saying the fourth line, Hairless the fifth line, Long Hair the sixth line, and on it went.

Mrs. Moody said, "They speak the Lord's Prayer all day, and most of the night as well. They say nothing else."

Ham frowned. "Do they eat?"

"Barely. Sometimes we have to put them on IVs."

On the other side of the room, Mrs. Moody stopped beside the bed of a young man who, face cradled in his hands, wept. He ceased for a moment to look at them and mournfully howled, a sound that deepened until it became unbearable. It was the wail of a child whose dog has died, a mother whose newborn has perished, a skipper whose crew has drowned. All at once, the howl ended, and the young man resumed weeping.

Mrs. Moody said, "You all know, 'Blessed are they that mourn: for they shall be comforted.' Well, the nanobots of Derek Chambers here slid off into an OCD loop. In fact, his nickname is 'Mournful.' He mourns day and night because his brain believes he will be comforted."

"Will he?" Tuck said.

Mrs. Moody allowed a cynical chuckle. "What do you think?"

The other residents in the front room slept, and Mrs. Moody didn't comment on their afflictions. As she neared the back door, her face became somber, as though she were reliving a painful memory.

"In this next room," she said, "I won't have to tell you anything."

She was right. It amazed Tuck how soundproofed this raucous back chamber was from the front room. In here, six beds set on each side, and verbal ravings slashed the air like teeth rending flesh. Strapped to their beds, the residents chafed against their bonds. But their mouths remained uncovered, as though they should be allowed this one freedom. They made the most of it, cackling, screaming, ranting, two of them croaking like frogs, one of them braying like a donkey, another gibbering like an ape.

And the faces, oh by all that is holy, the faces.

Even though CGI special effects could create the ghastliest movie visages imaginable, nothing could top madness to distort the human face into a caricature out of hell.

A middle-aged aide pushed in a medicine cart, its wheels squeaking, and he and his fellow aide checked the IVs. Both aides ignored the bedlam raging around them. Tuck supposed one could grow used to anything—or calloused to it.

He was not sorry when Mrs. Moody gestured for him, Ham, and Coach to leave.

Once outside, Ham asked, "Who were those two aides?"

"Homeless people I took in some time ago. They work for me in return for meals and a place to live—they stay in the barn, half of which has been converted into living quarters. I trained them myself. When my husband was alive, I was a CNA volunteer in a nursing home, and before I married, I worked as a licensed practical nurse."

The images in Tuck's head wouldn't shut off. "I can hardly believe what we saw in there."

Mrs. Moody sighed. "Yes, and it's all because of my son experimenting with the nanobots. As you can see, he's had many failures. The front room Leps, such as Krystal the Eyeless, keep to themselves. As for the livelier Leps in Romper Room—our nickname for our psycho ward—we could sedate them. We've done it before, and they are able to respond to simple directions. But why fill them full of drugs that may make them feel worse?"

Tuck said, "Do their families know they're here?"

"No." She twisted her hands. "My son won't allow it."

Tuck's guts churned in anger and disgust, and he turned to his high school mentor. "Coach, you and your outfit just let this go on without telling the families?"

"Yeah," Ham said. "What's up with that?"

Coach donned his best assistant principal's face, the one he had used when explaining controversial decisions to parents and the school board. "When we bring Brother Moody's church down, we'll return the Leps to their families. It's too dangerous to do so now. We need Mrs. Moody right where she is, and the Leps right where they are."

Mrs. Moody sighed. "Yes, I'm afraid Mr. Shimura is right. My son Grahammie—you call him Brother Moody—takes good care of me. He believes it is his biblical duty, James 1:27 and all. Believe it or not, he is actually quite generous with his money." A sly smile grew across her face, and a light shone in her eyes. "Little does Grahammie realize Mama is scheming to bring down his house of cards."

Tuck said, "How do you know he's not spying on you right now? Listening in somehow?"

Coach popped the joints in his neck. "We took

precautions. Made sure the compound's video cameras and audio bugs went dark before our arrival. They should stay that way for an hour."

Mrs. Moody added, "I'll just tell Grahammie it must have been some government organization trying to harass us. Grahammie believes every word I say." She chuckled. "Such a foolish boy."

"Speaking of which," Coach said, "not much time is left, Mrs. Moody, for you to share your vision with Tuck."

Her posture straightened, and her face donned an authoritative demeanor. "Agreed. Follow me."

They sat around the kitchen table, and Mrs. Moody lit a candle in a shot glass. She turned off the lights, apparently hoping to create an atmosphere. It worked. Tuck half-expected her to ask them to hold hands for a seance. Instead, she closed her eyes and furrowed her brow.

"Lord in heaven," she said, "please guide the path of your humble servant. Though I am an old woman, you have seen fit to let me dream dreams and see visions. Thank you for this dispensation of your Sacred Spirit. Let me speak words that are true to these men gathered with me and let us be blessed by the outpouring of your grace."

Silence reigned for sixty seconds, the candle that flickered in the shot glass casting eerie shadows across the faces of Tuck's companions. Dread uncoiled inside Tuck like a cold snake.

Mrs. Moody's countenance grew taut, then relaxed. "So be it." She opened her eyes. "Tuck Jameson, your brother Clay Jameson has purer faith than most, so pure that when he was a child, God healed his cat Gollum.

"Clay is destined to transform into Grahammie's herald. Once he drinks the nanbless wine, his faith will become limitless. The affliction of unbelief will have passed—He will be free to do great things in the Son's name, fulfilling Christ's words that those who followed him would do greater things than he."

Coach said, "What kinds of things, Mrs. Moody?" He glanced at his watch, apparently trying to move her along.

Mrs. Moody's voice remained calm. "Grahammie hopes everyone in the world will become a Good Sam. Indeed, he sees a time when he will help to usher in a new heaven and a new earth, with The Prophet—Clay Jameson—leading the way. It will begin in America.

"Clay will heal dozens, perhaps hundreds, maybe even thousands. In return, Grahammie will demand all political, military, and church leaders become Good Sams who acknowledge him as God's appointed Elder. If they refuse, The Prophet will make them rue the day they were born."

Mrs. Moody smiled, and her voice took on a disturbing timbre. "I see The Prophet calling down plagues on our nation in the name of God. Outbreaks of tornadoes in the Mid-West that will dwarf all previous cyclone cycles. Wreckage will toll into the billions, and even with modern weather forecasting technology, hundreds will perish, for the tornadoes will strike at a moment's notice.

"If that doesn't convince the country's leaders to accept Grahammie's sovereignty, The Prophet will call on hurricanes to ravage the East Coast, battering New York, and tsunamis to flood the coast of California, inundating L.A. and San Francisco. Thousands will die."

Tuck's cheeks burned—he didn't want to hear this. "Clay would never do anything like what you're saying."

Mrs. Moody's eyes widened, and a hideous grin stretched her face. "Perhaps you don't know him as well as you think. Your little brother may appear loving on the outside, but he harbors deep resentments inside. Resentments against the world. Resentments against you."

Tuck banged the table and stifled a swear word.

Mrs. Moody ignored him. "Grahammie will have your brother drink enhanced nanbless wine that will demand Clay's total submission to his eldership. A simple tweaking of Hebrews 13:17 is all that is necessary. Clay will feel compelled to submit to Grahammie as though he were submitting to God Himself."

Tuck rose from the table and frowned. "I've heard enough."

"No," Mrs. Moody said, voice as tranquil as ever, "you have not heard enough. In fact, the Holy Spirit wants me to tell you, to tell all of you, a new Word of Wisdom." She shut her eyes, and her words became labored, as though she were in a trance. "'Mary Moody, if The Prophet lives past the 352nd day on the Gregorian calendar of this year, your son will win.'"

Mrs. Moody's eyes popped open, and for the first time since she, Tuck, Ham, and Coach had sat at the table, she looked alarmed. "Oh, I am so sorry, Mr. Tuck Jameson. So very sorry. I didn't know what the Holy Spirit was going to tell me."

"But we all know now," Coach said, his tone grim.

Ham looked puzzled. "When is the 352nd day on the Gregorian calendar?"

"Tuesday. Two days away."

Ham frowned. "No way."

Tuck's blood frosted. "There has got to be a—"

"You think I like this any more than you do?" Anguish laced Coach's words. "God rarely makes it easy on us. Read the Old Testament lately?"

Tuck put a hand to his forehead. "Please, Coach, no junk about God telling Abraham to kill his son."

"But," Ham said, "God kept Abraham from killing Isaac."

Coach glowered. "We may not have that luxury." Coach's eyes filled with clear resolve. "The Prophet is Clay. God just told us if he lives past Tuesday, Brother Moody will subjugate first America, then the world."

Tuck chuckled nervously. "You can't be suggesting what I think."

Coach's eyes grew steely. "I'm afraid there's no other

way."

Tuck felt as though life had yanked a trapdoor out from under him, his feet left to dangle over the abyss.

Chapter 30

In Mrs. Moody's kitchen, Tuck glared at Coach. Shoulders trembling, Mrs. Moody dropped her face into her hands, and Ham, apparently trying to console her, touched her back.

"Our mission has changed," Coach said.

Anger clutching his bowels, Tuck grimaced. "I won't be an accomplice to my brother's murder."

"You don't have to be."

"I'm just supposed to sit and twiddle my thumbs while you assassinate Clay?"

"You won't be coming along."

"You going to stop me?"

"As a matter of fact, I am." Coach drew a SIG Sauer P226 Select from under his overcoat and trained the pistol on Tuck and Ham. Tuck's eyes widened.

Mrs. Moody raised her head. "Good heavens. Mr. Shimura, have you taken leave of your senses?"

Tuck put his natural tendency to shield an elderly woman from criticism on hold. "In the first place, high school mentor of mine, how do we know anything about Mrs. Moody's prophecies is true?"

"Because seventy-five percent of her prophecies have come true in the past."

"Which means twenty-five percent haven't. You're willing to kill my brother when you don't even know if her prophecy is true?"

"Can't take the chance. None of us can."

"When Mrs. Moody's prophecies are wrong, where did they come from? Obviously not God. Maybe herself? Crazy thoughts her son has planted in her head? The Evil One, if you believe in that kind of thing?"

Coach's eyes flashed with fear. "Oh, I believe, Tuckster. But you're missing the point."

Ham shook his head. "Wait a minute. Couldn't there be another way to interpret Mrs. Moody's prophecy?"

Relief swelling in his chest, Tuck rose to the occasion. "Yes. Her prophecy said if The Prophet lived past Tuesday, Brother Moody would win. But Clay isn't The Prophet yet—he won't be until he drinks the nanbless wine. If we rescue Clay before that happens, there won't be any Prophet to live past Tuesday."

Keeping the SIG Sauer P226 trained on Tuck and Ham, Coach snickered. "Oh, please." He turned to Mrs. Moody. "Mrs. Moody, is that what you think your prophecy means?"

Mrs. Moody's eyes widened. "Means? What do I think it means?" Her head wobbled. "Why, it means what it means. It means… I need a drink." She grabbed a whiskey bottle from the cabinet, poured herself a shot glass, and downed it in one gulp, as though she were a gunslinger in a Wild West saloon. Unbelievably, she poured herself another and knocked it back as well.

In a fatherly voice, Coach said, "Tuck, Clay is your own flesh-and-blood. That's why you can't see this thing objectively."

Tuck whipped his head back and forth. What did an only child like Coach know about a brother's love? "You mean the needs of the many outweigh the needs of the few?"

"I'm afraid so. If Brother Moody wins, the weather disasters Mrs. Moody saw in her visions will kill thousands across the United States—men, women, and children. And who knows how many will be injured?"

"I don't buy it."

"Innocent children have more of a right to live than Clay. He's thirty-six years old. But they have their whole lives ahead of them."

Tuck squinted at Coach and cursed.

"The health care system in the U.S. would be taxed beyond its capacity to cope. It would mean the end of America, and the beginning of Brother Moody's theocracy. Is that what you want?"

"Of course not." He spat the words. "But killing Clay is not the only way." Tuck fought to keep his rage in check but couldn't still the tremor in his voice. "Mrs. Moody's 'Word of Wisdom' may be full of hot air. Years ago, I heard a 'Word of Wisdom' that a friend would get a kidney transplant in time. He didn't. He died."

"Tuckster, on this one, we must err on the side of caution. That means your brother can't live past Tuesday." Coach smiled, amusement dancing in his eyes. "But it's not brotherly love that motivates you. You just want to be in charge."

The accusation stung, and Tuck struggled to smother it. "If you didn't have that gun in your hand, I swear to God I'd—"

"You want to control everything, like you did in high school. Or at least like you think you did."

He jabbed a finger in Coach's direction. "If you harm a hair on Clay's head—"

"Then what? You'll come gunning for me?"

"I'll kill you with my bare hands."

"Great. We can keep each other company in hell."

"There's something else, Coach. The God you speak of is practically working for Moody. But God is slave to no man."

Ham nodded. "Yeah."

Tuck continued. "If God is real, he wouldn't honor Clay's or anyone else's faith by having plagues ravage

America. A loving God would never do that."

Coach shook his head. "You pitiful back-slider. What do you think AIDS was? 9/11? God's plagues."

"You don't know that. Jesus rebuked his disciples when they wanted to call down fire."

"You don't understand the first thing about God. Moody does. And so do I." Coach's upper lip curled. "Even under the New Covenant, God will in the future pour plagues upon the earth. Believe in a weak-kneed God if you must, but the God of Revelation is a God of wrath. The same God who will honor Clay's faith."

By this time, Mrs. Moody had downed her third whiskey, and the kitchen stank like a barroom. "Please forgive me," she said to no one in particular. "I shouldn't be doing this."

Coach's expression softened. "God forgives you, Mrs. Moody. He always forgives you."

The quick change in Coach's demeanor startled Tuck. It was as though he had a stock of masks he pulled on to suit the moment's need.

At gunpoint, Coach ordered Ham to shelve the whiskey bottle and toss the shot glass into the sink. He marched Tuck and Ham to the Buick Century and commanded them to sit in the front, forcing Ham to bind Tuck's hands and feet with zip-ties and blindfold him. His world plunged again into darkness, Tuck's mind raced—there had to be a way out of this. But that's what everybody in a jam thought.

"Don't worry," Coach said as he apparently slid into the back, "I won't shoot either of you unless you give me no choice."

Coach ordered Ham to drive. Tuck wished he could somehow get a message to his friend—but how? And what could Ham do? Coach was telling Ham the directions back to the safe house, so there was no way Ham could deviate without Coach being wise.

The Buick Century apparently passed over many rocks in the road, and every jolt made Tuck wish he would awaken from a bad dream. Mrs. Moody had to be wrong—no matter what Brother Moody did to Clay, Tuck's little brother would not ask God to call down plagues upon America. Still, the notion of Clay completely freed from sin, his faith boundless in scope, made Tuck shiver. As a sinner, Clay's faith had probably brought a dead cat to life. What could hinder Clay's faith if he was a sinless saint?

But God would never honor Clay's request to shower judgment on America. Or would He? Coach seemed confident the Almighty would. What about all the torments promised in the Book of Revelation? What about the plagues God sent upon Egypt in Moses' day? After all, God had let The Body flower into being, and Brother Moody seemed to be on the winning side.

Of course, Tuck could see Clay's faith triggering Mrs. Moody's prophesied healings. But ordering a tornado to obliterate Winkdale, killing dozens if not hundreds of people he'd grown up with, people with whom he shared a small-town bond?

Never.

But Tuck couldn't quiet the lingering doubts that teased the corners of his mind. Was every man capable of performing great evil? If nanobots forced Clay to obey Moody, would Clay be himself anymore, or only a monstrous lookalike? What if Clay would actually be serving Moody's God, who might or might not be The Evil One? What if, somehow, Moody and Clay were connected to the last days, as Coach implied?

After what seemed like an hour, but was probably less, the car braked, and Tuck figured they had arrived back at the safe house. Coach ordered Tuck and Ham to stay in the car, and a car door slammed.

"Ham, what's going on?" Tuck said, cursing his blindfold.

"Coach is talking on the phone."

"We've got to get—"

The car door opened, and Coach ordered Ham to untie Tuck's feet and take him, still blindfolded, into the house. Next, Coach commanded Ham to strap Tuck to a kitchen chair using a zip-tie. Ham tightened it around Tuck's chest, and as he did, Tuck flexed his muscles, hoping Coach wouldn't notice and Ham wouldn't give him away.

Ham didn't.

Coach directed Ham to re-tie Tuck's feet and hands—both of which Tuck flexed as much as possible—and unlock his blindfold. Coach held them at gunpoint, but it surprised Tuck to see Coach's other hand holding a rag and a medium-sized bottle, both of which he gave to Ham.

"Soak the rag," Coach said.

Ham scowled. "And if I don't?"

"I've killed men before. I can do it again."

Tuck figured as much, but it was still something he hadn't wanted to hear. Killing was sometimes the only choice, but Tuck couldn't help but wonder if Coach's kills had been legitimate, or if they had been the shadow government's equivalent of hit jobs.

Coach smiled at Ham and gestured at the rag. "Don't think for a minute you'll be soaking the rag with chloroform. That only works in movies. In real life, chloroform would take a good five minutes to knock you out, and that's under the best of circumstances. Nanomeds have enhanced that bottle you hold in your hand. We call it chloroform N. It'll knock you flat in one or two minutes." Coach's smile vanished. "Hold the rag over your nose and mouth."

Ham shook his head. "No way, dirtbag. How do I know you won't shoot Tuck after I'm out cold?"

Calmly, Coach held the SIG Sauer P226's muzzle an inch from Tuck's temple. "If you don't, I will shoot him now."

Sweat popped out across Tuck's brow. "Don't listen to him, Ham."

Coach snarled at Tuck. "Shut up." The words stung like

a slap in the face.

To Ham, Coach said, "I'll give you five seconds. Four. Three."

"Okay, okay."

Ham saturated the rag and smashed it over his nose and mouth.

"Harder," Coach said. "Press it harder."

Ham did so, and in a little over a minute, the former Arkansas Razorback collapsed. Coach secured Ham's hands and feet with zip-ties.

To Tuck, Coach said, "Couple of minutes ago I talked to my superior. He wants me to find Clay posthaste. That's why I'm leaving you guys here."

"So," Tuck said, "you're not going to knock me out too?"

"Negative. Chloroform N can have unpredictable side effects, including death. Last night I looked up your medical records and ran a scenario where you had been knocked out with the stuff. Didn't look good."

"So, you already thought about knocking me and Ham out before you even knew about Mrs. Moody's 'Word of Wisdom' today?"

"I have to be ready for any contingency. So yes, it occurred to me at some point, I might have to knock you out. Didn't run a scan on Ham, though. But he should probably be out cold for twenty to thirty minutes. By then, a couple of my fellow agents will have arrived to guard you. We don't kill unless we must. But in Clay's case, there's no choice."

Tuck said, "There's always a choice."

"Not in the real world."

Coach took off in his Buick.

It couldn't go down this way. Tuck's mouth had dried into a desert, but he resolved to escape before Coach's black ops friends arrived.

And Ham? Hopefully, he would awaken sooner than twenty or thirty minutes.

No time to wait. Tuck started inching the kitchen chair

to which he was tied toward the wall. If this worked, he might yet save Clay's bacon.

Chapter 31

Tuck slid his kitchen chair backwards on a collision course with a corner wall.

By having flexed his muscles when Ham had zip-tied him to the chair, Tuck had some wiggle room, but not enough. Same with the ties binding his hands and feet.

But if he could scoot the chair to the wall edge and repeatedly scrape the hand-restraining ties against it, his bonds might break.

The patio door through which the late afternoon sun shone rocked back and forth as Tuck walked the chair rearward. Had other black ops victims been bound in this house? Had they lived—or died? If the latter, what happened to their bodies? Would Tuck and Ham become missing persons?

Tuck worried about the chloroform N that Ham had inhaled. The big guy's chest was rising and falling, a good sign. But had the drug damaged his organs? His brain? What if he didn't wake up?

By the time Tuck arrived at the corner wall, sweat slicked his forehead. Lifting his arms above his head, he vigorously rubbed his hands' zip-ties against the wall's edge for five seconds.

Ten seconds.

Fifteen.

More.

His arms ached, and his shoulders smarted. The flexing of his torso ripped his belly like fiery talons.

Keep going.

Sweat stung his eyes. Friction, do your stuff. Just a few more seconds. Almost. There.

Bingo.

The zip-ties binding his hands popped open, and he swung his hands free.

He sped the chair next to a kitchen cutlery drawer, pulled out a butcher knife, and severed the zip-ties from his feet and chest. He grabbed a water pitcher from the sink, filled it with cold water, and dashed the liquid across Ham's face.

No reaction.

Tuck refilled the pitcher and doused Ham.

Still nothing.

Twice more Tuck tried, each time loading the pitcher with water and ice from the freezer, but Ham remained dead to the world.

Tuck paced. He had to stop Coach, but leaving Ham would be like deserting a wounded comrade. Tuck had always respected combat vets, and though he knew he wasn't fit to tie their bootlaces, he aspired to emulate their fighting spirit, especially when it meant standing shoulder to shoulder with a brother, and to Tuck, that's exactly what Ham was.

Tuck felt a lump in his pants pocket—the burner phone Coach had given him the previous night. Probably in all the excitement, Coach had forgotten he had given Tuck and Ham burner phones yesterday. Or maybe he hadn't forgotten—maybe he figured it didn't matter. After all, regardless of who Tuck called, Coach's black ops cronies would arrive first.

Tuck ransacked the house for weapons. Padlocks barred two of the backrooms' doors. No doubt weapons were inside. Or perhaps not—Coach had apparently assumed Tuck wouldn't be able to free himself from his zip-ties.

But the kitchen boasted cutlery—butcher knives galore. The fire extinguisher on the counter might also come in handy.

Realization smacked Tuck in the head. What if video cameras filmed his every move? If so, Coach's cronies knew Tuck had freed himself and were barreling his way. Or if Coach knew, he might hightail it back to snuff out him and Ham. Tuck imagined Coach cursing the decency that had moved him to spare Tuck's and Ham's lives. No doubt he would be determined not to repeat the same mistake.

Tuck sliced the most wicked-looking butcher knife against his thumb. The blade stung, a drop of blood welling at the tiny cut. This knife would have to do.

From the living room, Ham groaned.

Tuck jostled his moaning friend. "Ham! Wake up!"

Slowly, Ham opened his eyes. "What, what's going on?" He sat up and rubbed the back of his neck. "Man, I feel like I've been run over by a truck."

Tuck said, "It was Coach. Remember? He made you put the rag with that stuff over your nose and mouth."

Ham nodded, his head apparently clearing up. "That's right." He held his stomach. "I'm sick." Ham turned his head and threw up, the ensuing stench revolting. "Help me up, beanpole."

Tuck did, and Ham sat on the couch, his shoulders slumped. As he recovered, Tuck told him two of Coach's cronies were on their way to guard them.

"Great," Ham said. "We gotta scoot."

Tuck cocked his head. "You up to it?"

"Do I have a choice?"

"Not unless you want the two of us to wind up in a lost landfill somewhere."

Ham shook his head. "Not my idea of a dream vacation."

"You good to go?"

"Gotta hit the john first."

The two minutes Ham spent in the bathroom seemed like

two hours, and Tuck was relieved when his friend hobbled into the living room.

Tuck and Ham donned their jackets, armed themselves with butcher knives, and fled. Outside, the sun was settling into a purplish twilight over the Ozark Mountains. Any other time, Tuck would have savored the sight, but under the circumstances, the fall of night promised danger. He shivered and turned up his collar.

Tuck and Ham decided to hike north on Highway 74, which ran beside the safe house, and stop when they got to Goodson's convenience store. Thick woods towered over both sides of the road, and even though Tuck and Ham stayed as close as possible to the tree line, Tuck worried the trees provided inadequate cover.

He yanked out the burner phone. Should he use it? He had to. He called Marv and briefly explained the situation.

"This is a lot to ask me to buy into, Tuck."

"Marv, you know I don't go off on flights of fancy. Can you pick Ham and me up at Goodsons' in ten or fifteen minutes?"

"Will do. In fact, I'm on my way. You say these Leps are on Mrs. Moody's farm?"

"Yeah. Ham knows how to get there."

"You can bet your life on that," Ham said.

Tuck continued. "Marv, we've got to break this story wide open. What do you think about a Little Rock TV news crew meeting us at Mrs. Moody's farm? You know one of the key reporters at Channel 29, right?"

"That's an affirmative."

"What do you think?"

"I think it's a peachy idea."

Tuck pressed the burner phone off and tossed it into a nearby thicket.

Tuck and Ham should run, but apparently recovering from chloroform N, Ham was doing well to walk. Goodson's was still one to two miles away.

As though Ham had read Tuck's mind, he said, "Bet you think I'm a slowpoke, huh, Mr. Flash?"

"Well, now that you mention it…"

Ham cocked an eyebrow. "Bet I can beat your sorry behind to Goodson's."

"You're on."

Tuck and Ham pumped their legs, and Ham appeared to push himself like a felon on the run. Tuck had to kick it into high gear to keep up with his husky friend. Tuck's lungs burned with the cold night air, and his still-tender stomach stung. But the exhilaration proved invigorating and helped Tuck temporarily forget the danger they faced.

An auto's engine roared as it grew near. Headlights washed over them, but the Ford pickup's driver, probably going sixty in a forty-five zone, ignored them. The vehicle left a burned oil smell in its wake.

A different engine snarled from behind them, and the driver of the vintage 1967 Ford Mustang—Marv, of course—screeched to a halt on the road's shoulder six feet ahead. Tuck and Ham stole into the car.

Marv rocketed onto the highway in the direction of Goodson's. Ham assured Marv he knew how to get to Mrs. Moody's farm, but Marv insisted on driving to Goodson's before surrendering his wheels.

"What's up?" Tuck asked.

Marv smiled. "A fine surprise."

Tuck hoped Marv wasn't being sarcastic.

Chapter 32

Tuck, Ham, and Marv reached Goodson's, the modest convenience store by the railroad tracks, and the store's lights that shone across the parking lot made Tuck squint. A weather-beaten Honda Civic was parked in front. Inside, a familiar rotund man—Brother Eli—was talking to the young male attendant behind the register.

Tuck said, "What's Brother Eli doing here?"

"Yeah." Ham smirked. "We're not exactly headed for a prayer meeting."

"Not exactly," Marv said, "but I'll let Eli explain why he's joining us."

Tuck recoiled. "Joining us?"

Seemingly ignoring Tuck's comment, Marv strolled into the store, and Tuck and Ham followed.

"So," the young cashier with the beatific smile was saying to Brother Eli, "if you become a Good Sam like me, Brother Moody will never let you down."

Brother Eli grinned. "Good to know. Now if you'll excuse me."

He hurried outside, motioning for Tuck, Marv, and Ham to follow. His back to the store, Brother Eli said in a stage whisper, "Good Sams—they're everywhere!"

"Thanks for the news flash," Tuck said. "Why do you want to join us?"

Marv gestured towards Brother Eli as though he were an

accomplished statesman. "Gentlemen, may I introduce you to The Anti-Bodies' leader, Maurice."

Ham whistled.

Tuck's eyes widened. "You're Maurice?"

Brother Eli smiled. "In the flesh, all three chins of him."

"So, what you told me yesterday about being afraid of The Body was just a cover?"

"That's the fact, Jack. What better cover than to publicly say I fear for my life? Which, in fact, I do. But you can't let fear win, now, can you?"

Ham said, "I'll drink to that. Er, I mean, figuratively of course, reverend."

Eli laughed. "Of course."

Marv noted the Little Rock news crew might not arrive for twenty minutes.

Tuck stroked his chin. "The black op guys will probably be here by then. We can't let them find us."

Brother Eli said, "I suggest we take to the open road."

"No," Ham said, "I say hide in the woods."

Tuck shook his head—Ham's suggestions always lacked foresight "Our cars will be a dead giveaway."

"I say the woods," Ham insisted. "If there's just two of 'em, we could climb up a tree and jump 'em."

Marv and Brother Eli agreed.

Tuck took a deep breath. "Okay, but we don't jump 'em unless they see us. That's the better plan. No offense, Ham." Tuck turned to Marv and Brother Eli. "You guys up for a little hide-and-seek?"

"Absolutely," Brother Eli said, "with one minor enhancement." He winked, strode to his car, came back with a Glock 17, and racked the slide.

Ham whistled. "Well, whaddya know?"

Within seconds, the four men climbed a nearby tree, and Tuck worried about Ham. Apparently still recovering from the chloroform N, Ham struggled onto an oak limb sturdy enough to support his bulk. Brother Eli, the heftiest of the bunch, had the hardest time scaling the tree. He crawled onto a broad limb that Tuck feared might snap. About Eli's marksmanship, Tuck wondered—should he have insisted Ham take the handgun? Ham was probably the best shot among them. But because of the chloroform N, his aim might be off.

Tuck felt an urge to pray, but would God listen? And if He did, would He do anything? He seemed to be a mostly laissez faire God, leaving the horrors of the world untouched while providing shopping mall parking spots for Christians.

From his vantage point, a grin spread across Tuck's face when a van with the Channel 29 logo pulled into Goodson's parking lot. A young reporter in a white shirt and dark tie jumped from the car, his scruffy cameraperson behind him.

Tuck was ready to give the order to meet the news crew when another vehicle, a Ford Taurus, pulled into the parking lot beside the news van.

Tuck's hands became clammy. Black ops.

Two men in flannel shirts and blue jeans got out of the Taurus and struck up a conversation with the reporter and cameraperson, but Tuck was too far away to make out any words.

Ham stage whispered, "What are we waiting for?"

Tuck shushed him. "Those guys are probably Coach's friends."

Ham's eyes went wide.

Tuck clenched his jaw—if only he could hear what the black ops guys were saying to the news crew. He looked at Brother Eli, who hoisted his Glock and mouthed the word *Now?*

Tuck shook his head. Didn't need to get into a firefight if they could help it. The ops agents had to be armed, and two guns against one were bad odds. Tuck inwardly sighed.

The black op guys went into the store. Tuck hoped they wouldn't stay long. What if they talked to the chatty clerk? Sweat slicked Tuck's forehead.

The agents left the store. More convo with the reporter and cameraperson. Lots of body language both ways.

Finally, the black ops guys shook hands with the journalist and his partner, got into their Ford, and took off.

Tuck squeezed his eyes shut. Thank God. But did he mean it literally?

He waited five minutes to make sure the agents weren't going to circle back.

Marv made a clicking noise. "Looks like the proverbial coast is clear, gentlemen."

Tuck and his three companions abandoned the tree, and Marv handled introductions to the reporter and cameraperson.

"So," Tuck said to the dapper reporter, "what did they want?"

The reporter smiled. "To know your whereabouts. Claimed you were fugitives on the run. We explained your two vehicles by saying you'd vacated them for a third car, a Lexus, and had headed west. You probably saw they went in the store. Cashier told them he didn't see you guys get into a Lexus."

Tuck pursed his lips. "But you convinced them otherwise?"

"Yep."

Ham whistled. "Lucky break."

Brother Eli cleared his throat. "Luck had nothing to do with it." He pointed up. "God decided to save our sorry behinds, that's all."

Marv chuckled. "You Christians always chalk up good luck as a godsend. Even if God is up there, I doubt He pays much attention to us."

Brother Eli raised an eyebrow. "Well, Dr. Gillespie, guess we'll have to agree to disagree."

Marv gave a thumbs up.

Tuck agreed with Marv, but he kept it to himself. He grinned at the reporter and cameraperson. "Appreciate your quick thinking."

The reporter smiled. "All part of the job."

Ham slid into the driver's seat of Marv's Mustang and nodded to the news guys. "Just follow me, y'all."

Marv climbed in the front while Tuck got in the back.

"No speeding," Tuck said. "We don't want a cop pulling us over."

Ham sighed. "Beanpole, you missed your calling. You should've been a juvey hall director."

"I'll second that," Marv said with a smile.

Tuck shook his head. "As they say, with friends like you two…" He let the sentence trail off as Ham followed Tuck's advice to hold the Mustang under the speed limit.

Tuck felt like whistling. He was pushing ahead, and comrades were following him into battle. The good guys were on the march, and it wouldn't be long before the walls of Brother Moody's cover-up came tumbling down, just like the walls around the Old Testament's Jericho.

But Marv had texted earlier he'd found some interesting info on Coach. Whatever. It could wait till after they'd blown the lid on Brother Moody.

In no time, from Highway 74, Ham turned left onto a dirt road. A padlocked aluminum gate barred their way.

"Crud," Ham said. "Wish we'd looked for bolt cutters before we ran off from that safe house."

"No worries," Marv said. Brandishing an extra pair of keys, he hurried to the back of the Mustang. Tuck craned his head to watch as metal tools jostled in the trunk behind the open trunk hood. Marv removed a pair of heavy-duty bolt cutters and slammed the trunk shut.

"Whoa," Ham said. "I'll bet those babies could cut through a tank."

"I don't know about that," Tuck said, "but I'll bet they can take out that gate's padlock."

They did. Tuck wanted to thank God.

A victorious Marv pulled the gate aside, and once he

darted back into the car, a convoy took off down the dirt road to Mrs. Moody's place—the Mustang in the lead, the Channel 29 van behind them, and though Tuck couldn't see it, Brother Eli's Honda Civic apparently bringing up the rear. Tuck smiled. The cavalry was on the offensive.

Tuck grimaced a few times as the bumpy ride jostled his still-tender belly. But no sweat. The trees whose branches joined overhead no longer seemed to blot out the stars, but rather to shelter this righteous caravan. He imagined what would happen when the Channel 29 news showed the Leps on TV and revealed Brother Moody's unjust treatment of them as human guinea pigs.

That would not only bust Brother Moody's enterprise wide open, but would no doubt convince Clay that Moody was a fraud. Who knew—Clay might even thank Tuck.

What if Channel 29 wouldn't run the story? The Body in Arkansas was controversial. But if Channel 29 squelched the story, Tuck and his friends could still get it out on social media.

The convoy arrived at Mary Moody's farm, and she waved from the front porch. Reminding Tuck of his long-deceased great-grandmother, Tuck regretted Mrs. Moody was mixed up in this, but the spotlight would be on the Leps, not her. Still, Tuck would have to coax her into an on-camera interview.

Tuck, Marv, Ham, Coach, Brother Eli, and the Channel 29 reporter and his cameraperson spilled forth, but Mrs. Moody looked unfazed. Tuck explained to her the Channel 29 news crew was there to shoot a story about the Leps, as well as interview her.

Mrs. Moody blinked in confusion. "Leps? I'm afraid I don't know what you're talking about, son."

Tuck frowned. "Sure, you do. They're kept in the nursing home behind your house."

"Oh, that old thing? That's a homeless shelter."

"Would you care to let the news crew go into the nursing

home?"

"I told you, it's a homeless shelter. But yes, they can go in, I guess."

She led them to the building. Inside, empty beds lined the walls.

Tuck's head swam. "Where are the Leps, Mrs. Moody?"

She frowned. "I told you before, I don't know anything about any 'Leps.'"

Tuck gestured to Ham and said, "My friend and I were out here not more than two hours ago. We saw them. They were here."

As if she were dealing with a mental patient, Mrs. Moody said, "If you say so." She made a dubious face at the clean-cut Channel 29 reporter.

Tuck forced himself to take a deep breath—this couldn't be happening. "Let's go to the back room."

Mrs. Moody shrugged. "Suit yourself."

The back room proved to be the same story as the front room—rows of empty beds lining the walls.

Confusion and outrage gripped Tuck. "Mrs. Moody, maybe your son has threatened you, or someone else has, but you and I both know the Leps were here."

Ham nodded. "I saw them too."

Elegantly, Marv arched an eyebrow. "Well, the Leps obviously aren't here now."

"Obviously," the news reporter said, an exasperated look on his face.

"Gentlemen," Mrs. Moody said, "I don't know what to tell you. I can't say what they think they saw. But I do know this homeless shelter has been empty for weeks."

Tuck's voice rose. "Where are you hiding them, Mrs. Moody? Are they stashed in the barn?"

"'They' are not stashed anywhere." She glanced at her watch. "Now, if you don't mind, it's late. I'd like to go to bed."

Feeling like a lawyer in danger of losing an important

case, Tuck turned to the reporter and spread his hands. "She's lying. Ask her to let you search the barn."

The reporter traded a knowing glance with his cameraperson. "Mr. Jameson, we are not police officers. And there's no probable cause."

"There is probable cause!"

To his cameraperson, the reporter said, "C'mon, Hal. Let's get out of here."

Marv shrugged at the reporter and offered a placating smile. "I apologize I asked you out here for what appears to have been much ado about nothing."

The reporter nodded. "You meant well, Dr. Gillespie. But I wouldn't put any stock in your friend's stories again." The reporter gave Tuck a dirty look, and he and his cameraperson headed for their van. But Marv's Mustang had them boxed in, so they'd have to wait.

Tuck could live with the disdain of strangers, but did Marv take him for a fool, too? "You believe me, don't you, Marv?"

Slowly, Marv nodded. "I know you well enough to know I must believe you. We have a mystery here."

"The Leps may be in the barn. We've got to—"

"What? Storm the barn with Brother Eli's Glock so Mrs. Moody can phone the police on us? I imagine the Leps, as you call them, are hidden elsewhere."

Brother Eli said, "He's right, blokes. I'm afraid we've lost the battle." He gripped Tuck's shoulder. "But we sure as all that is holy haven't lost the war."

Tuck wanted to believe that. But every battle he lost pushed Clay that much closer to the abyss. How many battles did he have left?

Mrs. Moody, an enigmatic smile on her face, wished Tuck, Marv, Ham, and Brother Eli a safe journey.

"What a croc," Tuck said as Ham slid behind the Mustang's wheel and Marv again rode shotgun.

The Channel 29 van followed behind them, Brother Eli's

Civic in the rear.

Tuck scowled. "Man, this whole thing blew up in our faces."

Ham snorted as he maneuvered the car over a major road bump. "Our faces?"

"What's that supposed to mean?"

"It was your idea we come out here to expose the Leps."

Tuck let out an exasperated breath. "I didn't hear you oppose it."

"How could I? You're such a know-it-all that—"

"Gentlemen," Marv said, the voice of serenity in the storm, "time is too precious for this nonsense. What should our next move be?"

Knowing he'd deserved Marv's gentle rebuke, Tuck relented. "Got to get some kind of lead on how to find Clay."

"May I suggest we drive to The Body's Temple?"

Tuck whistled. "That's almost seventy miles away."

"Astute. Got any better ideas?"

"Well… no." Tuck smacked a fist into his palm. "I just don't get it. Why did Mrs. Moody lie?"

Marv said, "Probably one or more threats from her son."

"But how did she know to hide the Leps before we got there?"

Marv shrugged. "Perhaps Mrs. Moody phoned her son and told him you and Ham and Mr. Shimura had been out there and had seen the Leps. He might have ordered her to hide them, just in case. My guess is they already had a contingency plan to hide the Leps if it looked like they might be discovered. Maybe they have a storm cellar."

Tuck tapped his chin. "Yeah. Sounds like something Brother Moody would do. But man, we were so close to exposing that jerk."

Marv's phone rang, and Tuck frowned. It wasn't a good idea for Marv to use his regular smartphone that could be traced, but the man's ensuing conversation snared Tuck's attention.

Marv said, "You heard what on the radio? ... I can't believe it... Yes, I understand... Okay, listen. I'm going to ask Ham to stop the car... Yes, that's right... When I do, they'll have to stop the news van. At that point, stop the Civic, use your Glock to blow out one of their tires... I'm totally serious... Well, you don't think he really did it, do you? ... Very good, I'll keep you informed."

Baffled, Tuck said, "What was that all about?"

"Brother Eli heard that the police have issued an arrest warrant in your name for the murder of David Freeman."

Tuck's spine iced over.

"The report said an unidentified eyewitness saw you leave Mr. Freeman's house not long after the police believe he was killed."

"Not true." Of course, April had texted him this might happen.

Marv said, "Tuck, I'm sure you are innocent. But we're going to need to hide you until we can decide our next move."

"You'd be willing to do that?"

"Yes. Now Ham, carefully bring the Mustang to a stop."

Ham eased to a halt slowly enough that the van behind them had time to stop without bumping into them. No doubt the news reporter and his cameraperson were fuming. Marv's phone trilled—probably the news reporter—but he didn't take the call. A gunshot rang out; that had to have been Brother Eli blowing a hole in one of the van's back tires.

From the Maverick's back glass, Tuck saw the news reporter and his cameraperson duck beneath the van's windshield.

Ham floored it, leaving the news van in the distance as dust and gravel spewed behind the Mustang.

"Okay," Tuck said as the car jostling came fast and heavy, "I'm going to duck and stay that way. Marv, if you could take Ham and me to a motel..."

Marv twisted to face Tuck. "The motel clerk might

recognize you if your picture has been on the news. I'll rent us a motel room for the night while you gentlemen stay ducked down in the car. Around midnight, I'll wave you inside." He shifted to Ham. "Stop at the gate."

Ham did so, and Marv took over driver duties. Tuck got in the front passenger seat, Ham in the back, and both ducked out of sight. Scrunching his head next to the glove compartment, a vinyl cleaner smell tickled his nose, and Tuck mentally sighed—so he was a murder fugitive. Could Brother Moody have had anything to do with this? No, he could have had *everything* to do with this.

Marv said, "Keep out of sight. But while we've got time to kill, and please forgive the play on words, there are some things about Adam Shimura—or 'Coach,' as you quaintly call him—you need to know. As I texted earlier, I've been doing some investigating. I'm an impeccable detective." He winked.

Tuck smiled. No brag, just fact.

Marv said, "Adam's dad was a doctor, but he worked for the government. He felt guilty about his father's role in World War II's Unit 731, and he wanted to atone for those sins. He thought working for the government might do so.

"More brilliant than his father, Adam's dad was one of the smartest medical professionals in the country. At first, he was pleased with the work he was doing because it benefited others. But he eventually got sucked into a bad place. The more ruthless leaders in government decided to enlist his expertise into questionable endeavors."

The car hit a pothole, causing Tuck's head to bang against the glove compartment. "Go on, please."

"To help atone for his father's crimes, Dr. Shimura, Adam's dad, wanted Adam to be a doctor, but Adam wouldn't have it. He became an educator, which you already know."

Tuck whispered, "What did Coach's dad do for the government?"

"What didn't he do? Let's just say he was involved in several clandestine operations. Some quite unsavory. A good example involved homeless flu sufferers. They became an involuntary study group for flu treatments, some getting the new treatment, some getting a placebo, but all of them thinking they were getting the real deal. Dr. Shimura probably rationalized that at least a few of these men were getting helped.

"But some of his assignments became darker. A couple involved bacterial warfare, another mind control. Dr. Shimura no doubt grew coarsened, for there is only so much any sane man can reasonably rationalize."

Tuck pushed his brows down. "Did Coach know about this?"

"Not while he grew up. He only knew he saw his dad less and less. When at home, his father often went into his study and closed the door for the night.

"On his deathbed, he told Adam all about his shadow government exploits. He apparently hoped this would compel Adam to work for the Agency, as it was nicknamed. But Adam refused.

"Meanwhile, Dr. Shimura told Trevor Lords, his superior, about his confessions to Adam. Dr. Shimura suggested Mr. Lords convince Adam to work for the Agency, noting Adam's splendid intellect and medical insight. You see, Dr. Shimura had saved Mr. Lord's life once, and Lords vowed that in return, he would fulfill any reasonable request Shimura made. So, Shimura called in the favor—spare Adam's life, even though Shimura had told Adam secrets no one should know.

"Dr. Shimura died, but Adam refused to work for the Agency. Due to his promise to Dr. Shimura, Lords didn't have Adam killed. But to show Adam he meant business, Lords did have Adam's wife Sondra killed. Lords told him that would only be the beginning of his sorrows if he didn't join the agency."

"Only the beginning?" Tuck whispered.

"Yes. Lords told Adam if he didn't work for them, someone else he held close to his heart would die. To prevent that, Adam went to work for the Agency."

Tuck whispered, "Who was it they also threatened to kill? An aunt? An uncle?"

"No. Coach's favorite high school student at the time—you."

Tuck gasped. This couldn't be true. Tuck didn't want to be the reason Coach had become black ops. All these years, his life had been spared because of a sacrifice Coach had made ages ago to work for a questionable government organization.

It was too much to process. But despite this revelation, Tuck couldn't back down from his mission to save Clay, even if it meant taking Coach's life. Could this mess get any worse? Tuck shut his eyes and told God he didn't really want to know.

Chapter 33

In the barn after midnight, Mrs. Moody buried her dread and smiled with all the sweetness she could muster. "Good news, children! Soon, we will be moving."

The Leps murmured in alarm, even those drugged, who stirred in the hay.

Gerald scowled and rubbed his stump. "Moving? Where?"

"Survivor Central. Also called SC. A wonderful place, just beneath The Temple."

Gerald snorted. "Anywhere close to The Temple can't be wonderful."

"Home is a wonderful place," Krystal the Eyeless said. "Are we going there?"

Mrs. Moody cleared her throat. "Why yes, my dear. In a manner of speaking, we certainly are."

"Oh, goody." Krystal hummed "Over the Rainbow." "We aren't going to be in Kansas anymore, are we?"

"Not at all. Where we're going is far better than Oz."

Gerald frowned. "Mrs. Moody, that's bull and you know it." He turned to his fellow Leps. "She wants to move us closer to Brother Moody, brothers and sisters. The man who made us the freaks we are today."

"Now, Gerald, how many times do I have to tell you? You are not freaks, not a one of you."

A drugged Lep shuffled forward. "Will our aides… be…

there?"

"Yeah," another drugged Lep said, his face askew, "will… Fred and Willis go… with us?"

"No," Mrs. Moody said. "I'm afraid I have to let them go."

The Leps moaned in disappointment: "They gotta come with us." "Can't leave 'em behind." "Must not leave." "Must stay with Fred and Willis."

"No," Mrs. Moody said, "that won't be possible. The vans will pick us up within the hour."

The Leps grew distressed: Several shouted, two cried, one tumbled into the hay.

Gerald gave a sharp whistle, and the Lep chatter ceased. "Mrs. Moody, what if we refuse to go quietly?"

Mrs. Moody trembled. "That would be just plain unreasonable, Gerald."

"In other words, you ain't got a back-up plan."

"I neither scheme nor connive. I've always told you the truth."

"I hope God don't strike you down for that, Mrs. Moody. 'Cause we all know you're lying through your false teeth."

"Gerald, please, don't do this."

"I got to, Mrs. Moody. I cut my hand off 'cause it led me into sin. I won't be led into sin again and lose the other hand."

"I'm not leading anybody into sin, least of all, you, my children."

"Not the way I see it."

"My eyes," Krystal said, frowning. "They made me sin. Delicious, wonderful sin. I hated every minute of it." Her lower lip trembled. "I wasn't blind, but now I don't see." Her hands played desperately over Gerald's hardened face, and he caressed her.

Between sobs, Derek Chambers said, "Behind my back, I know you call me Mournful. I don't want to sin. I only want to be comforted. God, please, please. Mrs. Moody, please,

please."

Mrs. Moody squeezed Derek's shoulder and sighed. "Children, why do you think moving to Survivor Central will cause you to sin?"

Gerald cradled a trembling Krystal as he spoke. "Because the closer I am to Brother Moody, the closer any of us are to him, the greater our desire to kill him. And killing is sin."

Is it? Though Mrs. Moody had thought about it before, she couldn't say. But once a meme got started among her children, it spread like flu. So, as the Leps wept, she motioned for Gerald to follow her to the barn door.

"Gerald, what in heaven's name is the matter with you? Temptation, desiring to kill, is not the same thing as actual murder. The Book of James tells us that."

"I'm not so sure, Mrs. Moody. I don't want to lose my other hand. Anyways, I think your son wants to move us to Survivor Central so nobody else can drive out here and find us. He wants to hide us from the world like we're incriminating evidence."

"Good heavens, no," Mrs. Moody said, "nothing could be further from the truth." After that lie, another slithered forth. "In fact, I know a secret about my son that will make all of you feel better about him."

Hope filled Gerald's eyes. "Really? Can you share it?"

"There's nothing I'd love to do more."

Gerald whistled. "Brothers and sisters, Mrs. Moody says she got something good to tell us."

"You mean," one of the drugged Leps said, "we're staying?"

Mrs. Moody smiled. "I'm afraid not, my dear. But I do have a wonderful surprise for you. My son swore me to silence, but I'm going to tell you the real reason you are being moved to Survival Central. He wants to make you better. And once you are better, he'll let you go home."

"Real home?" Krystal said, smiling weakly. "Not

Kansas?"

"No, not Kansas. Home to your loved ones, your families. The only reason my son hasn't already done so is he wants to make you well, so when you do go home, you will be almost as good as new."

"I'm going to get new eyes?" Krystal said.

Having lied twice made the third time easy. "I think that is a distinct possibility, Krystal. Yes, indeed."

Krystal clapped in joy. Her fellow Leps also displayed hope—nods, smiles, tears. Two danced in the hay. One started a singalong.

"I will return in a jiffy," Mrs. Moody shouted over the hubbub and shuffled toward her house. What would they think if they knew she was headed for a drink?

Mrs. Moody cursed, angered she had lied to her children. But it was for their own good. She had to get them to Survivor Central with as little fuss as possible. Otherwise, she feared her son would retaliate—once Grahmmie had known Tuck Jameson and his friends had seen the Leps, he'd considered putting the Leps to sleep. Humanely, of course. Her stomach wrenched. Hard to believe her own flesh and blood would consider such a thing. Grahmmie had to be stopped, the reason she was working as a double agent with Adam Shimura's shadow organization.

She downed a whiskey in the kitchen and wondered if the Leps would help her. The liquor burned down her throat, and a warmth filled her bosom. Yes, when they found out Brother Moody had no intentions of letting them go home, they would be more than happy to poison his well—perhaps literally.

Chapter 34

April gripped the phone and bolted from her living room recliner. "Kenny Rhodes?"

"Ms. Showers," he said, "this is my one phone call. Didn't want no lawyer."

Kenny landed in jail often, of course, but he'd never called April before. "What do you want?"

"Ms. Showers, could you come down to the jail? Got something I need to say. Private like."

"You can't tell me over the phone?"

"No, ma'am."

The plaintive quality in his voice touched her. "All right, Kenny. I'll be there soon."

As she drove to the jail, she wondered what Kenny wanted. Yes, when he had spent a semester at ARV Career School, she had tutored him a few weeks—sadly, he flunked out and never returned. Something about him sometimes scared her, and she shivered as she parked at the jail.

Inside, a small Christmas tree stood in the corner, icicles weighing down its scraggly limbs—April couldn't help but think of the homely tree in *A Charlie Brown Christmas*. Weight-challenged Deputy Sam Derleth, resembling a thirtysomething Santa Claus, tossed his newspaper aside and adjusted his gun belt. "Been expecting you, ma'am."

"Kenny said he wanted to talk."

"Yep," Deputy Derleth said. "He tell you what he's in

here for?"

"No."

"We're holding him for the murder of David Freeman."

April's breath caught in her throat. "What?"

"Mrs. Jenson and her granddaughter said they saw Kenny leavin' Mr. Freeman's house about the time the M.E. says the murder took place. And we got forensic evidence."

Confusion filled April's head. "What about the arrest warrant for Tuck?"

"It's been canceled." The deputy looked both ways, as though someone might be listening. "Frankly, ma'am, I'm glad to hear it. No way Tuck could have killed a man in cold blood."

April agreed, of course, and relief replaced her confusion. *Thank you, God.* But she felt guilty that she was more concerned about Tuck than her deceased fiancée. Her sinuses stung as she realized once again David was gone.

Deputy Derleth led April to Kenny's cell, and she wrinkled her nose at the musty air. Behind bars, Kenny sat on a foldout metal chair, shoulders slumped, head downcast.

"Kenny," the deputy said, "Ms. Showers is here."

Kenny looked up, his cadaverous face a study in despair, but when he saw April, his countenance brightened. "Ms. Showers. Thank you for comin'." He narrowed his eyes at the deputy. "Lawman, leave us be."

Deputy Derleth chuckled. "Anything you say, Mr. Rhodes." He winked at April and sauntered toward the front office, the keys on his gun belt jangling as he went.

Kenny smiled. Grime smeared his face, and he reeked like a man who'd sworn off deodorant for a month. He gazed at April without blinking, and she fought off a shiver.

"Kenny," she said, wondering why he had killed David, "you said you wanted to talk."

"Ms. Showers, I wanted to apologize for killin' David Freeman. I know the two of you were gonna be married."

"Yes," April said, a pang in her heart. Her throat

tightened.

"Ms. Showers," Kenny continued, "nothing I can say will change things. But hang it all, you were too good for David Freeman. Too good for any man."

Tears welled in April's eyes, and she didn't dare speak. Why was she here listening to this? She hadn't even had time to process her grief over David.

Kenny's look of defiance melted into remorse. "I turned myself in. I did it for you. When I die, that'll be for you, too." In the dim light, his eyes glistened. "You were always nice to me, you and Clay. Not like the rest of this lousy town."

April took in a deep breath and locked down her emotions. "Kenny, I'm sorry for the way this town has treated you. But there's no excuse for murdering a man."

Face twisting into a mask of rage, Kenny bolted from his chair, which clattered behind him. "Don't you think I know that, Ms. Showers? Huh?"

Deputy Derleth bustled into the cellblock and shot Kenny a reproachful look. "Hold it down, Rhodes." He turned to April. "Ma'am, maybe you ought to leave."

"No," Kenny said, clutching the bars. "Please, not yet."

To the deputy, April said, "It's all right."

"Well, okay. But y'all need to finish up quick."

The deputy left, and April turned to Kenny. "Did you want to tell me something else?"

A curious mix of emotions played across his face, settling into fear. "Ma'am, I work for Brother Moody."

April cocked her head. "You work for Brother Moody? How do you mean?"

"I'm one of his acolytes, workers of his who ain't Good Sams. Acolytes do awful things, like torture." He dropped his chin. "And sometimes worse."

"Kenny, no offense, but that's pretty hard to swallow."

"Deputy Dawg out there? He's an acolyte too. Better watch him."

Trying to ignore a shudder, April straightened her back.

"I'm confident I can hold my own with the deputy."

Kenny grunted. "Don't go being cocky, Ms. Showers. Brother Moody won't let no one stand in the way of what he wants."

"What does he want?"

Kenny smiled sourly. "Clay. Sad what Clay is gonna wind up doing for him."

"Which is?"

Terror sprang into Kenny's eyes, and he backed away from the cell bars. "Please don't ask me, Ms. Showers. Just be careful. For God's sake, be careful."

Deputy Derleth ambled into the cellblock and hooked fingers into his gun belt. "Rhodes, Ms. Showers has been with you longer than any lady needs to be." To April, he tipped his cap. "Ma'am, you should go."

"All right." She turned toward Kenny, moved by the tears streaming down his face. "Kenny, I'll remember you in my prayers."

In a thick voice, he said, "Thank you."

April nodded, but as she left Kenny's jail cell, she thought she heard him say, "I'll be gone real soon, Ms. Showers."

On the way home, she considered Kenny might have a crush on her. She shivered, feeling guilty that Kenny repulsed her. But at the same time, she pitied him—he reminded her of Gollum from *The Lord of the Rings*. She wondered if Kenny's defense would call her as a character witness at his trial. And if it did, what would she say?

Once she arrived home, she called Tuck, but only got his voicemail. She texted him. Mandy had parked herself beside her food dish and meowed impatiently while April poured Purina One into the bowl.

"What do you think, Mandy?" April said as the cat crunched into its meal. "Who else should I try?"

She emailed, texted, and called all twenty-five of ARV's Student Services staff, even Dr. Pritchard, but no one had heard from Tuck. However, Dr. Pritchard suggested April call Farris Steel, Stribling Hall's RD.

"Ms. Showers," Farris said, "I wish Mr. J had contacted us. Me and the guys are worried sick. We're afraid something bad has happened."

"I hope you're wrong, Farris."

"Anything we can do to help?"

"No."

Now what? April knew of only one other person she might call, someone she had avoided for years—June, Tuck's ex-wife.

Funny how back in high school, the senior class had chosen Tuck and April, star basketball player and star cheerleader, as The Couple Most Likely to Succeed. Then, just one month before the prom, Tuck ditched April for June.

Tuck and June had married six weeks after graduation. Five years later came the divorce, partially for the usual reasons—youth, naivete, overconfidence—but also because of June's serial adultery. In addition, June wanted money and all that came with it. That she had cheated on Tuck hadn't surprised April, nor that after June's divorce she had wed a bank president twenty years her senior.

Despite April's best attempts to avoid June, in a town as little as Winkdale, April had run into her occasionally at the grocery store or a social event, their small talk rivaling the stature of the title character in *The Incredible Shrinking Man*, one of April's favorite classic sci-fi movies. After a deep sigh, April looked up June's number and called.

"April," June said, "I haven't heard from you in ages. I assume you're calling because you want something."

Same old June. "Well, actually, that's true." She told her Tuck was missing and had been incommunicado.

"What makes you think Tuck would call me?"

"You were close once."

"I was also a virgin once."

"I understand the divorce was amicable."

"So people said. Tuck was weak. Only a loser goes into a low-paying field like education."

"Or someone who wants to make a difference in kids' lives."

"Oh, I forgot—you're a teacher yourself. I intended no offense. But if any was taken, not my problem."

"Haven't changed much, have you, June?"

"No. And I'm fine with that. I'm sorry it sounds as though we're having an argument. Of course, the only place we never argued was on the tennis court. As doubles partners, we were unbeatable. Remember?"

"How could I forget?"

"You never answered my emails about playing doubles in the Arkansas River Valley Tennis Association. Course, I knew you were still sore over me taking Tuck away from you."

"June, our differences aside, I happen to be concerned about Tuck and hoped you might know where he was."

June laughed. "You haven't gone googly eyes over him again, have you?"

"I don't think that's any of your business."

"If you have fallen for the jerk again, nothing to be ashamed of. Tuck's a good-looking man with charm to spare—until you find out what a loser he is."

"I can't believe you're still so bitter."

"If you should choose to tie the knot with him, you'll think 'bitter.' He was always telling me I needed to 'broaden my horizons,' that I needed to get a degree in interior design because that was one of my 'gifts.' He thought he knew what was best for me and everybody else. From what I hear, the big jerk hasn't changed."

"I wouldn't know."

"I think you would."

"Look, June, I'm sorry I called. I was hoping against hope you had heard from Tuck."

"Well, I haven't, and that's not the last verse." A pause.

"But believe it or not," she said, a slight tremor in her voice, "I pray he turns up."

"Thank you."

April ended the conversation and sighed. Did Tuck feel the same way about contacting her that he did about phoning June?

She leaned back in her recliner and wondered if Tuck was in danger. Could he be hurt? Spread-eagled in a ditch somewhere, dead?

"No, April," she said aloud, "he can't be dead."

But David was dead. A week ago, she'd have said he couldn't be deceased either. Everything was happening too fast.

What about Kenny's strange story of Brother Moody using acolytes to do his bidding? Was he telling the truth? She was only starting to admit her anger towards Brother Moody for having changed David into a Good Sam. But dark deeds? Kenny had even said torture— *"and sometimes worse."* Just what did "worse" mean?

The phone rang—Mom. April rolled her eyes.

"April," Mom said, wound up as usual, "you won't believe it."

"What, Mom?"

"You know Kenny Rhodes? That loser you used to tutor? They arrested him for David's murder!"

"Really?" Mom must have been using her police scanner app again.

"That's not all. I just heard he killed himself in jail."

April sat up straight—how was this possible? "Killed himself? How?"

"Had a visitor who apparently slipped him a belt, and he hung himself."

"The deputy wouldn't let that happen."

"Deputy Derleth? He's the biggest doofus in town."

Kenny had said the deputy was an acolyte, meaning the lawman must have given the belt to Kenny, maybe even egged him on. Poor Kenny—she should have stayed at the jail longer. "Mom, you may be right about the deputy."

"I'm glad we agree on something."

"Another thing."

"What's that, muffin?"

"Kenny Rhodes was not a loser."

"Are you kidding me? Not a loser? He was—"

"He was abused as a child."

"April, he killed your own fiancée."

April took a deep breath, still finding it hard to believe David was gone. "And nothing excuses that. But Kenny had so much going against him."

"Muffin, sometimes you see the good in people when there isn't any. Just like your father."

She wanted to say, *Hurray for Dad*. But instead, she said, "Mom, so much has happened. I'm just trying to take it all in."

Mom's tone softened. "I know. David's dead, Kenny's killed himself, and who knows what might happen next?"

"Who knows," April said. Someone knocked at the door. Maybe the police? "Mom, gotta go."

"Call me. I mean it."

Both relieved and guilty her conversation with Mom had ended, April couldn't imagine who might be knocking. One of Tuck's Student Services colleagues who had heard from him? Had to be—she needed some good news.

April opened the door, and what greeted her wiped the smile from her face.

Before her stood a mountain of a man, at least six and a half feet tall. A ski mask over his face, he was dressed in black. She had wondered when she might need to use the self-defense moves Kurt Ambrose, a retired Navy Seal, had taught her, and it looked as though that time had come.

"Good evening," Ski Mask said in a shrill cartoon voice that belied his burly looks. "Are you Ms. April Showers, and is that a real name?"

April laughed nervously. "Yes, I am she. And that is a real name. You'd have to know my mom to understand."

"Is that so?"

He grabbed her, spun her around, and pressed a wet cloth over her nose and mouth—it happened too fast for April to use any self-defense moves. He mashed the rag so hard over her face that her nose hurt. She fought to escape, but breathed in more of the sweet, noxious stuff. Was she about to join David? Head spinning, she tried to scream, but couldn't.

Her ski-masked assailant said, "I knew April Showers was your real name, just like to have my fun." He broke into a high-pitched giggle, and goosebumps sprouted across April's arms. As consciousness faded, she remembered Kenny saying acolytes sometimes did things worse than torture.

The world went black.

Chapter 35

In a nanotechnology lab beneath the Temple, Brother Moody drummed his fingers. Get on with it.

Dr. Sloan's lecture held Clay spellbound, but Moody knew Clay's true interests, and he itched to get to them.

"So," Clay said to Dr. Sloan, motioning to the Atomic Force Microscope and its attached monitor, "the AFM allows you to measure atomic surfaces, and also alter them?"

"Correct," Dr. Sloan said.

"But most of the work goes on in the cleanrooms because there's almost no dust or other particles. Right?"

"Correct again."

Moody rolled his eyes. Regarding the stainless steel and plastic state-of-the-art lab equipment surrounding them, its only relevance was to help usher in a new heaven and earth.

"Clay," Moody said, "Dr. Sloan is a busy man with work to do. Right, Dr. Sloan?"

The slender scientist with the salt and pepper cowlick locked eyes with Moody. "Yes." He turned to Clay. "Sorry."

Clay raised an eyebrow. "One more question?"

Dr. Sloan looked Moody's way, and Moody nodded. Better to indulge Clay than to irritate him.

To Dr. Sloan, Clay said, "Are you a Good Sam?"

Dr. Sloan flinched. "No."

Adrenaline shot through Moody's veins—that stupid pencil-necked geek.

Clay continued his Dr. Sloan conversation. "Why not? What could be better than total commitment to God?"

"Nothing… if one believed in God."

"You're an atheist?"

"Yes."

Moody imagined breaking Dr. Sloan's neck.

Clay smiled. "I won't hit you over the head with a Bible. But why don't you believe in God?"

Moody cut in. "Clay, as I said, Dr. Sloan has urgent work awaiting."

Clay ignored Moody. "Dr. Sloan, as an atheist, I'm sure you have a set of important values."

"That's a reasonable appraisal."

"If there was a nanbless wine that would free to you live out your atheistic values to their fullest, would you drink it?"

"A fair question," Dr. Sloan said. "I'd have to think it over."

Moody gritted his teeth. "Dr. Sloan, your work."

"Yes," Dr. Sloan said too sharply for Moody's tastes, "of course."

Like a drum major in a marching band, Dr. Sloan pivoted for his office. Moody's face heated as though from an internal furnace—the scientist had disrespected him, and he would pay.

Forcing down his rage, Moody turned to Clay. "The only part of the lab complex left is the break room. Care to join me?"

"Sure." Clay sighed. "Also, I have some issues with the nanbless wine."

"No worries, Clay. We'll talk it out." Moody's voice shook, but his self-control grew second by second. *Thank you, Holy Spirit, that you empower me above other men.*

Once Moody and Clay sat across from each other in the break room, Moody waded in. "What troubles you, Clay? Having second thoughts?"

"Yes."

"Why? The nanbless wine will allow the Holy Spirit not only to bring the Strong Man to his knees, but to flush him from your life like an unwanted cancer. Becoming a Good Sam is the perfect blend of science and spirituality, making science subject to the gospel."

Clay pushed his eyebrows down. "You sure about that? How do I know it's not all science and no gospel?"

"Would that be so bad if the result made one more obedient to Christ?"

"Maybe for some. But I don't want to be a zombie."

"Don't you? During our Purge sessions, you said you'd welcome being brainwashed for Christ. Have things changed?"

Clay picked at a scab on his hand. "No. I do want to live for the Lord. But I also want to make Tuck proud. Guess you could say I have mixed motives."

Alarm screamed in Moody's head—how had he failed to drag this out of Clay during the Purge? He suppressed his anxiety and patted Clay's knee. "When we are living out Romans 7, we always have mixed motives. So what if you want to make Tuck proud? More important is your desire to live for the Lord. When you drink the nanbless wine, you will live 100% for Christ."

"That's my hope."

"When you were a boy, you prayed for your cat's healing, and God heard your prayer. Once you drink the nanbless wine, you will ask God and He will do more, yes, far more than that."

Clay cocked his head, a confused look on his face.

A familiar peace settled over Moody. "Clay, I feel the Spirit moving within me. Once you are a Good Sam, your faith in God will heal many. Your words will flatten mountains. You will be the Lord's Prophet."

Clay's look of puzzlement morphed into alarm. "The Lord's Prophet? No way."

"Isn't that what Moses and others in the Bible said? I

have seen a vision of you as a Prophet."

"I don't believe it."

Moody smiled. "Let me show you something." Feeling led by the Spirit, Moody called Leon King and asked him to come down. Should Moody warn Clay about Leon's disfigurement?

"Leon," Moody said to Clay, "is a very special Good Sam." There. He'd sounded a quasi-alarm.

When Leon entered the room, Clay had the micro-second startle reaction most did upon seeing Leon's face for the first time.

"Leon," Moody said, "I'd like you to meet Clay Jameson. He will join The Body during our Tuesday night service."

Clay and Leon exchanged pleasantries. Leon's looks didn't deter Clay—quite the contrary, Clay's smile was natural, his eyes unafraid to look into Leon's.

"So," Leon said, his deep voice gravelly, "you're a librarian?"

Clay nodded.

"What's your favorite book?"

"*That Hideous Strength.*"

Leon's eyes smiled. "Mine too. You a C. S. Lewis fan?"

Clay grinned. "Born and bred."

The two were hitting it off, but Moody had seen and heard enough. "Leon, thank you for coming down. Now I need to speak with Clay privately. If you will excuse us."

What was left of Leon's face struggled to smile. "Nice to have met you, Clay."

Clay said, "Same to you, Leon."

Leon departed, and Clay looked at Moody with a mixture of surprise and resentment. "Why didn't you tell me?"

"About Leon's appearance? I have my reasons. Several years ago, his house caught on fire. He tried to rescue his dog, to no avail. For his efforts, he got burned by the flames, but lived through it. You've seen the result."

"How did he become a Good Sam?"

"He found out about us through one of our ads, and eagerly desired to live among people who didn't care about his appearance. Once he became a Good Sam, he started working full time on the Temple's landscape crew."

"So, sort of a happy ending."

Moody smiled. "Yes, sort of. Because the nanobots imprinted Romans 8:28 in his head when he was initiated, he now joyfully accepts his fate as God's will."

"Don't know if I could do that."

"Oh? With the perfect faith you will have after drinking the nanbless wine, there is something you could do. You could ask God to give Leon a new face." He paused to let his words sink in. "Nowadays, Leon refuses to seek a relationship. But with a healed countenance, he could take a wife and raise a family."

"I'll never have that kind of faith."

Moody placed a hand on Clay's shoulder. "But you will, Clay. The Lord will hear your prayers, and you'll be able to heal the afflictions of many. That's why on Tuesday, you must drink the nanbless wine."

Clay twisted his hands, and Moody sensed a war raged within him. He prayed God would move Clay to accept his destiny as a Prophet under Moody's guidance.

A familiar but unwelcome voice whispered in Moody's head. *Tell him the whole truth.*

Moody clenched his jaw. *Begone, diseased spirit.*

Tell him he will not only heal but also kill.

I refuse to listen.

I am not the Evil One. I am much closer.

Father of lies.

You have twisted me beyond recognition.

No more of this nonsense about you being my conscience.

If you prick us, do we not die?

In the name of the Lord God, I cast you out!

A screech filled Moody's head, quickly silenced as though sucked into a wormhole.

Thank you once again, Lord God, for your timely deliverance.

Clay was staring at Moody, his eyes wide. "You okay, Chief Elder?"

Moody smiled. "Couldn't be better. Just another skirmish with the Evil One in the recesses of my soul. Happens all the time."

"I'm not used to this level of spiritual warfare."

Moody patted Clay's shoulder. "You will be. If you drink the nanbless wine."

Clay said, "I will."

Moody embraced him, tears wetting the lad's tunic. "Thank God in Heaven."

"Hallelujah," Clay said.

Moody smiled. Yes. Hallelujah, indeed.

~

Dr. Sloan cringed behind his desk as Moody towered over him. "What were you trying to do out there?"

"Do?" the scientist said in a shaky voice, his chair squeaking as he rolled it backwards.

"Showing disrespect for me in front of the young man who will soon be our Prophet."

Sweat popped out across Dr. Sloan's forehead. "I, I was only trying to answer his questions."

Moody sneered. "'Only trying to answer his questions.' You should have lied and told Clay you were a Good Sam, or at least a believer in God. Your confession of atheism could have ruined everything."

"But it didn't."

Moody's sneer deepened. "Fortunately for you. From now on, when I give you the signal, you will shut up at once. Understood?"

"Yes, Brother Moody, u-understood."

"Don't forget we have Sandy."

The scientist chuckled nervously. "How could I forget that? You remind me every time I see you."

"Sandy will remain unharmed, as long as you cooperate. Besides, you may be an atheist, but you are doing God's will. His good, righteous, and perfect will. Nothing is more important."

Moody had, of course, considered forcing Dr. Sloan to drink designer nanbless wine, but he feared that might affect the scientist's intellect and initiative. Besides, since Dr. Sloan would create the nanbless wine he drank, he might give himself a harmless batch and only pretend to be a Good Sam.

Moody left the scientist's office and strode down one of Survivor Central's corridors, where smiling Good Sams greeted him.

"Hallelujah, Brother Moody!"

"Blessed day, Chief Elder!"

"Glory be to God, Favored One!"

Moody smiled—"Favored One" was the name Good Sams had coined for him. It fit, for just as Mary was favored in the Lord's sight two thousand years ago, so Moody was favored today.

As Moody stole into his prayer closet, the darkness startled him, as usual. He hung his head, again regretting the need to kidnap Dr. Sloan's twelve-year-old daughter Sandy to insure the scientist's cooperation. Sloan's being a widower helped. The man ranked at the top of his field, proven by the advent of the nanobot-driven Good Sams mere months ago. Sloan and his staff had sworn an oath of secrecy, but Moody knew some of them had no doubt squealed to spouses, friends, siblings.

Didn't matter.

Once Clay took the Last Step, he would be the first Prophet in two thousand years, one who could call down plagues upon America if necessary. Foreign governments would tremble as well. One day in the future, airborne nanobots would transform the entire human race into Good Sams, and Moody would reign as their Chief Elder, second in command only to the Godhead.

That hated voice sounded in Moody's head again. *Prideful pretender.*

Back so soon?

False Messiah.

Look who's calling who false.

Hypocrite.

Begone, diseased spirit. A burst of energy crackled through Moody's veins like lightning, and this surge had to be his lifeline to the Almighty. *I will cast you out once and for all.*

If you do, birds will burn, and angels will weep.

"Out!" he said aloud. "Satan, strong man of this world, you will fail in turning me against The Plan. I deny the false guilt you try to stir in my heart. Dr. Sloan's daughter is one person—one person! If she must be sacrificed for the new heaven and earth, so be it."

Moody fell prostrate upon the floor. "Holy Father, thank you that you have not made me like other men who let the Evil One deter them from the truth."

The energy surge in Moody's limbs dampened to a pleasant tingle, and a blinding inner light dispelled the darkness. Moody smiled—more than ever, God was on his side, and woe be to the man or woman who wasn't.

Chapter 36

Knuckles rapped against the car window, and Tuck bumped his head against the glove compartment. *Ow!*

Marv yanked the door open. "The coast is clear."

Under cover of the night, Tuck and Ham hustled into Marv's motel room. Marv bolted the door and gave an OK sign. "Mission accomplished, gentlemen."

Tuck thanked Marv and rubbed the bump on his head, surprised the bed table clock showed it was after midnight.

Ham frowned. "You sure nobody saw us?"

Marv said, "As sure as is possible under these less-than-ideal circumstances."

"'Cause if somebody did see us, it could be bad news."

Tuck pushed down his brows. "Lay off, Ham. Marv stuck his neck out for us. You ought to be grateful."

"Point taken," Ham said. "Thank you, Dr. Gillespie."

"Don't mention it. Hungry?"

"Starved."

Marv gave Tuck and Ham packages of cheese and peanut butter crackers, and Tuck, savoring the saltiness, devoured his as though he hadn't eaten in days.

As Tuck and Ham munched without restraint, Marv handed them Cokes. Tuck took a long swallow, disappointed by the lukewarm temperature, but glad for the familiar acid burn. Ham downed half his can in one gulp.

Marv said, "Got the Cokes an hour ago, thinking you two would be in by eleven. But the motel manager chose that time to take a stroll."

Tuck cocked his head. "Think he's suspicious?"

"Don't know. Maybe he always makes the rounds before midnight. But we'd best be wise."

"Absolutely," Ham said before belching.

Tuck shook his head. "Nice."

"Hey, burping is a sign of politeness in Arab countries."

"Actually," Marv said, "that's inaccurate."

Ham looked sheepish. "Oh."

"Marv," Tuck said, "sorry I've mixed you up in this."

"No sweat, as they said back in the day. However, time for that age-old question—what now?"

A bed squeaked when Tuck sat on it. "Way I see it, as a murder fugitive, I am a definite liability. I should set out on my own come morning."

"Indeed? And what are Ham and I supposed to do in the meantime?"

"Well, Ham might choose to follow me." Tuck looked Ham's way. "Or not."

Ham rolled his eyes. "Yeah, right, like I'm going to bail on my best friend. Course I'm going with you. You need a nursemaid."

Tuck grinned. "Yeah, yeah."

"And where, pray tell," Marv said, "does that leave yours truly?"

Tuck pulled off one of his shoes, got a whiff of sock stench, and slid the shoe back on. "You've gone above and beyond. I can't involve you further."

"It's a little late for that. By hiding you, I'm already an accomplice to murder—"

"—I feel awful about that—"

"—and I say we get four to five hours of sleep, then head for The Temple in the wee hours of the morning."

"Marv, we don't know for sure Clay's there."

"Got any better ideas?"

Tuck shrugged—from what Coach and Mrs. Moody had said earlier, Clay had to be at The Temple.

Ham crumpled his empty Coke can and hurled it into the trash. "Got an idea. Dr. Gillespie, why not let me and Tuck make a getaway in your car, just the two of us?"

Marv said, "With you as driver, I suppose."

"Or Tuck. Doesn't matter."

"And how do I figure into this grand scenario?"

"You could say we stole your car. That would leave you in the clear."

"I am not interested in being 'left in the clear.'"

Tuck frowned. "It's a bad idea anyway, guys."

"And then some," Marv replied, raising an eyebrow at a chastised Ham.

"Okay," Ham said. "How about this—Tuck, you and I turn ourselves in."

Tuck laughed and pitched his own Coke can into the trash. "You gone nuts?"

"Look, the cops are probably going to find us, anyway. Maybe we can get 'em on our side. Or steal a squad car."

"Worst idea you've ever had, Ham, and that's really saying something."

"Okay, okay, beanpole. Then how about this—we steal a car and leave Marv here."

Marv said, "Mr. Crouch, the multitude of your ideas is exceeded only by their absurdity."

Tuck tapped his chin. "Maybe Ham's right. I'm already charged with murder. What's grand theft auto on top of that?"

To Marv, Ham said, "Gotta admit he has a point."

Marv crossed his arms. "So you say."

Tuck looked at Marv. "You're a good friend. I don't want you to throw away your career on my account. I refuse to let that happen."

"Oh, you do?" Marv grinned. "Tuck, I normally put up

with your occasional attempts to tell me what to do, because I know it's not my skin color—you have a habit of telling everyone what to do, black, white, brown, or polka-dot. But neither you nor anyone else tells me how far my commitment to a friend goes. Capiche?"

Feeling rebuked, Tuck nodded. "No offense intended."

"None taken."

"Dr. Gillespie," Ham said, "got any idea what happened to Brother Eli?"

Marv sighed. "He hasn't texted, no doubt to keep the police from tracking us down. Channel 29 has probably filed charges against him."

"Which means he may be in jail." Tuck hung his head. "Man, I hate that." All the innocent people now up to their necks in trouble for Tuck's sake.

Marv shrugged. "As Super Chicken once said to his lion sidekick Fred, Eli knew the job was dangerous when he took it."

"You make it sound like a joke."

"Hardly that. But Eli understands The Body is a serious threat, and he's willing to pay the price to see it decommissioned, even if it means jail time."

"And losing his pastorate?"

"Possibly, yes."

Ham snapped his fingers. "Wait! Got another idea. Why not go back to Winkdale and gather up a posse?"

Tuck cocked an eyebrow. "A posse?"

"We could get the Stribling Hall RD and RAs and a bunch of other residents and arm them. Heck, I imagine they own handguns anyway, and I know they have rifles. We could probably rally thirty or more of 'em."

"And," Marv said, "lay siege to The Temple?"

"Exactly," Ham said.

Tuck frowned. "Ham, they're just kids."

"Okay, then we get a bunch of adults from town. Vinnie and his Pizza Palace crew, plus guys in Rotary—you're their president, Tuck—and a bunch of others. They could come armed to the hilt."

"Ham, The Temple would have the law on their side."

"Besides," Marv said, "you can't be too sure who's trustworthy in Winkdale these days." He glanced at the closed motel room blinds. "There are more acolytes in Winkdale than the two of you gentlemen may imagine."

An unsettling feeling wormed into Tuck's gut. "You're saying Vinnie is an acolyte?"

"Yes."

The single word raised the hairs on the nape of Tuck's neck.

"Vinnie is one of many acolytes in Winkdale. They aren't all disaffected military and law officer veterans."

Ham sighed. "So, you're saying thumbs down to an armed militia from Winkdale?"

"Way down."

Tuck said, "Back to the drawing board." Snatches of unsatisfactory ideas flitted through his head, most incoherent—except for one. "Marv is right, Ham. We should all get some shuteye, then head out early in the a.m."

Ham looked as though he'd been sucker punched. "But I thought—"

"—that I don't think Marv should go with us. But it's his decision."

"Gentlemen," Marv said, moving to the bathroom, "if you'll excuse me, and even if you won't, I have a shower to take."

"No offense, Marv," Tuck said, "but I think Ham and I will stay grungy."

"Suit yourselves. Doesn't surprise me in Mr. Crouch's case, but I am a little disappointed in you, Tuck."

As soon as Tuck heard the shower water running, he spoke to Ham in a low voice. "This is our chance, here's what we got to—"

"—how did you know he was gonna—"

"—he told me he always takes a shower before bed. Here's the plan. We get up at 5:00 a.m., and while Marv's asleep, we hightail it out of here."

"How do we get the keys to the Mustang?"

"We won't be taking the Mustang. We'll get out of here and head out to Walmart. When we see a chance, we'll steal a car."

Ham's eyes widened. "Steal a car?"

"Keep your voice down. I can wake myself up without an alarm, done it for years. Then I'll get you up, and we'll make tracks."

Marv stepped from the bathroom, and the clean smell of body wash wafted through the air. "Sure you gentlemen don't want to shower? I brought several changes of clothes, just in case."

"Nah," Tuck said, "we're good."

Minutes after Marv had switched off the lights and reclined on the bed, Tuck lay on the scratchy carpet, turned to Ham, and gave him a thumbs up before shutting his eyes. He wanted to appear confident for Ham's sake—but inside, thinking about tomorrow knotted his guts. Everything that might go wrong could go wrong, and Tuck feared Murphy's Law hungered for a fresh victim.

Chapter 37

Ham, holding his hand over his eyes to block out the sunrise, motioned Tuck to follow him into Jonesburg's Waffle House. "Wanted man or not, you gotta eat."

Tuck shook his head. "You're nuts."

"Where I go, you go. I say we chow down on a mess of pancakes and hash browns." He opened the door, and the heavenly aroma of bacon poured forth.

Tuck turned and ran down the Jonesburg Lane sidewalk, his shoes clattering on the concrete. He looked back—Ham was catching up. Stubborn jerk.

A siren wailed, and adrenaline blasted to the roof of Tuck's skull. His mouth dried up. How could he be this unlucky?

A police sedan pulled beside him, and a buzz cut officer who looked all of sixteen stepped out. "Mr. Tuck Jameson?"

Tuck saw no reason to lie. "Yes, officer."

"Sir, you are under arrest." He read Tuck his Miranda rights and eased him into the cramped back of the police sedan.

Ham insisted he was Tuck's accomplice, and Buzz Cut gave him the same Miranda treatment.

"Officer," Tuck said. "This man is innocent."

"Sorry, sir," Buzz Cut said. "Sargeant says your buddy tipped us off about you."

The blood drained from Tuck's face, and he stared at Ham in disbelief. Ham turned away. Had Ham become a Perf? Had he been a Perf all along? Was this a bad dream?

The police sedan took off. Inside, a steel mesh cage and bulletproof glass protected the two officers in front. No doubt metal plating prevented the police from getting stabbed from behind. But suppose the backseat prisoners got into a fight?

Tuck trembled, and he said, "Look at me, Ham."

Ham kept his head turned away.

"I said, look at me."

Ham did, his face guilt-soaked. He wasn't a Perf—Perfs couldn't lie. But turncoats could.

"Ham, you told the cops to find me by the Waffle House. That's why you wanted us to eat there. Right?"

Ham hung his head and nodded.

"That bathroom break you took before we left the motel room. You were calling the police?"

"Yeah."

"For heaven's sake, Ham, why?"

Ham glanced at Tuck, eyes moist. "Had to." His voice was thick. "You might as well hear all of it."

"Yeah," Tuck said, baffled and enraged, "I think I'm entitled."

Ham shut his eyes. "I've been having an affair with a volleyball coach in another town."

Tuck's stomach knotted. "You've been what?"

"Look, you want to hear this or not?"

"I do." And it better get better.

"Somehow, Brother Moody found out about my affair. Said he'd tell Molly unless I did what he said. That meant she'd fight for sole custody of Jake." He pressed the heels of his hands against his eyes. "I couldn't bear losing Jake. So, I did what Moody said. I deliberately tried to steer you from finding Clay."

Blood thudded in Tuck's ears. "And the Leps at Mrs.

Moody's place? Did you warn Brother Moody about us coming down with Marv and the press?"

"Yeah."

"When? How?"

"When I went to the bathroom at the safe house, I didn't need to go. I called Moody and let him know he needed to hide the Leps, since I figured you would bring in the media."

Tuck scowled. "And after Moody's goons beat me to a pulp a couple of days ago, your quick arrival to untie me was no coincidence, was it?"

Ham shook his head.

"You were working with them the whole time." Tuck's upper lip curled, and he clenched his fists. "Think you know me pretty well, right? So, what did you think I'd do if I found out about your cozy little relationship with Brother Moody? Huh?"

Ham shrugged and turned away. "You weren't supposed to find out."

Shaking, Tuck sucked in a deep breath and struggled to collect his thoughts. The good times they'd had, the shared confidences, the laughs—all of it gone south. Ham's betrayal was the last thing Tuck had expected, now or anytime. But coming now made it worse.

In a rising voice, Tuck said, "Why did you lie about the affair?"

"Because," Ham said, "you made a federal case last time. You made me believe it was my 'husbandly duty' to tell Molly about my two affairs. That got me kicked out of the house." Ham snickered. "You know exactly how everybody else should live their life, what's best for them so they can 'reach their full potential.' Yeah, right. If I had told you about my affair with the volleyball coach, you would have insisted I tell Molly. And that meant I would lose Jake."

"Ham, you can't be suggesting adultery is okay."

Ham grimaced. "Sometimes you don't listen so good. I know I need to be faithful to my wife. I also need a friend who can help me see the light without shoving it in my face."

A storm of emotions thundered in Tuck's chest. Could it be he was partially to blame for his friend's betrayal? Did Tuck really appear to know what was best for everyone?

Ham said, "I ended the affair two weeks ago. I've decided I'll tell Molly. Let the chips fall where they may. She deserves that much."

"But you told the cops you helped me kill David. So, you're going to prison with me."

"You won't understand this, but I had to say I was an accomplice."

"Don't tell me—for the sake of our friendship?"

Ham nodded.

Tuck swore. "You're a real piece of work, Ham."

The police sedan braked to a stop, and the officers escorted Tuck and Ham into the station. One of the two lawmen was a grizzled middle-aged bear of a man, and to him Tuck said, "I'm sure you won't believe me, officevr, but I didn't kill David Freeman."

"We know that, dude."

Tuck did a double take. "You do?"

"Sure. Some guy in your hometown confessed to the murder, and two eyewitnesses saw him leaving the house at the time of the crime." Griswold glared at his partner. "Owens, didn't you tell this man what you were arresting him for?"

"Sir, I, I guess I forgot."

"You forgot?" Griswold tore into his partner. "Being a greenhorn don't excuse your sloppiness. Your grandpa may be the attorney general of the state, kid, but that don't cut no slack with me."

"No, sir. Of course not, sir."

Griswold rolled his eyes. "Of all the rookies in the world, I would get stuck with Barney Fife, Jr."

His head swirling, Tuck said, "If we're not being arrested for murder, what's the charge?"

"Kidnapping."

"Officer, who am I supposed to have kidnapped?"

Buzz Cut, apparently hoping to make amends with Griswold, jumped in. "Sir, you were arrested for suspicion of kidnapping Ms. April Showers." He looked at Ham. "You too, sir."

Tuck's jaw dropped. "April?"

"Yes, sir," Buzz Cut said. "An eyewitness saw the two of you forcing her into an SUV while she screamed for help. Speculation is you might have sexually accosted her."

Tuck dropped his head to his chest—could this day get any worse?

The police hustled Tuck and Ham inside, booked and fingerprinted them, confiscated their belongings, and locked them in a cell. Tuck's insistence that neither of them owned an SUV or had been in Winkdale for two days got no traction.

Tuck wanted to spit. "I'd bet my bottom dollar Brother Moody is behind this."

Ham said, "Why?"

"To get me out of the way. Bet the 'witness' who supposedly saw us kidnapping April is one of Moody's acolytes."

"Could've been a Good Sam."

"Nah. Those goody two shoes can't lie." Tuck clutched the cell bars. "April probably really has been kidnapped. Otherwise, she could just go to the authorities and report she was safe."

"If that's true, what has Moody done with her?"

"Who knows." Tuck turned to his former friend and curled his lip. "Or maybe you would, since you're working for the man."

Ham spread his hands. "Tuck, nothing I can say will make things better—"

"Then keep your mouth shut." Tuck shook the cell bars, longing to be the Incredible Hulk. Where was a blast of good old gamma radiation when you needed it? "April's in danger. I can feel it."

Ham stepped beside Tuck. "She's probably all right. Why would Moody kill her?"

"Why would Moody do a lot of things?"

"But we can't lose hope. Sometimes, miracles happen, man."

Tuck snickered. "Do they?" But for the first time in weeks, despite what had happened today, or perhaps because of it, Tuck prayed without irony. *Please.* He wondered if anyone upstairs was listening.

Chapter 38

April awoke with a shudder—before her loomed Brother Moody and the ski-masked man mountain who had abducted her.

Brother Moody smiled and affected a grandfatherly tone. "Miss April, you are prettier in real life than on Facebook. And no worries. I assure you, Mace didn't have his way with you."

The cloying smell of the drug that had knocked April out clung to her nostrils, and she wiped her nose. Puzzled by a stainless-steel table in the middle of the antiseptic room, she said, "What's this about?"

Putting his hands behind his back, Brother Moody swayed. "Well, I can tell you what it's not about. You're in no danger."

April smirked. "Yeah, right."

Brother Moody chuckled. "So, you're intent on being disagreeable? Fine. Like Burger King used to say, have it your way. But you are as safe here as anywhere on earth."

"Where is here?"

"You are in Survival Central, a multi-story underground complex built to protect five hundred survivors in the event of a national or worldwide catastrophe like nuclear war or asteroid impact. This shelter also serves as The Body's HQ—it's beneath our Temple."

"I know you're rich," April said, "but you can't be rich

enough to afford all this."

"Quite perceptive, my dear. T.J. LeMay financed most of it. He's a big believer in the Good Sam movement."

"Thanks for the news flash."

"His son-in-law—"

"—became a Good Sam and started treating LeMay's daughter like a queen."

Brother Moody cocked his head. "You sound out of sorts, Miss April. No doubt you wonder why I've brought you here. No, it isn't to be Mace's love slave."

"I also hope it's not to be your wife."

Brother Moody looked stricken, as though she'd skewered an old wound. "I am beyond marriage. Even if I wasn't, you are—I'm sure you've heard the saying—not my type."

"That goes both ways."

Brother Moody laughed. "Spirited, aren't you? But you don't fool me, missy. I know deep down, you're terrified."

He was right—her hands had gone clammy, and it felt as though a fingernail were scraping across the inside of her belly.

"To put your fears to rest, I've brought you here to marry Clay Jameson. He doesn't know yet. But he will thank me for it."

April recoiled. "Look, Brother Moody, I'm not some concubine from the Middle East. I've got a mind of my own."

"I know you do, and that's wonderful." He smiled. "With Clay's faith and your intellect, you should have specially endowed kids."

"Would I have to become a Good Sam?"

"Don't insult my intelligence. Of course, you would have to become a Good Sam. Against your will, if necessary. But you must marry Clay first. He needs to see that you are not marrying him because you are a Good Sam and have to, hence the reason we won't force you to drink the nano wine until after the two of you are wed. I will simply coax him to ask you if you're a Good Sam. He knows a Good Sam can't lie, so when you tell him you are not a Perfect, he will know that you are still acting of your free will."

"You think Clay will go along with that?"

"You're missing the point, my dear. This would be the best thing for him and the new heaven and earth." His face hardened. "Besides, if you refuse, I can't be held responsible for what might happen to your parents."

April sprung from her seat.

Mace moved so fast he seized April's throat before she could speak. His grip choked her, and his hot breath moistened her cheek.

"Let her go, Mace," Brother Moody said.

Mace released her, and she dropped. Coughing, she clutched her throat as she staggered to her feet.

"For someone with a mind of her own, that was a pretty stupid thing to do, daughter of the South." Brother Moody's expression became kindly again. "Now, I don't want to harm your parents. But just as in war, sometimes a Southern gentleman must do things he regrets. So, please understand why I had to order what you are about to see."

April's head raced. What was he talking about now? Mace left the room, and April prayed he wouldn't bring back Mom and Dad in chains.

He didn't.

But he did bring back a pet carrier, and a skeletal man, gloved and garbed in a white smock, followed him. Mace pulled a house cat from the pet carrier and slammed it on the stainless-steel table, and the feline yowled in displeasure. The hapless cat sported the same orange tabby stripes as Mandy. In fact, it had the same glittery collar.

"Mandy?" April said.

The cat meowed at her—it *was* Mandy.

April leaped at the surgery table, but gripping her arms, Brother Moody blocked her. "Let me go."

Mandy hissed as she struggled to escape Mace's grip. Meanwhile, the man in the white smock inserted a catheter into Mandy. The feline yowled at this violation, and White Smock injected something into the catheter.

April fought against Brother Moody. "What are you doing to her?"

Mandy grew weak until, thirty seconds later, she went limp.

Brother Moody smiled. "Nothing to worry about now. Jimmy just gave her propofol, which has put her to sleep. Your cat won't feel a thing."

As April continued to tussle, White Smock inserted a different substance into Mandy's catheter.

"Jimmy just gave her an overdose of pentobarbital, a feline sedative. She'll be dead in no time."

"Dead?" April struggled more fiercely, but Brother Moody held her in a vise-like grip. Minutes later, he released her.

Heart pounding in her ears, April ran to the table and touched Mandy—the cat was already losing body warmth. Through hot tears, April glared at White Smock, Mace, and Brother Moody.

Brother Moody said, "I am sorry, Miss April. But your cat didn't feel a thing."

The look of sympathy on his face stunned her, as though he'd done nothing wrong.

"I had to show you that your future marriage to Clay is not up for discussion. What I just did to your cat, I did painlessly."

April glowered. "What about her fear? What about her terror?"

He shrugged. "Couldn't be helped."

"Couldn't be helped?"

"I wanted to assure you I have the spiritual fortitude to do what must be done. If it means eliminating your parents, I will do so. You can keep this from happening by agreeing to marry Clay."

April had never wanted to kill a man, but there was a first time for everything.

"So, will you give me your word you will marry Clay?"

April had no qualms about lying to this man. "Yes. You have my word."

Brother Moody smiled. "I'm glad you are seeing reason, Miss April. God will bless you for this."

The man was a monster—April imagined raking her nails down his cheeks.

"Don't even think about escaping," Brother Moody said as he stashed Mandy's dead body in the pet carrier and White Smock picked it up. "Mace is here to guard you. Don't make him do more than that."

Moody and White Smock left, and Mace stood rigid as a sphinx.

April had few options. Short of marrying Clay, she had to hatch a plan to save Mom and Dad. She could take her own life. But Mace would undoubtedly stop her, so there had to be another way.

She looked at the stainless-steel table and thought of Mandy. The table blurred. What a horrible death, what a horrible man. She wiped her eyes and decided she could grieve later—for now, she had to devise an escape plan.

She scrutinized the walls. Nothing of interest there. Besides, with Mace guarding her, how could she hope to escape?

Wait—what if she pretended she was attracted to Mace? Maybe she could win him over.

April centered herself with several deep breaths and prayed.

God, please help me escape. And please stop Brother Moody. Forgive me for wanting his death, but right now, I could kill him.

She opened her eyes and smiled at Mace. "So, how did you get the name Mace? Is it a nickname, or were you born with it?"

Arms folded across his chest, the ski-masked man mountain remained silent, but like the elements had worn down the sphinx, so April would wear down Mace.

Chapter 39

Tuck brooded on how to escape the jail cell, and Ham said, "Beanpole, if we get out of here, I can get us inside The Temple."

Despite his newborn contempt for Ham, Tuck's ears perked up. "How?"

Ham smiled. "An acolyte—big dude named Mace—showed me a secret entrance in the woods."

"Really?" Tuck rubbed his chin, coarse with unshaven whiskers.

"That's probably where Moody has Clay and April."

Tuck crossed his arms and narrowed his eyes. "How do I know you're not lying again?"

"Tuck, I'm trying to make things right."

"You can't."

Ham swore, a rarity. "You gotta give me another chance."

"Says who?"

"God, for starters."

Tuck rolled his eyes and did his best to ignore a pinprick of guilt.

Ham continued his sermon. "You say you're a Christian. Well, how many times did Jesus say you had to forgive your brother?"

Tuck hesitated. "Seven times seventy." The pinprick of guilt broadened into a Bowie knife.

"Then give me another chance. What I did stunk. But even if you hate my guts for the rest of your life, I want to help find Clay and April."

Tuck shook his head and sighed. "If only I could believe you, big guy."

"You can." Ham spread his hands. "You've got to."

Tuck sniffed. A subtle cologne spiced the air. Marv's?

As though in answer to his query, the jailer brought Marv in. Tuck flinched. What the—?

"So, Tuck," Marv said after being locked in with them, "you're finally captive for my interview with you." He added he knew about the dropped murder charges. "But the deputy has informed me you've both been incarcerated for kidnapping."

"Of April, no less," Tuck said.

"But," Ham added, "Dr. Gillespie, you could be our alibi. We were with you yesterday and this morning. All you gotta do is tell the cops."

"I have. They don't believe me. Seems the two eyewitnesses who supposedly saw you abduct April were white, and I obviously am not."

As though it was the most natural thing in the world, the jailer stepped into the cellblock with Coach.

Tuck's stomach flipped.

"Gentlemen," the jailer said in a tinny voice, "the higher ups have given this man, Mr. Adam Shimura, the right to take you with him." As the jailer unlocked the cell, Coach pulled out his Sig Hauser P226 semi-automatic.

"As the saying goes," Coach said, motioning Tuck and Ham out of the cell with his weapon, "don't try anything funny."

Marv stood in Coach's way. "I suppose that adage applies to me as well."

"Bingo, Dr. Gillespie. It's not a racial thing. I'd feel the same about an old white guy."

Marv put hands to hips. "How broad-minded."

Coach said, "I want you to march into the jail cell, and I don't mean tomorrow."

"If I refuse?"

"Unwise. You are an accessory to Mr. Jameson's and Mr. Crouch's crime of kidnapping."

Marv laughed. "Ridiculous."

"Not ridiculous, my man. I have the authority to have you jailed." Coach's features hardened. "If you refuse, bad things could happen to your grandmother in El Dorado."

Marv's face grew livid. "Scum." Posture ramrod straight, he stepped into the cell, which the jailer locked.

Coach looked at Tuck and Ham. "You two have one smart friend."

Marv said, "I demand my phone call."

A smiling Coach said, "Well, you're not getting it, Dr. Gillespie. If you don't like it, sue me."

Coach marched Tuck and Ham from the cellblock. Tuck couldn't believe this was happening—Marv locked up on trumped-up charges, Coach taking custody of Tuck and Ham at gunpoint. Was his former high school mentor going to drive them out in the sticks and shoot them? But if he'd wanted them out of the way, why not leave them behind bars?

Outside the jail, a chilled gust of December wind smacked Tuck in the face like an icy fist. A higher power trying to get his attention?

Coach's Buick Century was parked in front of the county courthouse, and a few townspeople had apparently noticed Coach's semi-automatic pistol trained on Tuck and Ham.

A middle-aged woman pointed at Coach and said, "That man's got a gun!"

A couple of bystanders screamed, several ran, and an old guy with a white goatee and Razorback cap trotted towards his pickup, perhaps to retrieve a firearm.

Could Tuck sway these folks to his and Ham's side?

Coach said, "No worries, folks! I'm a federal agent

taking these two fugitives in for questioning! Just ask the sheriff!"

That seemed to quiet the onlookers, though several pulled out their smartphones, some no doubt to verify Coach's story, a couple to record the federal agent and his prisoners.

The ancient clock on the courthouse tower clanged four times.

Frowning, Coach said, "Need to make a fast call. If you even think about trying to escape while I'm on the line, you're dead men."

"You're bluffing," Ham said. "You wouldn't shoot us in broad daylight in front of all these people."

Coach grimaced. "Just try me, fat boy."

Fear welled in Ham's eyes, but Tuck struggled to appear blasé—Coach was no doubt trying to spook them. At least, Tuck hoped that's all it was. Perhaps there was still some way he could reach his former high school mentor. Or was Coach past the point of no return?

During his phone conversation, Coach's voice rose. Tuck whispered to Ham, "When we get in the car, one of us has to make a distraction."

Ham nodded.

Coach shouted into the phone for ten more seconds, then jammed it into his pants pocket. A small crowd of spectators gawked.

Coach ordered Tuck and Ham into the car—Tuck behind the wheel, Ham in the passenger seat. Coach slid into the back, where he probably figured he had greater latitude with the gun.

To Tuck, Coach said, "Take her out, slow and easy."

Tuck obeyed. "Where we headed?"

"I think Ham knows."

Ham said, "I do?"

"Yeah," Coach said, "I hear you know a way into The Temple."

"Who told you that?"

"A 'Word of Wisdom' Moody's Mom had."

Tuck shook his head. "Naturally, you believe her."

"I believe her." Coach held the muzzle of his semi-automatic inches from the back of Tuck's head. "And if your friend doesn't tell us how to get to the secret entrance, I may be forced to lodge a bullet in your skull."

Ham took the hint. "Turn on Highway 22 up the way. Drive about five more miles. You'll see a sign for a curvy road. We'll stop there, turn east, go the rest of the way on foot. I know the markers for us to follow."

Per Ham's instructions, Tuck maneuvered the Buick Century onto Highway 22. Minutes passed, the only sounds were those of the humming engine and a Porsche screeching past them on the crest of a hill. Two tears of sweat streamed down Tuck's cheek. "Coach, guess you haven't changed your mind about Clay."

"No," Coach said, regret in his voice.

"Who were you talking to on the phone? Sounded like an argument."

"No point in not telling you, I suppose. It was my Agency superior. He wants me to kidnap Clay, not shoot him."

Tuck perked up—a ray of sanity. "And?"

"And I still plan to shoot him. Only time I will have disobeyed orders."

"So, your boss must agree with my interpretation of Mrs. Moody's Word of Wisdom."

"He does. He's wrong."

"How do you know?"

"Tuckster, we've been over this before. There's too much at stake. The forfeiture of your brother's one life is better than the risk of thousands of others."

"What will your Agency superior do if you shoot Clay?"

Coach chuckled. "Buy me a one-way ticket to hell. And no, I don't mean Toledo."

Tuck dismissed Coach's show of bravado. Would they kill Coach? Or put him in a secret government prison somewhere? If there was only some way to change his high school mentor's mind.

As the woods flashed past, Tuck envisaged steering the car into an oak. But he had read that a vehicle traveling only 35 mph could crash into a tree and injure if not kill the car's occupants.

Ham moaned. The groan was so realistic, Tuck fell for it, until he realized Ham was play acting.

"Ham," Tuck said, stringing along, "what is it?"

Ham shut his eyes and gripped his chest. "Hurts bad. Think I'm having a heart attack."

This was great—Coach had said before he hadn't run a scan of Ham's medical records, which meant he didn't know if Ham had heart disease.

Coach said, "Why should I believe this isn't a trick?"

A realistic edge to his voice, Tuck said, "Heart disease runs in Ham's family. His doctor warned him about losing weight."

Eyes shut, Ham's moans continued to sound genuine. His head dropped to his chest.

"Ham," Tuck said, shoving his friend's shoulder. "You okay?"

Ham went limp, his head lolling to the side.

"He needs CPR."

"Pull over and give him CPR, then."

"No. I'll pull over, and *you* give him CPR."

"Are you nuts? I could blow your head off."

"If you do, you won't have anybody to drive. If Ham dies, you won't be able to get to The Temple's secret entrance."

"I'll bet you know the way."

"Nope."

"If Ham is really in danger, you won't let him die."

"Better him than Clay."

"You wouldn't do that."

"Wouldn't I?" Tuck pulled onto the side of the road and braked. "If you don't give Ham CPR, I'm gonna gouge my eyes out." Tuck reached for his right eye and clutched the skin around its socket.

"You nuts?"

"I can be an unpredictable cuss. Remember when I broke my little finger to get Cindy to go to the prom with me?" Flushed with adrenaline, Tuck turned his back to Coach. "Here goes the first one." He made a mewling noise and hoped Coach would buy it without him having to gouge out at least this eye.

Coach cursed. "All right, all right." He stepped onto the shoulder of the road, leaving his car door open.

Tuck floored it, and the Buick sped off, spewing gravel. In the rearview mirror, Coach aimed his Sig Sauer P226. Two pops sounded. Tuck pushed the Buick beyond eighty, and soon Coach faded from view.

"Ham, it worked!" Tuck turned to his friend.

Ham's face was a mask of blood.

"Aw, no… Ham."

"Been shot," Ham said weakly.

"Gotta get you to a hospital."

Tuck floored the Buick. If they didn't stop Clay from drinking the nanbless wine, he would become The Prophet. But if Ham was badly hurt, he could die.

"Gonna take a look at you, bud," Tuck said, swerving onto the shoulder. He examined Ham's head—a bullet had grazed the scalp, the laceration almost two inches long. The blood on the wound was thickening.

"You need stitches," Tuck said.

"No. We gotta get to Clay. Can't let him… drink that wine. Also, got to find April."

"How close are we to the secret entrance?"

"A mile. Maybe two. Traffic sign with a curvy road is ahead. Must go the rest of the way on foot."

"Can you do that?"

"Got to." Ham used his shirt sleeve to wipe blood from his face, and the coppery tang that hung in the air made Tuck queasy.

Tuck screeched the Buick back on the road, and in a short while, there it was—the wavy road traffic sign at the top of the ridge. He pulled onto the shoulder and helped Ham from the car.

"Can do this… myself," Ham said.

Ham twisted away from Tuck and dropped to the asphalt. Holding his head, he moaned.

"Look," Tuck said, "you're not gonna make it on your own. Can you tell me how to get to the secret entrance from here?"

"No… have to… show you… many landmarks… too hard to describe."

"Okay, then, we're gonna do things my way."

"Since when is… that… news?"

A trace of humor, so maybe Ham was still lucid enough to help Tuck get to The Temple.

"Ham," Tuck said, "can you stand?"

"Yeah."

Tuck helped him up. "Gonna have to use the fireman's carry."

Ham faced Tuck, and Tuck braced his right foot between Ham's legs. With his left hand, he grabbed Ham's right hand and pulled it over his shoulder. He put his head under Ham's armpit and clasped his other arm under Ham's right knee. Next, he squatted and maneuvered Ham's body atop his shoulders. Finally, he rose to his full height, and felt as though a cruise ship's anchor was draped over his back.

"Hey," Tuck said, steeling himself for the task. "You're gonna have to steer me."

"Okay," Ham said. "No… no cracks about my weight."

Tuck blew out a breath. "We're wasting time."

"Go east. In a mile... a marked oak tree."

Thankful he kept himself in shape, Tuck tromped forward, twigs and leaves crunching underfoot. Tuck cursed the noise but didn't know how to avoid it with a former Razorback offensive lineman atop his shoulders.

Tuck paced his breathing to each step—in, out, in, out. He wondered when Coach would find the ditched Buick. But would he know where they'd gone? Yes, because in the car Ham had mentioned the curvy road sign and then going east. Plus, Coach could follow the trail of crunched leaves and underbrush. Tuck hoped he wasn't leaving that big a path.

What about blood? Though Ham's laceration was clotting, a few drops might have fallen. But they'd be hard to see, and Tuck crossed his fingers that Coach didn't have any high-tech goggles in the trunk of the abandoned Buick.

Wondering what had become of his deist convictions, Tuck prayed for strength to get him and Ham to The Temple.

As Tuck crunched underbrush, a mild droning filled his ears. Someone else in the woods? No, it was Ham—the heavier than a blue whale former Razorback was gently humming one of his favorite songs, "He Ain't Heavy, He's My Brother," and Tuck grinned at the irony.

Years ago, when a contestant had performed the song on *The Voice*, Ham's eyes had moistened, and Tuck's first reaction had been to tease his friend. Before he could, Ham started singing along with the singer, belting out the tune as though it were a confession. At the finale, his cheeks wet, Ham turned to a dumbfounded Tuck, smiled, and offered a fist bump. Tuck obliged him, marveling at this side of his friend he'd never seen before.

The woods before Tuck wavered, and he chuckled, because now it was his turn to be teased.

In a halting voice, Ham started singing the song's chorus.

"Hey, big guy," Tuck said, "better hold it down. Might be Temple sentries out here."

"Yeah," Ham answered. "Humming is safer."

Ham switched to this less noisy verbalization and kept it

low, and though Tuck considered shushing him, he realized his footsteps through the woods were louder than Ham. As he marched, he began softly humming the tune along with Ham, and he wondered what the angels must think about these two tone-challenged Bozos.

They approached a gigantic oak with a small cross spray-painted in white on its trunk, and Tuck said, "This the tree?"

"Yeah," Ham said, "turn north… go another mile."

Tuck obliged. He wasn't sure he could forgive Ham for his betrayal. Yet the more he carried the big guy humming "He Ain't Heavy, He's My Brother," hope seemed less impossible.

What if Clay had already drunk the nanbless wine and become The Prophet? What then?

Breath in—step. Breath out—step.

Ham seemed to get heavier, and Tuck's legs ached. But he pushed on. Despite what Ham had done, Tuck had wronged him, and he realized he had also wronged his little brother.

Clay's determination to join The Body no longer seemed so mysterious. For just as Tuck believed he had inadvertently helped push Ham into betraying him, he feared he had likewise pushed Clay into joining The Body. As with Ham, Tuck had always assumed he knew what was best for Clay, offering what he thought was loving counsel to guide his brother into using his God-given gifts. But now he realized his counseling had probably seemed more like badgering, his guidance browbeating. He had to tell Clay he was sorry. And survive to live out his apology.

Please, God.

Tuck's stomach tied in knots, and the night darkened as he continued.

If he failed Clay this time, there would be no second chance.

Chapter 40

S o," Brother Moody said as he showed Mother the last of the three Survival Central apartments for the Leps, "what do you think?"

She fixed him with a bland smile. "I think you believe you have spared no expense."

"I haven't. Look around you." Moody gestured about the spacious room with multiple beds. The walls featured an expansive blue-sky mural, angels and bluebirds flitting in and out of puffy white clouds. The air smelled of pine trees, but it couldn't hide the stink of fresh human waste.

A Good Sam nurse was bundling up a Lep's excrement in a biohazard bag. She smiled at Mother. "Mrs. Moody, praise God, it's so nice to see you!"

Mother appraised the nurse with a puzzled look. "This sort of work doesn't bother you, my dear?"

The nurse shook her head. "Why should it? It's all part of God's wonderful order."

"Do the Leps bother you at all?"

Now it was the nurse's turn to look puzzled. "Why should they?"

"Did you know they were involuntary test subjects for my son's nanobot experiments?"

The nurse frowned. "Oh no, Mrs. Moody. Chief Elder would never do such a thing." She touched Mother's shoulder. "Why, of all people, you should realize he is second only to The Godhead."

"Who told you that?" Mother said.

"He did, of course, during his sermon series on obedience." She regarded Mother as though she were sizing her up for an Alzheimer's ward.

Mother glared at the nurse. "Don't look at me that way, missy. I am not senile."

The nurse smiled. "Oh, but Mrs. Moody, I'm afraid you are."

"Did Chief Elder tell you that too?"

With a sunny smile, the nurse said, "Of course!"

Moody touched the nurse's hand. "Nurse Nadine, that will be all. Thank you, as always, for a job well done."

The nurse left the room smiling, a bounce in her step as she toted the reeking biohazard bag.

"Hmph," Mother said. "I'll bet she would keep smiling even if you told her to eat the dung."

Moody shook his head. "Oh, Mother. Point is, the Leps are in the best of hands. Realistically, what more could I do?"

"You might consider their dignity."

Moody laughed. "Their dignity? Mother, that's a secular humanist concept. Men and women have no dignity. In the sight of God, they are disgusting slugs beyond contempt."

"Then why did Jesus die for them?"

"Enough." Moody planted fists on hips. "What's this really about?"

"You will let the Leps go back to their families once your order is established, won't you?"

"You mean, once the Lord's order is established. Yes, I will. I said I would."

"You say a lot of things. Once upon a time, I would have believed you. No longer. You've changed."

"How so?"

Mother grinned. "You can really stand there and pretend your precious Nurse Nadine didn't just spill the beans? You believe you are second only to The Trinity."

Moody chuckled, an artificial laugh he abruptly severed. "Only The Prophet will be second to The Trinity."

"But not if you have your way, Grahmmie, oh, dearie me, no." The air became thick, as though polluted with an unseen contaminant. "I can see things, you know." Her face stretched into a cheerless smile, and her eyes became dark pools bubbling up from an alien sea.

Moody hated it when Mother's eyes took on this ethereal cast, and wings of ice spread across his shoulders. But this time, he refused to yield to fear. A blinding light pulsed through his skull, and for a moment, he feared it might be God Almighty himself. But he regained his mental footing and realized it was instead The Enemy.

"You don't scare me, Mother," he said, struggling to convince himself. "You prophesy not in the service of God, but of The Evil One."

"Yes," she said, that unearthly glint still in her eyes, "that is what you must believe, isn't it, Grahmmie?"

"Don't call me that!"

"I will call you whatever I choose, son of mine."

Flushing with anger, Moody said, "Suppose you were right. Why shouldn't I think of myself as being next to divinity? Look at all I've sacrificed, woman. The burn scars—I could have them fixed, but I don't, out of humility and devotion to the Lord. My impotence—I could have had that fixed too, but for God's sake, I chose not to."

The dreaminess left Mother's eyes, replaced with an earthbound sadness. "Anything you say, Grahmmie. But the truth is closer to home. You don't want to be anything like your father."

Moody sneered. "Dad is burning in hell at this very moment, Mother Dear. By becoming second only to The Trinity, I can make sure every man, woman, and child on earth becomes a Good Sam, with no chance of going to hell."

Mother's eyebrows rose in the middle. "I know you must believe that, my son." Her eyes sparkled. "I wish you hadn't been the one to find him."

A light pulsed through Moody's head, and a decades-old vision became as clear as an unsullied conscience. He had heard something fall in his father's study, so he had run upstairs to investigate. And there Dad was, twitching, suspended from a rope tied to a ceiling fan. Purple splotches freckled Dad's face, excrement fouled the air. And when the body stopped twitching, the son started screaming.

"Grahmmie," Mother said, "you don't know how many times I wished I had been the one to find your father."

Moody considered answering, but no—they'd had this conversation one time too many. "Visions of my father's suicide spurred on by The Evil One won't stop me. I'm not weak."

Mother tapped her chin. "We are all weak, Grahmmie." A sly look creased her face. "Do you still plan to imbibe Good Sam nanobots after Clay becomes The Prophet?"

"Possibly."

"If you are not weak, why do you need them?"

Moody wagged his finger in Mother's face. "Ah, no, Mother Dear. Truth is, it's none of your business when or if I plan to become a Good Sam." He felt a burst of inspiration. "Question is, are you with me, or agin' me?"

Fear displaced sadness in her eyes. "Grahmmie, I wouldn't be counseling you if I wasn't with you."

He smirked.

"Please," she said, the light glinting off her eyes. "You must believe me."

He grinned, delighted by her shift from haughtiness to humility. "Better watch your step."

As he strode from the room, he contemplated dear old Mom's fate. Turning her into a Good Sam would be too easy. But maybe he could make her an example for all who defied him. After all, once Clay became The Prophet, who needed her?

Chapter 41

Tuck," Ham said, still draped over Tuck's shoulders, "what if Clay doesn't … want to leave?"

Crunching through the woods, his nose and ears stinging in the chilled air, Tuck ignored Ham. "What's The Temple's next marker?"

"Ten yards… itty-bitty chalice… spray painted on a pine tree. You didn't… answer my question."

Tuck frowned. Here he was doing his best to keep marching through the woods while toting a redneck Godzilla on his shoulders, and all Ham could do was repeat the same query. "If Clay is already The Prophet, I'll force him to leave."

"You mean… you'll kidnap him?"

Tuck hesitated. "Would I have any choice?"

Tuck expected Ham to ask the logical follow-up question but was glad he didn't. For if Clay had already become The Prophet, then Mary Moody's prophecy of plagues and destruction had a 75% chance of coming true. The needs of the one against the needs of the many? Tuck cursed even to consider Coach's favorite saying. But if it came to that, was there a painless form of murder?

No, Tuck wouldn't go there—fratricide was too much to ask of anyone. A good God wouldn't allow such a thing. But God had allowed plenty of other morally ambiguous events through the ages, such as the choice of evils between war and totalitarianism. Maybe Tuck's predicament qualified as war.

Tuck spotted the small chalice on the pine tree trunk and stopped, his legs aching. "This where we turn?"

"Yep," Ham said. "East."

In the stillness, underbrush crunched behind them, getting louder as it advanced. Tuck's eyes went wide. Coach.

"Ham," Tuck whispered, "we got to hide."

Tuck's eyes scanned the woods for cover. Nothing.

"Ham, can you climb a tree?"

"Sure."

Tuck set Ham down, and the big guy collapsed to his knees. Tuck helped him up.

"Get up the… tree," Ham said. "Don't worry… 'bout…"

"Stop right there." Coach's voice. With both hands, the black ops agent trained his Sig Sauer P226 on Tuck and Ham. Coach was panting, no doubt from having run to catch up, and his face was flushed.

"Nice stunt back there," Coach said. "Fake heart attack—an oldie but goodie. Shouldn't have fallen for it. I've let sentimentality cloud my better judgment. But no longer."

Tuck said, "How'd you find us?"

Coach rolled his eyes. "Give me some credit, Tuckster."

Ham lunged for Coach, but apparently his sluggishness threw off his aim. Coach sidestepped the former Razorback, who tumbled head-first into the brush.

"Don't try that again," Coach said as Ham struggled to his feet, wiping leaves from his jacket. "If you make me shoot you, I swear to God I'll also take down Tuck."

Ham glared at the black ops agent. "To think I thought you were an all-right guy."

"We're wasting time," Coach said. "Take me to the secret entrance, fat boy."

"C'mon," Tuck said, offering again to haul Ham in a fireman's carry.

"No," Ham said, scowling at Coach. "I can walk."

Coach's jaw clenched. "This better not be a stalling tactic. If you don't walk fast enough, I'll make you ride Tuckster's back. Now get going."

Tuck and Ham marched through the woods, Coach behind them with his semi-automatic pistol trained on their backs. Surprisingly, Ham kept up with Tuck—the former razorback's anger against Coach appeared to have strengthened him. Tuck respected his companion's grit. Maybe, if they got out of this alive, they could be friends again.

Maybe.

But for now, Tuck had to get that gun away from Coach.

He prayed for at least the fifth time that day.

God, you better be listening.

Chapter 42

From The Temple's pulpit, Brother Moody savored the lavender scent, which he believed made people more trusting. He raised his hands before the congregation of three hundred Good Sams.

"Praise God?" Moody said.

"Praise God!" the throng of Good Sams thundered back.

"When?"

"Today! Tomorrow! Forever!"

"At noon?"

"Yes!"

"At night?"

"Yes!"

"At dawn?"

"Yes!"

"Praise God?"

"Praise God!"

The Good Sam congregation burst into spontaneous praise, each lifting a different psalm to God—their babbling sent delightful tingles down Moody's spine, and his smile stretched his facial muscles to capacity.

After sixty seconds, the throng yelled "Hallelujah!" in unison, the sound carrying in the high-ceilinged edifice that could seat up to 2,000. Royal tones of red, purple, and violet dominated the interior, replete with stained glass windows depicting key biblical characters, most of them resembling

Brother Moody. The Good Sams were dressed in white robes, just as their ancient first century counterparts might have worn, and Moody's heart bloated with satisfaction.

"Brothers and sisters," Moody said, "I bring you here this evening because The Body is under attack."

The congregation gasped.

"Please turn your attention to the screens." The 144-inch flat screen monitors burst into life and displayed still photos of three men. "These fellows are acolytes of The Evil One. Their names are Adam Shimura, also known as Coach, Tuck Jameson, and Ham Crouch. Our sentries spotted them in the woods, took their pictures, and sent the photos to me. This godless trio plans to stop the initiation of Clay Jameson into The Body."

A Good Sam cried, "May God have mercy on their souls!"

"Yes," Moody agreed, "mercy is God's way. Yet we must also protect ourselves. Romans 13:4 says those in authority do not wield the sword in vain."

One of the Good Sams looked puzzled. "But Chief Elder, Scripture says if an enemy slaps us on one cheek, we should turn the other."

His peers murmured in agreement.

"Quite true, Brother Osbourne. Your knowledge of Scripture is commendable. But when men were about to stone the adulteress, what did Jesus say in John 8:7?"

"He said whoever was without sin could cast the first stone."

Moody smiled. "Because of The Purge and your final sanctification through the Lord's blood and flesh, you are sinless, every one of you! Some Good Sams have not reached perfection—their faulty spiritual wiring allows an occasional transgression. But not you. You are the cream of The Body's crop, and the Lord's nanotechnology at work in your brain won't allow you to sin. You with me?"

The congregation responded with "Amen!" and "Praise

God!"

"Since you are without sin, you *may* throw the first stone. Christ's admonition was to sinful men, not sinless saints like yourselves. Therefore, as your Chief Elder, I command each of you to take a stone from the courtyard. Go out in the woods, find these three men, and when you do"—he gestured at the two church monitors—"stone them until they are dead."

Brother Osbourne rose his arms. "Thank you, Chief Elder! God continues to anoint you with wisdom for your humble servants."

"Now go," Moody said, fervor burning within his chest. "Stone them until when?"

"Until they are dead!" the throng answered in unison. Good Sams poured from the building, greeted by an armed acolyte who would lead them to the trio's location.

Mr. Shimura may have blacked out the cameras and ground sensors, but he hadn't avoided Moody's human sentries. The latter had the trio under surveillance and kept track of their every move. Mr. Shimura and his two friends must have realized Moody kept the grounds monitored not only electronically but also physically, but apparently, they felt they had no choice but to push on. Mr. Shimura had a gun, as well as a backpack—did it contain gas? Hand grenades? Plastic explosives?

Moody could order his armed acolytes to take out the trio, but he wanted to test his CCs—Cream of the Croppers—to see if he could persuade them to obey commands that stretched biblical limits. Stones were biblical, and hence a form of execution the CCs could accept. Guns were another matter altogether. But if for any reason the CCs didn't stone the trio, he could order the acolytes to shoot the three men.

Mother appeared beside Moody. "You and your 'sinless' CCs."

Moody scowled but refused to let her presence dampen

his good spirits. "How long have you been here?"

"Long enough."

"Well, enjoy your freedom while you can, old dear."

Mother seemed to ignore his threat. "You've forgotten the sin of self-deception. The dark nature still exists in each of your so-called 'saints.' Arrogance hides itself in the soul's shadows, where your nanotechnology cannot reach."

"You're wrong, as usual. The three hundred Good Sams at the top of the heap are free from sin—any of them that Tuck or Ham or Mr. Shimura kills will at once meet his Lord. When Clay becomes The Prophet tonight, he will help usher in a new heaven and a new earth."

Mother smirked. "Or an old hell and an old earth. Here it is, the 21st century, and you have asked your own parishioners to stone men to death, an inhumane torture long condemned by Christians."

Moody glared at her. "You pitiful old fool." He wanted to slap her until she begged for mercy. The image made him smile, and as his joy grew, something dark and irresistible welled within him, flooding every recess of his soul like warm sludge. Ancient tendrils, familiar but never this intimate, slithered into his heart and brain and told him what to say. "Why couldn't you have been the one to commit suicide instead of Dad?"

Mother's look was precious—hands clenched at her cheeks, brows raised in the middle. Moody smiled at the wreck he'd made of her. Yet, for a moment, regret flashed across his mind. But the darkness soon smothered that weakling sentiment, and he laughed as Mother fled the sanctuary in tears.

Chapter 43

At gunpoint, Coach ordered Tuck and Ham to stop in a clearing. Someone or something was trampling through the woods toward them.

Tuck frowned. "Perfs?"

Coach nodded and motioned Tuck and Ham behind a thicket of bushes.

The marching crunched only yards away.

Tuck's hands turned cold. Perfs wouldn't bear arms, given the biblical command to turn the other cheek. Yet Sheriff Dunn had become a Perf, and he carried a firearm.

In the clearing, a hooded, white-robed figure holding a huge rock emerged from the woods. Behind him, dozens of stone-carrying lookalikes followed. Tuck thought of Shirley Jackson's short story "The Lottery," and his mouth dried up.

Another man appeared, this one in camo fatigues and toting a Colt AR-15 rifle. He said something indecipherable to the white-robed leader, motioned to where Tuck, Ham, and Coach were hiding.

Before his army of peers, White Robe raised his rock. "When will we stone them?"

"Until they are dead!" came the unison response.

Tuck swallowed. Oh, great.

With White Robe in the lead and stones upraised, they traipsed into the woods.

Semi-automatic in hand, Coach motioned Tuck and Ham to run, goading them to zig-zag.

The Perfs speeded to a slow trot, but that still gave Tuck and his companions time to dash ahead.

"Scatter!" White Robe said from maybe twenty yards away.

"Hey," Tuck whispered as he and his fellows came to a stop, "why not climb this tree?"

Coach shook his head. "Too risky. We stay put."

Crunching footsteps approached, and Coach waved Tuck and Ham behind a bramble bush. The footsteps seemed few—three men? Four?

"Guys," Coach whispered, "ever seen *The Wizard of Oz*?"

Tuck said, "You lost your mind?"

"Only a few of them coming this way. We take 'em out, put on their robes, and join the other Perfs."

"What if the robes don't fit?"

"We gotta chance it. On the count of three, we'll jump 'em."

Tuck thought this was nuts, but he nodded along with Ham.

Five white-robed Perfs, all males, strode into view, each carrying a large stone hoisted above his head. Coach silently mouthed *one, two, three*. Tuck, Ham, and Coach moved:

Tuck's elbow struck a Perf's temple. The guy went down, stunned, but still conscious. From Tuck's peripheral vision, he saw Ham sock one of the Perfs on the jaw, knocking the man out cold. With catlike speed, Coach smashed three of the Perfs in the temple with his pistol butt—all three dropped in succession.

Coach also bashed Tuck's stunned Perf in the head with his pistol butt.

"Quick," Coach said, "get their robes on."

Tuck and Coach did so, but Ham, still weak, struggled with his. "Mine won't fit."

Coach frowned. "Try another one."

Ham writhed into the tallest Perf's robe, but it wouldn't fit either. "Too small." Given Ham's bulk, Tuck wasn't surprised. He knew this plan was nuts.

"All right," Coach said. "Tuck and I will get in line with the Perfs. Ham, you hang back out of sight. Don't even think about hightailing it to the highway to get help. If you aren't still behind us when we get to The Temple, ole Tuckster here becomes collateral damage."

Tuck pulled the sash around his robe and turned to Coach. "But won't their leader notice not all the Perfs who went out came back in?"

"Probably. But by that time, we should be inside."

Coach trained his firearm on Tuck. "Pick up a stone. We'll fall behind the other Perfs when they start to go back." Coach holstered the semiautomatic pistol under his robe and hoisted a stone himself.

Nearby, White Robe said, "Regroup in the clearing, Good Sams!"

Tuck and his two companions made their way to the clearing, and Tuck whispered, "Why are they giving up so easy?"

"Evening church service starts soon," Coach said. "Clay'll be there. If there's any justice in the world, so will we."

Tuck said, "So you can shoot him."

Coach tightened his jaw.

Dozens of Good Sams holding stones faced White Robe. Tuck and Coach hung in the back. Fortunately, the hoods obscured their faces.

"Time to return, brothers," White Robe said in a regretful tone. "When we get there, leave your stones in the courtyard. We may have lost the unbelievers in the woods, but tonight we will all witness the glorying of Clay Jameson."

They yelled "Praise God!" as one and marched in single file. Tuck and Coach took the last positions in line, Coach motioning Tuck to go in front of him.

The image of the four Perfs smashed in the skull with Coach's gun flashed in Tuck's head—they might be dead, injured, brain damaged. Tuck's stomach churned.

Ham was apparently following them from a distance. Good—Tuck would need his friend's help inside. Friend? After his betrayal? Tuck shrugged the concern aside—he could deal with it after they'd rescued Clay. When they did, Tuck planned to apologize to his younger brother for trying to run his life. If he'd accepted Clay for who he was long ago, they might not be in this mess.

The Temple loomed ahead, looking less like a modern mega-church than a grand cathedral from the Middle Ages, complete with regal stone spires. Tuck had always thought it had been retouched in Body publicity, but now he knew it wasn't.

Coach pressed Tuck in the back—he must have dropped his stone and unholstered his Sig Sauer P226. He motioned Tuck to fall out of the Perfs' line and follow him into a grove of pecan trees. Ham emerged from the woods and joined them.

From his backpack, Coach pulled out his scrambler and punched a few keys. "Okay," he said, "that should keep their sensors messed up a while longer. Ham, is the secret entrance near?"

"Yes," he said, rubbing his head.

Coach said, "Lead the way."

Coach kept his gun at their backs, and Tuck thanked God that Ham's being a covert agent for Brother Moody would allow them access.

In an area overgrown with cloying honeysuckle, Ham bent over a manhole cover, punched a button beside it, and a panel opened. Ham pushed a sequence of buttons—the code, no doubt—and another panel opened, this one with a camera that apparently read Ham's eye. Within seconds, the manhole cover flipped open.

Coach said, "Retinal scan?"

"No," Ham said. "Iris scan. There are video cams down there."

"No worries. At this close range, my scrambler should've knocked 'em out." Coach pulled two packages of earplugs from his backpack and handed them to Tuck and Ham. "You'll need these if there's gunplay."

Holding his semi-automatic on them, Coach motioned for Tuck and Ham to climb down first. Tuck scrambled to the bottom, his nostrils rebelling against the musty odor radiating from the mold-splotched walls—it made him want to sneeze, but he held it back. He shed his robe. Coach did likewise.

"Follow me," Ham said.

Apparently almost recovered, Ham kept a steady pace. Somehow, from somewhere, he drew strength. Tuck figured it was anger against Coach.

As he strode beside Ham, Tuck wondered whose side God was on. Was the Almighty a radical fundamentalist's deity who sided with Moody's insane ambitions? If so, their efforts were doomed.

On the other hand, if the Almighty was the same God who'd written the golden rule and had offered mercy to tax collectors and prostitutes, there might be hope.

Ten yards in, a steel door bared their way, a panel beside it apparently another iris scan. This camera read Ham's eye, but the door didn't open.

"Good Sam," a remote voice sounded from a speaker beside the door, "some of our sensors are down. As a security measure, please swipe your Temple ID."

Panic sprang into Ham's eyes. To Tuck and Coach, in exaggerated pantomime, he silently mouthed the words, *I don't have it with me.*

Chapter 44

In the room where Mandy had died, Mace loomed over April, snickering. "You don't want me."

Although the ski mask hid Mace's face, April imagined him smiling behind it. He clutched her hand, his palm leather tough, and squeezed until she thought bones would break. She cried out, and he cast her hand aside.

He deepened his reedy voice. "I know about pretty girls like you. Your type made fun of me in school." He spat in her face.

Wiping away the spittle, April realized her original plan was toast. Apparently, he'd sooner kiss a spider than her—assuming he had lips. She shivered. Perhaps he couldn't help what he was. Yet even if he was a reluctant outcast like Kenny, she refused to let him or Moody off the hook. She would wait for the right opportunity to use her elbow strike. *Please, God, make it happen.*

A frantic Brother Moody rushed into the room, his usually coiffed hair a mess. "Mace, I need you."

The man-mountain followed Moody, replaced by a medium-sized young guy in camouflage bearing a Colt AR-15 rifle and reeking of cigarettes. "Name is Clint Matthews, retired Army. I won't hurt you. Promise."

Clint's statement was weird, and April pursued a hunch. "You seem like you might have been a nice guy once. Why are you working for someone like Brother Moody?"

"The big bucks, of course." He flashed a boyish grin.

April figured he was joking, but she didn't return his smile. Still, much as she hated to admit it, he possessed a certain aw-shucks charm.

"Seriously, ma'am, Brother Moody is the best hope for Arkansas. We're a state divided, have been for years. Brother Moody offers a non-political solution, and I think it's right."

"You think using technology to force people to be moral is a good thing?"

"Ah, but those people are choosing to let that technology be planted in their brains. I'm all about choice. Ain't you?"

"That depends on who's making the choice and why." She raised an eyebrow. "If you're on Brother Moody's side, why haven't you become a Good Sam?"

"Because, ma'am, I can better serve Arkansas by bearing arms on Brother Moody's behalf."

"What if Brother Moody ordered you to shoot me?"

"He won't."

"But if he did?"

"Like I said, ma'am, he won't. I don't shoot innocent folks."

"You do realize Brother Moody had me kidnapped?"

He paused. "Yes."

"You'll work for someone who kidnaps innocent civilians?"

Clint looked conflicted. "I trust his decisions."

April's hunch had been right. Clint was not your typical mercenary—he was light years from Mace, though he rationalized Brother Moody's wrongdoings. Maybe Moody's vetting process was less than infallible, or perhaps it wasn't easy finding acolytes. In any event, Clint might be persuadable. *Please, God.*

"So, Clint, you from around here?"

He chuckled. "Small talk's not gonna work, ma'am."

"I get it. If you have to waste me, the less we know each

other, the easier it'll be."

"I don't plan to waste nobody."

"Brother Moody does. He got rid of my cat, just to prove a point. He said he'd get rid of my parents if I caused any problems. What if he ordered you to kill them?"

"All this talk of killing ain't gonna come to nothing."

"There might be a lot of killing before this is over. You may have to do some of it."

He winced—apparently, she'd struck a redneck nerve. "That's not what Brother Moody said. He said his mama had a prophecy that everything would turn out all right."

"His mama?"

"Yeah. The Holy Spirit gives her visions."

April probed his faith. "What has the Holy Spirit given you, Clint?"

He shrugged. "Don't rightly know, ma'am. My stepdad preacher always told me I was going to hell."

"Is that what Brother Moody tells you?"

As though ashamed, Clint averted his eyes. "He says I might have a chance. But only if I follow his orders."

"He's lying, Clint."

The young mercenary furrowed his brow.

April said, "Are you familiar with the hymn 'Amazing Grace'?"

"Sure."

"Its message is genuine. God's grace can save you. Moody can't. He's using you. Don't you see that?"

Clint craned his neck, and April prayed she was about to crack his armor.

But to her surprise, an elderly woman staggered into the room who looked like Margaret Hamilton in *The Wizard of Oz*.

Clint looked puzzled. "Mrs. Moody. What are you doing here, ma'am?"

"My son has asked me to speak with Ms. Showers. In private."

"I didn't hear nothing about that."

"My son is busy with other matters. There's been a break-in."

"Well," Clint said, "okay, ma'am. I'll be right outside." Before he left, he said, "Don't try anything funny." His threat sounded half-hearted.

After he was gone, Mrs. Moody's expression changed from amiable to anxious. "Ms. Showers, I'm here to help you escape. In return, please help me stop Clay Jameson from joining The Body tonight."

This was coming too fast. "Wait, please, who are you? Brother Moody's mother?"

"Yes. We're in danger, all of us." Mrs. Moody informed April about her prophecy concerning Clay, Brother Moody's grand scheme, his framing Tuck for April's kidnapping, and the Leps.

"April," Mrs. Moody said, "if we show the Leps to Clay before he drinks the nanbless wine, he might not do it."

"Okay," April replied, "I get it. But how do we escape with Clint outside?"

"Good question."

"Wait," April said. "I know some self-defense moves. An elbow strike might take Clint out. But he would see it coming a mile away."

Mrs. Moody smiled, her face crinkling like parchment. "Unless I distracted him."

April worked out a scenario with Mrs. Moody.

"Clint!" April cried. "Help! Mrs. Moody is in trouble!"

Clint rushed into the room, and when he saw Mrs. Moody lying on the floor, his eyes went wide. He looked at April. "She breathing?"

"No," April said. "Do you know CPR? Oh, please say you know CPR!"

Clint squared his shoulders over Mrs. Moody's chest. While he joined his hands to give CPR, April rotated her hips and shoulder and smashed her elbow into Clint's temple.

Stunned, the acolyte fell on top of his AR-15 rifle.

April fumed because she couldn't get to the rifle but had no time to waste. "Let's find the Leps."

Clint groaned as April and Mrs. Moody fled the room, and April felt a pang of guilt for the misguided acolyte.

"First," Mrs. Moody said as she walked as fast as she probably could, "we need to get Dr. Sloan on our side."

"Will that be tough?"

"Probably. But where there's a will, there's a way."

"Amen to that."

Chapter 45

There a problem?" the speaker beside the locked tunnel door said.

"My ID," Ham said. "Don't have it. I am an acolyte. Name's Ham Crouch. I have vital information for Chief Elder Moody."

"We can't just take your word for it."

"Okay. But Mace could ID me."

"We'll see if we can find him."

Ham motioned Tuck and Coach into a huddle. "Inside," Ham whispered, "there are two guards with Tasers."

"Why not guns?" Tuck said.

"Moody doesn't want to accidentally kill a Good Sam. Their Tasers can take you out for thirty seconds."

"Must be Taser Bolts," Coach replied. "I've got something similar. Also, better put in your earplugs, just in case."

From his backpack, Coach pulled a Taser stun gun. He pressed down a yellow button until he apparently got a reading he wanted, let go, flipped off what Tuck assumed was the safety switch, and gave the Taser to Tuck. "Tuckster, I'm trusting you. Don't even think about using it on me. Aim it at the bad guys like you would a handgun." Coach held his Sig Sauer P226 at the ready.

The speaker beside the locked tunnel door squawked to life. "Mace is here. We're opening the door."

"Roger that," Ham said.

Taser-toting Tuck and pistol-packing Coach crouched to the door's right. It opened, and a man who looked like the Hulk's ski-masked stunt double lumbered into the tunnel, clutching a .44 Magnum. "Ham," he said in a screechy tenor, "what are you—"

"Freeze!" Coach cried, holding his semi-automatic on Mace.

Mace fired his handgun. The bullet hit Coach in the chest, and at the same time, Coach fired. His aim was off, and the bullet tore into Mace's right shoulder. The thundering shots deafened Tuck, despite his earplugs, and as Mace clutched his wound, Coach fell.

Tuck pressed his Taser. *Fry, dirtbag.* Twin electrodes hooked into Mace, delivering 50,000 volts. Mace gurgled, dropping his handgun as he collapsed. Tuck smiled.

Snap.

Tuck's body charley-horsed, the pain blinding. Growling, he fell. Couldn't move. Couldn't speak. But could think—a guard had tased him. *It can't end like this.*

Another gunshot. *What the—*Coach, somehow still alive, had shot the guy who'd tased Tuck. A guard tackled Coach from behind, and the two men grappled for Coach's pistol.

Mace had recovered from his Taser shock, but Ham delivered an uppercut to the goliath's chin. The unfazed juggernaut socked Ham in the jaw, knocking the big guy flat. Mace turned toward Tuck, recognition in his eyes. Tuck willed his body to move, but it wouldn't—the Taser hadn't worn off. *God, please.*

Mace snatched Tuck from the floor. "So," the mammoth acolyte said, his shrill voice penetrating the post-gunplay fog in Tuck's ears, "I see you took a licking but kept on ticking. Well, you won't be so lucky this time, pretty boy."

A massive fist smashed into Tuck's jaw—pain tore through his face, and a coppery tang filled his mouth.

"Care for a second helping?"

The Taser had worn off, and Tuck spat blood on Mace's ski mask.

Trembling in rage, the man-mountain yanked off his soiled hood.

To Tuck's shame, he gasped at a countenance that would have even given a mother nightmares.

"Are. You. Happy. Now?" Mace said, each word punctuated like a rifle report.

Apparently having disabled the guard he'd been wrestling, Coach slammed his pistol butt into the side of Mace's head.

The giant scowled and lunged at Coach, but the black ops agent dodged and again smashed his pistol butt into Mace's temple. The giant's head drooped, and it looked as though tears were streaming over Mace's warped cheeks.

The injured colossus dropped Tuck.

For a third, fourth, and fifth time, moving like a Tasmanian devil, Coach bashed Mace in the skull. The man-mountain's attempts to grasp Coach slowed until, wobbling, Mace dropped, Goliath to Coach's David.

The most recently tased Temple guard recovered and fired at Tuck. Tuck dodged. Shoved his palm hard into the base of the guard's nose. The man howled, giving Tuck a triumphant thrill.

Coach smashed his pistol butt three times into the guard's temple, and the man sprawled to the floor.

Tuck rose. "Coach, how did—"

"Bullet-resistant vest. I'm sure I have a nasty bruise."

Ham had struggled to his knees and rubbed his jaw. He cocked an eyebrow at Coach. "Why didn't you just shoot Mace?"

"Didn't want to waste the ammo. May need it later."

"You should have wasted him."

"Like I said, no need."

"Think you know everything, don't you?"

While Ham argued with Coach, Tuck slipped out of

Coach's visual range, grabbed one of the Temple guards' Tasers, and fired. The electrodes hooked into Coach's torso. With an agonized growl, Coach hit the floor and stiffened. Tuck tried to pry the Sig Sauer P226 from Coach's clenched hand but couldn't force the frozen fingers open. He swore. Ham grabbed one of the Tasers. Tuck took Mace's .44 Magnum and plucked up the other Taser.

Tuck said to Ham, "Thanks for distracting Coach."

"No sweat. Love arguing with know-it-alls." He motioned forward. "Follow me to the sanctuary."

Before leaving, Tuck tased Coach again, which meant he'd be decommissioned for another thirty seconds. Tuck couldn't bring himself to fire the .44 Magnum at his former high school mentor. There had to be a line a civilized man wouldn't cross—for Tuck, this was it. Would he regret his show of mercy?

Shrugging his ambivalence aside, Tuck tailed Ham into a bright hallway smelling of pine trees. Obviously pushing himself, Ham's head no doubt pounded, but guts apparently powered him on.

"Beanpole," he said, "pray."

"You got it," Tuck said.

Except for the gravity of the situation, it was almost like old times. Tuck could nearly forget about Ham's betrayal. Of course, at this point, he'd accept even Dr. Pritchard's help.

They rounded a corner, and to Tuck's surprise, Ham picked up the pace.

"How much further?" Tuck said.

"Not far."

It hit Tuck that Coach had killed Mace, as well as the two Temple guards. Tuck hadn't killed them himself, but he was still complicit in their deaths.

And where was April? Brother Moody had no doubt arranged her kidnapping, and she might be anywhere in this place. Once again, Tuck prayed—for April, for Ham, for

Clay. The more he prayed, the more right it seemed, and he felt his cynicism melting.

Yet it wasn't lost on Tuck he held a semi-automatic pistol. What if he had to shoot Brother Moody? Then there'd be no one to command Clay to bring judgment upon the United States. Still, cold-blooded murder? He'd drawn the line with Coach just a few minutes ago, but would circumstance force him to cross it?

Ham came to another locked door that read his iris and let them through.

"Not far," Ham said. "Get ready."

His body stoked for action, Tuck prayed for strength—and wisdom.

Chapter 46

April and Mrs. Moody rushed into the nanlab as Dr. Sloan hurled a beaker against the wall. Glass shattered, releasing disinfectant that stung April's nostrils.

"Dr. Sloan," Mrs. Moody said, "what's wrong?"

"My daughter is dead. That's what's wrong." He clutched a chair and smashed it into a computer monitor.

"Oh, doctor," Mrs. Moody said, "I am so very sorry."

He glared. "A Good Sam accidentally gave me a message intended for your son. My daughter choked to death while being held captive by your son's thugs." He giggled and wiped his eyes. "She choked to death on a chicken bone. A *chicken bone*." He burst into sobs.

April touched his quivering arm.

Dr. Sloan stared into space. "Of course, Brother Moody doesn't know I will get my revenge." He turned to April and Mrs. Moody. "After Clay drinks the nanbless wine, I will force Moody to drink wine especially designed for him. I've worked on it for months, tweaked its nanobots so Moody's guilt over sin will be three times that of a normal Good Sam." He smiled and yanked a capped chalice from a refrigerator. "His conscience will eat him alive."

April said, "Won't you need help to get Brother Moody to drink it?"

"Help?" Dr. Sloan raised an eyebrow.

"Yes," Mrs. Moody said, "the Leps could help."

Dr. Sloan looked at her as though she'd lost her mind. A second later, his pinched expression relaxed. "Yes. If the Good Sams see the Leps—"

April jumped in. "Then they'll know Brother Moody has been involved in unethical experiments."

Mrs. Moody said, "I can take us to the Leps."

Adrenaline coursed through April's veins as they stole into the hall, but Clint the acolyte blocked their way. AR-15 rifle at the ready, his eyes locked with April's.

Clint said, "That elbow strike could have killed me, ma'am. I admire your guts. But you ain't getting past me."

April took a slow, deep breath. "Clint, you don't know what Brother Moody is capable of." She told him about the Leps.

Clint shook his head. "Don't believe it."

"What if you're wrong, Clint?"

"You're trying to trick me again."

Mrs. Moody frowned. "No, she is not. I am oh so sorry we tricked you before. But the Leps are as real as you or I."

Clint narrowed his eyes. "Fool me once, shame on you. Fool me twice, shame on me."

April struggled to control her voice. "You've got the gun, Clint. What do you have to lose to follow us to the Leps?"

"My job, for one thing."

"Moody can't be paying you that much."

"It ain't the money, miss." Earnestness anchored Clint's gaze. "It's the cause."

"But if we're right about the Leps, that means Moody is not the great hero you think he is."

"So you say."

"It wouldn't be the first time a leader has used his followers to do his dirty work."

Mrs. Moody said, "Clint, I had a prophecy that a young man who looked like you would help me free the Leps. You know Grahmmie—Brother Moody—has said my prophecies, most of them anyway, are from God." Her eyes flashed a warning. "Want to take a chance on defying the Almighty Himself?"

Clint gulped.

April smiled—Mrs. Moody was no doubt lying about this prophecy, but she may have hit pay-dirt.

"All right," Clint said. "I'm probably a danged moron but take me to the Leps."

April thanked God. With Clint behind them, she, Mrs. Moody, and Dr. Sloan hurried to the Survival Central apartments, where the scent of fresh pine greeted them.

When Clint saw the Leps, his jaw dropped.

Nurse Nadine, the Leps' guardian, put hands on hips. "I don't know what this is about, but if you've come to harm the Leps, you'll have to get through me first."

Mrs. Moody smiled. "The young man is holding his gun on us because he doesn't accept the truth about the Leps."

"Oh. Really?" Nadine narrowed her eyes. "And just what is the truth about the Leps?"

Mrs. Moody explained, identifying the Leps by name for April's benefit.

Nadine shook her head. "Uh-uh. Brother Moody would never do such a thing."

"You're wrong," April said.

Nadine crossed her arms. "The Leps are God's mistakes, not Brother Moody's."

Dr. Sloan said, "For heaven sakes, Ms. Showers is not lying. The Leps are Moody's guinea pigs. He had my daughter kidnapped, so I would test nanobots on Good Sams." He chuckled grimly. "They thought they were getting a flu shot."

April moved back as the Leps who could stepped forward. The Lep with only one hand—Gerald Garson—pointed his stump at Nadine. "You wouldn't believe me before. Maybe you'll believe me now."

The Lep without eyes—Krystal—removed her sunglasses and grinned. "Yes, Nurse Nadine. Maybe now."

Nadine's face blanched. "All right, all right. But if you're wrong—and I'd bet my bottom dollar you are—I'll tell Brother Moody y'all threatened to kill me."

April nodded—good enough. "Clint," she said, "what more proof do you need?"

Clint shook his head. "I just can't believe Brother Moody would allow something like this."

"But he did. You have family?"

"Sure. Except for my Stepdad, we're all real close."

"Well, every one of these Leps is somebody's family, somebody's child or spouse or parent."

Dr. Sloan glowered. "My daughter died while Moody's thugs held her at some undisclosed location. What if she had been your sister?"

Clint groaned. "Okay. So help me, I believe you. What now?"

"Son," Mrs. Moody said, "we need to get to the sanctuary before time runs out."

April cocked her head toward the Leps. "But who can lead them since they're—"

"Crazy?" Mrs. Moody smiled. "They'll listen to Gerald. Always have."

Nadine took Gerald Garson's remaining hand and moved close to him, speaking just above a whisper. April strained to hear.

"Gerald," Nadine said, squeezing his hand, "please tell the Leps to follow us."

Gerald, his eyes intelligent and angry, said, "Why should I?"

"Because they'll listen to you."

"I'll help you, Nadine, on one condition."

"Yes?"

"That you guarantee each of the Leps will be returned to their loved ones."

Nadine furrowed her brow. "I don't know if I can—"

"Yes," Mrs. Moody said. "I guarantee you, Gerald."

Gerald's expression hardened. "I don't believe you."

"I admit I've lied to you before. To all of you. For which I am deeply ashamed."

Krystal's eyeless face dropped to her chest. "No new eyes?"

Mrs. Moody frowned. "I'm afraid not, my child. I should be horse-whipped."

The Leps murmured, and Gerald nodded.

"But I can get you back to your families."

Gerald sneered. "How?"

"By turning The Body against my son. Once Good Sams see what has happened to you, they will turn on him."

Krystal lifted her chin and smiled. "Really?"

"Really. My son is the reason I haven't been able to get you back to your loved ones, but once he is gone…"

The Leps raised their heads, many of them smiling.

Gerald sighed. "All right." He turned to Nadine. "Looks like we've got your back."

A couple of the Leps pumped their fists.

April, Dr. Sloan, Clint, and the Leps followed Mrs. Moody through Survival Central corridors. The Lord's Prayer Leps rolled their wheelchairs. With his one hand, Gerald led Krystal the Eyeless, and Derek "Mournful" Chambers trailed behind them, weeping as he awaited comfort that would never arrive. Nadine had to coax the dozen drugged Leps—the ones who, without medication, involuntarily acted out—to follow her, which they did in a shuffling gait like the zombies from 1968's *Night of the Living Dead*.

April shivered at the callous way Brother Moody had treated the Leps. But were she and her comrades any better? Were they taking advantage of the Leps by herding them to The Temple sanctuary as though they were pathetic one-offs? In 1932's *Freaks*, the film at first depicted its sideshow characters sympathetically, then later as vengeful murderers. Were she, Mrs. Moody, and Dr. Sloan likewise guilty of exploitation?

As Mrs. Moody negotiated a corner and April followed, Clay came to mind. Could someone as kind as Clay become a wrathful Prophet ravaging the land with divine plagues?

And what about Tuck? Where was he? She regretted having played games with him and wondered if she'd ever have the chance to atone. But more was at stake here than her and Tuck's future, much more, just as Humphrey Bogart had told Ingrid Bergman at the end of *Casablanca*.

April prayed God would use the Leps to stop Brother Moody before it was too late.

Chapter 47

Tuck's pulse knocked against his head as he and Ham crouched before another closed Survival Central door.

"Okay," Ham whispered. "This close to The Temple, the guards in the next room will have real guns. As soon as we get inside, crouch behind me. I'll make nice with the guards. If you get an opportunity, taser the dirtbags."

Tuck nodded.

The iris scan read Ham's eye and clicked. As Ham stepped into the room, Tuck crouched behind him. The room's two guards, over six-two apiece, leveled their Glock 22s on Ham and Tuck.

Ham smiled at the guards. "Hey, I'm on the home team. How else could I have gotten in?"

The bigger guard shook his head. "Brother Moody warned us about you two." He turned to Ham. "Moody wants your friend alive. But you, Paul Bunyan, aren't so lucky."

Dropping to the floor, Tuck thrashed his arms and legs, gagged, hoping his performance was Oscar caliber. Tuck's fit distracted the guard for a second, and Ham grabbed him and wrestled for his gun. The other guard sought an opportunity to fire. Tuck rolled and tased him, and the guy collapsed, immobile.

The bigger guard lunged for Tuck. Tuck maneuvered behind him. The spent gas cartridge was no good, but Tuck held the Taser trigger down and pressed the weapon against the back of the sentry's neck. Growling as he shook, the man dropped beside his motionless partner.

Tuck inwardly cheered, shifted his Taser to his left hand. Picked up one Glock with his right. Ham grabbed the other Glock, stuck it in his pants, but kept the Magnum in his good hand. He and Ham locked eyes, and Tuck knew they were thinking the same thing—should they waste these guys?

Ham ransacked the room's desk and found handcuffs and zip-ties, no doubt to subdue unwanted trespassers. He and Tuck bound both men, rolled them on their stomachs. Tuck pressed the Taser's back-up stun gun hard against the backs of both men's necks before he and Ham fled.

In what seemed like minutes to Tuck but might have been seconds, he and Ham reached the sanctuary's backroom. Ham held his finger to his lips. The two men whose backs they saw faced outward into the sanctuary. A young woman, raven hair flowing down her back, sang "Nearer My God to Thee" to the congregation. A sad song, but beautifully rendered in a rich alto—like many churches, The Temple apparently had its own resident Ms. Good Voice.

The backroom, reeking of incense that slightly turned Tuck's stomach, teemed with chalices and hymnal stacks. Sweat slicked Tuck's gun hand. He steeled himself for what was coming—and how long before Coach caught up with them? Considering the iris scans, would he get through?

As "Nearer My God to Thee" approached its finale, Tuck mouthed to Ham, *After the song is over*. Ham gave a thumbs up. Tuck pointed to one of the guards and back to himself, indicating that's the sentinel he would take out. Ham nodded.

The singer finished, and instead of applause, the congregation roared with shouts of "Praise God!" and "Hallelujah!"

Tuck nodded to Ham.

Ham pressed his Taser at the same time as Tuck, and electrical wires hooked into the two guards, shooting 50,000 volts through each of them. Immobile, they fell to the floor.

Tuck and Ham sprinted into the sanctuary. Before them sat perhaps a thousand white-robed Good Sams, and overhead the vaulted ceiling soared heavenward. Ms. Good Voice pulled a hand to her mouth, and Brother Moody, standing behind the pulpit, smiled. Clay stood nearby, dressed in a bulky black robe, especially thick in the chest. Upon seeing Tuck, Clay's eyes widened, his expression a mixture of surprise and confusion.

"So, brothers and sisters," Brother Moody said, "it appears the blood brother of Clay Jameson has decided to join us for The Prophet's initiation. We welcome him as we would any stranger. For we are One Body, Many Hearts."

In unison, the congregation echoed the slogan.

Tuck dropped the Taser and, using both hands, trained his Glock 22 at Moody's chest. Sweat stung Tuck's eye. It could be over in a second—but Clay, arms outstretched, ran in front of Moody.

Clay said, "I won't let you shoot our Chief Elder."

"Clay," Tuck said, "you don't understand."

"No," a familiar voice—Coach's—said, "he doesn't."

Coach stood to Ham's left, aimed his Sig Sauer P226 at Clay, and fired, the gunshot deafening.

Clay went down.

Brother Moody grimaced. Ms. Good Voice screamed. Ham lunged for Coach.

Tuck bolted to Clay, who lay beside the altar, eyes shut. This couldn't be happening. *God, how could you?*

Chapter 48

As from a distance, Tuck saw Ham smash into Coach's shoulder, twist Coach's gun hand toward the ceiling, and wrench free the Sig Sauer P226. He punched Coach in the solar plexus, toppling him. Coach stayed down.

Clay's eyes opened.

Relief washed over Tuck. "Clay?"

Clay nodded. "I'm okay."

"Well," Brother Moody said, standing over Tuck and Clay, "mostly okay. I thought Mr. Shimura might come gunning for Clay. So, under his robe he's wearing a Type IIIA body armor vest. Still, the gunshot probably felt like a wrecking ball, eh, lad?"

Tuck helped Clay to his feet but kept the .44 magnum trained on Moody. "I suppose you're wearing body armor too."

"Bingo, brother of The Prophet."

"But," Ham said, holding the Sig Sauer P226 on Moody, "we could still blow your head off."

Moody shrugged. "You could. But I don't think you will. Amen?"

Three acolytes in camo sprinted into the sanctuary, each brandishing a Colt AR-15 assault rifle—Moody must have buzzed for them. Two trained their weapons on Ham, the third on Tuck.

Moody said, "Tuck, if you don't set your weapon down, my acolytes will make sure Ham meets his Maker posthaste. Ham can't shoot both of them before one of them gets him."

Tuck's mouth went dry. He placed his firearm on the carpet. Ham did likewise.

Moody turned to the congregation. "Brothers and sisters, violence must always be the last resort for Christians. But Scripture tells us those in authority don't brandish the sword in vain. I only use the sword when I must, and today's initiation of Clay Jameson into The Temple is a godly event men must not quench."

Tuck seethed. "Don't listen to him. Your chief elder will kill anyone who gets in his way."

"Not anyone," Brother Moody said, "only those who threaten the new heaven and earth." He raised his hands and looked to the back of the sanctuary. "Bring in the communion table!"

Two stout-looking Good Sams carried in a beautifully finished medium oak table and set it beside the pulpit. A banner across the front read "In Recognition of the New Heaven and Earth" in place of the traditional "Do This in Remembrance of Me." Reverently, Ms. Good Voice draped the table with a corpse-white tablecloth.

From beneath the pulpit, Brother Moody presented a chalice and set it on the communion table's center, the vessel's earthy crimson contrasting with the fabric's ivory. "This," he said, "holds the nanbless wine, the means by which Neophyte Clay Jameson will become not only a Good Sam but also Our Prophet."

"Our Prophet," the congregation echoed.

"Who will usher in a new heaven and earth," Moody added.

The congregation again repeated his words.

Moody continued: "Praise God and The Temple of the Body of the Lord Jesus Christ in the highest."

The congregation: "Praise God and The Temple of the

Body of the Lord Jesus Christ in the highest."

"Clay," Tuck said to his brother, whose brow was furrowed, "hear me out."

Brother Moody waved his hand. "Talk all you want." He turned to Clay. "Your brother will say The Body has harassed him, that he's been falsely accused of kidnapping, that I am a narcissist trying to manipulate you. All lies."

Tuck said, "He's full of garbage, Clay."

Moody ignored him. "Clay, your brother will say or do anything to make you take his side. He wants to steal your free will and mold you in his own image."

Moody's accusations lanced Tuck's conscience, because he *had* tried to force his will on Clay—not once, not twice, but often. He winced at his well-meant but toxic arrogance. "Clay, is drinking the wine what you really want?"

"Yes."

"Why, little brother?"

"So I can die to myself and live one hundred percent for the Lord."

"That's what Brother Moody has told you?"

"Yes."

"And you trust him?"

A hesitation. "Yes."

Tuck shook his head. "Clay, trust yourself. Don't let him or anyone else run your life. That includes me."

Clay furrowed his brow.

Moody bristled. "See how desperate he is, Clay? He's trying to trick you."

Tuck sneered. "Really, Chief Elder? I am trying to trick him, and you're not a manipulative hypocrite?" He turned to Clay. "What do you think Brother Moody is going to do with me and Ham after you've become a Good Sam? Let us go our merry little way?"

To Clay, Moody spread his hands. "We'll have to detain your brother and his friend, of course."

Clay frowned. "For how long?"

"As long as necessary."

"Jesus wouldn't do that."

A tic marred Brother Moody's smile. "I know he's your brother, but he is just one man. Once you drink the nanbless wine, you'll be able to help *all* men. Think of the blind who will see, the lame who will walk, the hungry who will be filled. Amen?"

As the congregation echoed "Amen," Tuck turned to Clay. "Moody's mother had a prophecy, and in it, she said his Prophet will call down weather disasters to force America to join The Body."

Moody snickered. "Nonsense."

Tuck continued. "All churches will be forced to submit to The Body, which will wield as much power as the Roman Catholic Church did before the Reformation."

Moody said, "Ridiculous."

"Eventually, Brother Moody's scientists will perfect airborne nanobots that will force everyone on earth to become Good Sams. Dr. Sloan is only a few years away from this breakthrough."

"Dr. Sloan is working on no such thing."

"As for the nanbless wine you're about to drink? It won't just enslave your mind to the Gospel—it will also enslave your mind to Brother Moody."

Clay turned to the chief elder. "Is this true?"

Moody fumed. "Of course not! Like the Evil One, your brother is full of lies."

From behind Tuck, Mrs. Moody said, "These are not lies." She, Dr. Sloan, a young guy with a rifle, and April—*thank God!*—led the Leps into the altar area, provoking the congregation to murmur.

Tuck's eyes met April's. Relief exploded in his chest. She was alive, thank God. She smiled. How he wanted to run and throw his arms around her.

Moody's three acolytes trained their rifles on the young guy with the AR-15. "Drop it," one of them said.

The young guy shook his head. "I don't think so, boys."

An acolyte said, "Then the girl gets it." He aimed his weapon at April while his two companions kept the young guy in their sites.

The young guy sighed. "All right, you win." He laid his rifle on the carpet.

Mrs. Moody turned to the congregation and gestured toward the Leps. "My son experimented on these followers. They didn't know they were guinea pigs."

While Mrs. Moody introduced each of the Leps to the congregation, Tuck, weaponless, took two quick steps toward April.

One of the weapon-wielding acolytes shook his head.

"We're engaged," Tuck said, knowing no such thing was true—yet.

"Okay," the acolyte said, "go ahead. But watch yourself."

Tuck raced to April and crushed her body against his, her warmth wonderful. He wanted to hold her forever. "Thank God, April, thank God."

Her tears dampened Tuck's cheek. "I'm so sorry."

"There's nothing to be sorry about."

Mrs. Moody cleared her throat. "April, I think you have something to tell the congregation, don't you, my dear?"

Brother Moody jutted out his chin. "She most certainly does not."

Ignoring him, April turned from Tuck to the congregation. "Your chief elder had me kidnapped and threatened to kill my parents."

Clay's eyes widened, and his lip curled. The congregation erupted: Some yelled. Some wept. Some tore their robes. Two men got into a shouting match.

Moody waved his arms. "She's lying. This is The Evil One's plot to destroy us."

Clay said, "April has never lied to me."

"She's a woman! The first woman lied to Adam, and

they've been deceiving men ever since. That's what the 'me too' movement is all about."

Clay raised his voice. "How could I have been so blind?" He gestured at the chalice on the communion table and shook his head. "We're done here."

Chapter 49

Tuck inwardly cheered Clay on as the congregation roared at his little brother's defiance.

Moody's face turned red. "You can't change your mind. You can't thwart divine will."

Clay said, "But is it divine will? The Holy Spirit would never tell one of God's followers to kidnap someone and threaten to kill their parents."

"Wouldn't he? He ordered the Israelites to slaughter the Canaanites."

"That was before Christ's coming."

"Yet Christ whipped the moneylenders out of the temple."

"Not the same."

"Then what about my mother's prophecies?"

"I don't know," Clay said, frowning. "I have to pray through this before I'll even think about drinking that wine."

"Acolytes," Moody said, "aim your weapons between Tuck Jameson's eyes."

The men complied. Tuck's hands turned to ice.

Moody rose to his full height. "I'm sorry it's come to this, Clay, but you've left me no choice. You will—you must—drink the nanbless wine, or your brother dies."

Gasps sounded from the congregation. Someone said, "What's happened to Chief Elder Moody?"

Tuck gazed at Clay, perhaps the last time he would see

his brother, and regret consumed him. "Clay, it's okay if they shoot me. Like Moody said, I'm just one man."

"And," Moody added, "in ten seconds, one dead man."

His chin trembling, Tuck forced himself to focus. "I am proud of you, Clay. A library assistant is as noble a calling as any other." Clay's face blurred. "I love you, little brother."

The light glinted off Clay's eyes.

Moody said, "Time's wasting. Two seconds. One second."

"Stop," Clay said.

Moody commanded his acolytes to stand down.

"Clay," Tuck said, wiping his face, "no."

Moody glowered. "Do it or else."

Without hesitation, and apparently without the intended ceremony, Clay drunk from the chalice.

Tuck shook his head. "Oh, Clay…"

Moody turned to the agitated congregation. "Silence, brothers and sisters! Lift your hands toward heaven. Let the nanbless wine graft Neophyte Clay Jameson onto the Living Tree of The Body."

Tuck didn't know how long the nanobots needed to set up cranial housekeeping, and for fifteen minutes, nothing discernible happened to Clay. Based upon the congregation's subdued reaction, this was typical. On the other hand, Clay had imbibed what were supposed to be the most potent nanobots ever. Maybe the delay was intentional. Or, being experimental, perhaps the molecular brain architects were duds. Please, God.

Clay's expression changed—or did it? Yes, in a strange and subtle way. It was as though a miniscule artist working at the micro-level were airbrushing the skin pores on Clay's face, manipulations that would dazzle under a microscope, but remain mysterious at the macro level. Tuck prayed as Clay massaged his temples for five minutes. His little brother's hands dropped. His face looked serene, like a man for whom bliss had erased every spiritual conflict, a born-again Buddha. Clay's transformation from Christian to Good Sam appeared complete, and Tuck's hopes for a misfire crashed in flames.

Moody smiled. "Brother Jameson, welcome into The Church of the Body of the Lord Jesus Christ."

In a ragged unison, the congregation echoed, "Welcome, Brother Jameson."

"Brother Jameson," Moody said, "your first task for The Body is to take your brother's weapon and shoot him."

Tuck's pulse quickened. Clay gripped the .44 Magnum and looked at Tuck as though he were a sacrificial lamb. As Clay aimed the weapon with both hands, he flinched. A tic tugged at his mouth, and Clay had never had a tic in his life. He must be fighting against the implanted nanobots. Attaboy, little bro.

Moody turned to Tuck. "Do you accept The Body's premise that all sins must be confessed for one to go to heaven?"

Tuck said, "No. God's grace takes care of our sins once and for all."

Moody smiled. "Clay, you just heard the evidence. Any Bible scholar knows to die with unconfessed sin is to burn in hell forever. Your brother is an apostate. Shoot him."

Clay's aim wobbled, and sweat popped out across his forehead. It appeared a war raged within his soul.

"Clay," Moody said in a flat tone, "shoot him."

Clay squeezed the trigger. The shot boomed in the sanctuary, and the bullet zinged through the communion table. Tuck knew Clay was a crack shot, meaning his brother had deliberately missed.

Moody mopped his forehead with a handkerchief. "No shame, Brother Jameson. Put the gun to his head."

Clay held the muzzle of the .44 Magnum inches from Tuck's temple, so close the nanbless wine on his breath soured the air.

Clay's spiritual battle against Moody shattered Tuck's

denial, and in his mind's eye, Moody's face morphed into a visage Tuck knew all too well—his own. Tuck had plunged this realization beneath his consciousness for months, but now he saw Moody as his spiritual twin. Like Moody, Tuck had aspired to be nothing less than a god in Clay's life. From this point on, he prayed to be nothing more than a brother.

Questions, not commands. The three words popped into Tuck's head, and he knew what to do.

Moody trembled with rage. "I said, shoot him, Brother Jameson."

To Clay, Tuck said, "Does Scripture say to worship God alone?"

"Yes."

"According to Scripture, is any mortal man equal to God?"

"No."

"Is Brother Moody a mortal man?"

"Yes."

Moody clenched his teeth. "Don't listen to him. He is the devil's envoy."

Tuck continued. "Would God order you to shoot an unarmed man in cold blood?"

"N-no."

"But Chief Elder Moody has ordered you to do so—does that contradict Christ's teachings?"

"Yes."

"Then, as a Christian, can you obey Chief Elder Moody as though he is God? Or can you obey God alone?"

Moody stomped beside Clay. "Don't listen to him."

Clay said, "I can obey God alone."

By now, Moody screamed at Clay from inches away, spewing spittle on Clay's face. "It is God's will you obey me!"

A tic tugged at Clay's lip, and a successive tic pulled at his eye, his cheek, his other cheek. "It is God's will I obey the Lord alone."

Moody clenched his fists. "God will punish you for disobeying me, Brother Jameson. Save yourself from His wrath by shooting your brother!"

"No," Clay said. His face erupted into a mass of spasms, as though worms traveling at jet speed zig-zagged beneath the skin. His eyes rolled up into his head, blood dripped from his nose, and he dropped to the floor, convulsing.

Tuck knew what had happened—Coach's analogy of *Forbidden Planet*'s Robby the Robot freezing up when faced with two contradictory commands, in Clay's case obey Moody rather than God, or obey God rather than Moody. Coach had said two of the Leps had also become mentally frozen when given two contrary directives. According to Coach, months later, they still dwelled in that land of vacuous oblivion. Had Clay become a resident as well?

Chapter 50

Moody seethed. Look at what this apostate Tuck Jameson had done to The Prophet. And the congregation—they buzzed. Several shook their heads. Some walked out.

Moody waved his arms and said, "Stay where you are, brothers and sisters! This is just a minor setback!"

Dr. Sloan, a strange smile on his face, brought a chalice to Moody and said, "Brother Moody, perhaps it's time you got a taste of your own medicine."

"Yes," Mother said, stepping beside Moody, "I think you would be wise to take Dr. Sloan's advice before the congregation deserts you."

Maybe Mother was right. Moody cried out to the Good Sams leaving the sanctuary. "Wait! I am going to become one of you."

"Go ahead, Grahmmie," Mother said. "Drink."

"Drink," echoed one of the Leps behind Mother.

"Drink," said another.

The other Leps joined the chant and clapped in time. "Drink. Drink. Drink." They surrounded Moody at the communion table.

The trio of acolytes raised their rifles, but Moody ordered them to stand down. One of them looked confused, but all three obeyed.

Moody took Dr. Sloan's chalice and turned to the few

Good Sams remaining. "See! I drink from the same cup you drank." Moody swallowed the wine, perplexed by the nauseating taste and the scalding sensation as it flowed down his throat. "Tastes like fire."

"Well," Dr. Sloan said, smiling, "it isn't exactly the same wine your Good Sams drank."

Moody frowned. "What do you mean?"

"This wine is three times as potent."

Ice fanned across Moody's shoulders. "More potent? In what way?"

"Let's just say in a few minutes, your conscience will eat you alive." Dr. Sloan winked.

Mother must have seen a look of dread on Moody's face, for she chuckled.

"What's so funny?" he said.

"You'll see soon enough, my only son."

Moody frowned at Tuck, who was punching keys on his smartphone, no doubt dialing 911.

"Jameson," Moody said, still feeling like himself, nanobots to the contrary, "put that phone down."

Tuck said, "You aren't getting away with any of this, Moody."

"I'll deny it all. Say it was Dr. Sloan's doing. And Mother's."

"Suit yourself."

Moody planned to do just that, but he felt... funny. His head... something was crawling in his head... it was as though something, or some Things, were creeping inside his skull with flamethrowers, torching his soul, blistering his brain.

"Stop it. Stop it!"

As the cranial blaze spread, giggling engulfed Moody's head.

"Who's laughing?"

He clutched his skull. The sanctuary spun. Revelation incinerated his carefully built justifications, scorching them into cinders, casting torchlight on his sins:

As amoral as Niccolo Machiavelli, he had sought to force a man to kill his own brother.

As depraved as Charles Manson, he had blasphemed he was akin to the Godhead.

As merciless as Josef Mengele, he had used human beings—created in God's own image—as guinea pigs.

"Oh, my Lord," he said, hot tears spilling down his face. "I have sinned too much. Too much." He turned to Mother. "Mother, forgive me. Please."

Her eyes widened. He reached out to her, but she backed away, as though repulsed.

"Dr. Sloan," he said, falling to his knees before the scientist, his tears wetting the man's shoes, "please forgive me. I am so sorry about your daughter."

The scientist remained stone-faced. "Tell it to your God."

Guilt fanned the flames of self-loathing—an inferno offering only one way out.

Moody dropped to his knees before the communion table. He struggled to tell the Leps how sorry he was, but the time for confessions was past. In a tight circle, the Leps surrounded him, Krystal the Eyeless giggling.

Moody smashed his forehead into the edge of the communion table. A jolt of pain shot through his cranium. He crashed his forehead again.

And again.

And again.

Each time, pain crackled through his skull. Warm blood ran down his face, stinging his eyes. Some of it spattered on the white tablecloth.

With his hand and stump, Gerald tried to stop Moody. Tuck and April struggled to get to him, but most of the Leps blocked them. For this, Moody thanked God. Wobbling, he again smashed his forehead into the table, relished the lance of pain, and dropped to the carpet. The world went dark.

Chapter 51

Tuck felt for a pulse in Moody's neck. Nothing. No breathing either. The man was dead, but Tuck forced CPR on him anyway, his compressions timed to an internal "Stayin' Alive." Moody couldn't be dead, he couldn't. He deserved justice, not release. But after several minutes, Tuck gave up.

Someone tapped his back, and he turned to see a frowning Ham. "They took him, Tuck. They took Coach."

"Who took him?"

"Guys in suits. Said they were federal agents."

Tuck cursed under his breath. Maybe Moody was beyond getting justice, but Coach wasn't.

April touched Tuck's cheek. "It's okay, babe. It's over."

He nodded. "Yeah." He walked to Clay, who had stopped convulsing, though his eyes remained closed. Tuck took his brother's hand. Thank God for the warmth. But what came next? If Clay did wake up, would it be as Clay, or as a Perfect?

A man cleared his throat, and Tuck turned to see Dr. Sloan. "Mr. Jameson, I might be able to help Clay."

"Really?"

Dr. Sloan nodded.

Sirens wailed from outside, and police officers hurried into the temple. They would be full of questions. But then, who wasn't?

Chapter 52

In the ICU hospital room where his comatose brother lay, Tuck awaited Marv's TV interview with him, April, and Ham. Marv had also contracted with a known academic publisher to write a book about The Body.

In the past week, The Body and Brother Moody had become hot news in Arkansas and around the nation, abounding with juicy tidbits for news channels to exploit. However, thanks to connections, Marv had conducted his interview on behalf of PBS. Tuck fidgeted in his hospital recliner as he waited to see the edited version, but he'd have to wait a couple more minutes.

Dr. Steinberg had diagnosed Clay's unconscious state as toxic-metabolic encephalopathy, but he didn't pretend to know what had caused Clay's coma. Working on behalf of the federal government, Dr. Sumiko Nakajima and Dr. Justin Tezuka, both experts in the medical applications of nanotechnology, confessed Clay's situation baffled them—nanobots teemed in his brain yet were inert. Tuck wondered if these imminent MDs would solve this mystery. Dr. Sloan had shared his research with them, and they had injected Clay with designer nans they hoped would return him to his non-Perfect self, assuming, of course, he ever woke up.

Tuck's watch chirped—April should be here soon.

"Clay," Tuck said, "there's an interview coming up with me and April. Wish you could see it. Of course, you can hear it. Hope I don't come off sounding too dumb. If I do, I'm sure you'll tell me when you wake up." He chuckled. "What am I saying? You'd be too nice to say I'd blown it. But boy, let me tell you, April won't be."

Various poles and machines surrounded Clay, and tubes snaked in and out of his arms. Doctors had found no evidence of brain damage, but no one knew when, or if, Clay would revive. Fortunately, Mrs. Moody was paying Clay's medical bills, given that she'd received a generous inheritance from her deceased son. Of course, she was doing this from a jail cell, having turned herself in as an accomplice to her son's kidnapping of the Leps, all of whom had been returned to their loved ones.

Meanwhile, Mom's prayer group had pledged to pray for Clay eight hours a day. She insisted he would awaken soon. For everyone's sake, Tuck hoped she was right.

The TV interview started, and Tuck punched on the sound.

At first, Marv asked Tuck, April, and Ham questions about The Body, how they became involved with it, what happened the night of the cult's collapse in which Brother Moody had killed himself. Next, Marv turned to the delicate subject of Moody having blackmailed Ham.

Marv: "How did your wife Molly react to this revelation?"

Ham: "I've asked her to forgive me. We're separated. If she divorces me, I take the blame."

Marv: "And the two of you have a young son, correct?"

Ham: "Yeah. Jake. Great kid."

Marv: "We reached out to Molly, who declined our invitation to an interview, but she did say she won't fight for sole custody of your son. How does that make you feel?"

Ham: "Grateful."

"Good for Ham," Tuck said aloud, even though he already knew what Ham was going to say.

Next on the TV, Marv turned to Tuck.

Marv: "I understand you've been reinstated at ARV, Mr. Jameson, and that starting in January, you will be the new dean of students."

While the Tuck on the tube blabbed, the real-life Tuck said to Clay, "Dr. Pritchard will work under me in the spring. Can you believe that? Have to tell you, I'm tempted to give him a hard time. But I'm going to handle the situation with grace, like you would. If there's anybody that's grace-filled, it's you, little brother."

On the TV, Marv asked how Tuck, April, and Ham felt about nanotechnology. April and Ham said ban it—but the editor cut out Ham's expletive. Tuck heard himself say it should be banned conditionally, because further research could help the Leps and Clay.

Marv: "So, what about the Good Sams? Should they remain as they are?"

Tuck admitted that was a tough call, but he, April, and Ham agreed the decision was up to the Good Sams and their families.

Marv: "But the Good Sams aren't able to act on their own prerogative, so the argument goes, because of the nanotechnology in their heads. Should their loved ones get to decide for them?"

Tuck, April, and Ham expressed mixed feelings, noting the complex ethical and legal challenges. Marv thanked the trio for their time, and the screen faded to an exterior shot of The Temple.

April whipped into the hospital room. "The interview. Is it over?"

Tuck said, "'Fraid so. You came off good."

April sat beside Tuck. "How did you fare?"

"Well, I don't think I embarrassed you too bad."

She smiled. "Better be telling the truth, babe."

"Don't I always?"

April shook her head and turned to Clay. "Do you believe this guy, Clay? But of course you do—you had the misfortune to grow up with him. My condolences times infinity."

"You really know how to hurt a guy." Tuck took April's hand, pleased when she looked into his eyes. "Course, it's not as though Clay doesn't have every right to hate me for the way I rode him in the past."

April arched an eyebrow. "That's the past, babe." They kissed.

A voice said, "Tuck."

Tuck turned toward the bed. "April, did you hear that?"

"Yeah," she said. "I can't believe it, but yeah."

Tuck's elongated grin could have set a world's record. "Do you know what this means?" He rushed to Clay's bedside. "Clay, can you hear me, little brother? Was that you?"

Silence.

"Course it was you."

April disappeared and brought back Nurse Smithers. "We both heard him say it," April told the RN.

"Now, don't go getting your hopes up," the nurse said. "There's no telling when he might talk again..." She stopped, apparently aware Clay could be hearing this. "But he might be fine in just a few days."

Tuck jumped on the nurse's optimism bandwagon. "Hear that, Clay? You might be chewing your big bro's ear off in no time."

A half hour later, not surprised but disappointed Clay had said nothing else, Tuck walked April to her car. "I don't care what the nurse says. Clay saying my name was a sign he'll come back to us, sharp as ever."

April smiled. "I hope you're right."

Tuck returned her smile. "I am. Course, it could be a long wait."

"You won't be alone." April took his hand.

They kissed for the second time that night.

As she drove away, Tuck answered his phone. It was

Avery Olson, the student afraid of failing his Algebra final and having to drop out of school.

"Mr. Jameson," he said, "I bombed the final."

"Sorry to hear that, Avery."

"Should I take out a personal loan so I can come back in the spring?"

Tuck smiled. "That depends on you."

"But I don't know what to do."

"Tell you what. Meet with me on January 2 at my office. I'll help you list the pros and cons of taking out a personal loan, then you'll decide what's best. Sound like a plan?"

"Yes, sir. Thank you."

"You're more than welcome."

After hanging up, Tuck prayed God would give Avery, and himself, guidance in the new year.

Epilogue

Twelve months later, in one of First Christian Church's waiting rooms, Tuck, clad in traditional tux, checked his phone again. No word from Clay.

Ham, looking dapper in his own tux, frowned. "Sure you don't want me to sub for Clay as Best Man?"

Tuck scratched at his stiff collar. "I'm sure."

"Okay," Ham said, "it's your call. But the clock's ticking."

All the groomsmen—Marv, Ham, and Farris Steel (no longer a Stribling Hall RD but now an AVR Assistant Dean of Residence Life)—were here. But no Clay.

At the rehearsal dinner, Clay had only tripped over a few words from his planned reading for today's wedding. Nine months ago, Clay had awakened from his coma, and thanks to dedicated medical treatment and his own tenacity, three months later, he had recovered his cognitive faculties and motor skills—a blessing Tuck haltingly attributed to God.

Brother Eli, accompanied by his loud cologne, rushed into the room. "Hey, guys. Showtime in five minutes."

Tuck nodded. "Got it."

"Where's Clay?"

"Here." Clay stood at the door, resplendent in his tux.

Tuck inwardly sighed. Worried that Clay might not arrive in time, he was glad to be wrong. He squeezed Clay's shoulder. "Ready to roll?"

Clay smiled. "Sure thing."

Inside, Tuck thanked God, a practice that over the last year had started to become natural.

Minutes later, the processional began. Tuck assumed his place before the congregation as Clay and the groomsmen lined up behind him. Nearby flowers graced the sanctuary's steps, their fragrance redolent.

As Tuck waited for April to arrive at the end of the lengthy processional, guests filled the pews. Two former Leps—Gerald and Kristy, who wore sunglasses—sat midway back. Aunt Dolly and Mom, who used a tissue to dab her eyes, took seats in the family pews.

Then April appeared, escorted by her father.

The organ played "Here Comes the Bride," but the music and all other sights and sounds faded as April walked up the aisle in her beautiful white dress, a vision from heaven too good to be true. Or, as Dad had said about grace, too good not to be true.

Once April stood across from Tuck, their eyes met, and they couldn't hide their smiles.

Brother Eli stood before them and said, "Welcome, everyone, to this blessed event."

Yes, Tuck and Eli had buried the hatchet.

As Eli shared thoughts about the sanctity of marriage in his booming bass voice, Clay cleared his throat. He was probably nervous about his upcoming reading, but Tuck had faith in him.

Eli introduced him, and Clay stood before the congregation. "Brothers and sisters, it's not every day you lose a big brother to a wonderful woman like April. She has always been like the first rose blossoming in the spring." That line elicited smiles from the ladies. "And Tuck—what can I say about Tuck?" He stopped, sniffled, and waved his hand. "Sorry. What can I say about Tuck? Of all the big brothers in the world, I thank God daily for having blessed me with the finest of them all. I have always prayed to the

Lord to grant Tuck the hopes of his heart, and today, that prayer has been answered."

A gentle buzz filled the sanctuary. Tuck's throat tightened as Clay stepped back behind him, and April's eyes misted.

Next came the exchange of vows and rings, sacred in its solemnity, and the invitation to kiss the bride. Tuck lifted April's veil. Tenderly, their lips touched.

"And now," Eli boomed, "I pronounce you husband and wife."

Next came the reception (smartly organized by Clay), the well wishes, and the goodbyes.

That night, Tuck grinned at April in their wedding suite bed. "How could one guy be so lucky?"

She looked coy. "Luck had nothing to do with it, babe."

"No?"

"No." She smiled. "But grace had everything to do with it."

After midnight, when Tuck and April drifted into sleep in one another's arms, Tuck dreamed of having a son and daughter.

Two years later, his dream became reality.

Jake and Lila, the manic twosome, loved visits from Uncle Clay, and they filled the Jameson house with mischief and laughter. The family dog followed their impish ways by tracking muddy paw prints across the carpet. Between shaken heads, weary smiles, and wagging fingers, Tuck and April did their best, and Tuck realized April had indeed been right—grace had everything to do with it.